Fate of Gray

A Murder Mystery Amateur Sleuth With A
Past

Jodi Walter

THIRTEEN PAGES

To anyone who has persisted through tough times and questioned the hardships of life. Life experiences help us become who we are destined to be.

CHAPTER 1

JED STIRRED.

Adrift in the foggy no-man's land that marked the boundary between sleep and waking, he heard a dim voice calling out to him. Was it from his dream, or did it come from the real world? He could not tell.

And he did not care.

Her face floated before him, her ash-blonde hair framing that dimpled smile which never failed to send his heart into a mad frenzy. In the dream, it was difficult to tell where they were. The only thing Jed knew for certain was that the place was some sort of lush meadow, and it was afternoon. Warm, radiant sunbeams poured over Christie's face like melted butter, making her locks glimmer and sparkle. Her cherry-red lips were parted into a wide, unrestrained smile, and her mouth was slightly open, as if she was about to say something. Or confess something.

Do it. Jed silently urged her, feeling his pulse beating staccato rhythms in his palms and neck. *Do it. Say what's in your heart. I know I'm not the only one feeling this way. I can't be.*

As if she had guessed his thoughts, the smile on Christie's face widened even further, revealing the remainder of her perfect, even teeth. Her mouth opened, and Jed felt such an intense wave of giddiness surge up from within him that he feared he would drown in its depths. He swallowed and put a hand on his chest to steady himself.

I can't die. Not now. Not before I hear her finally confess what I've secretly known all along. Jed's eyes were fixated like magnets on Christie, as if he were terrified that she would disappear the moment he averted his gaze. The very air around him seemed held taut in anticipation, waiting for this moment to unfold. Christie's mouth opened in slow motion, the first word of her confession beginning to slip out. Jed waited, every hair on his body standing on end, his heart teetering on the edge of his chest. He watched as her mouth moved, and the word—

—was lost in noise.

A deafening noise, like a thousand church bells clamoring at once, filled Jed's ears. Frowning, he put his palms against the sides of his skull and looked around. The rich green meadow they were standing in was quickly fading away to black, fragmenting into pieces as the dream began to break down.

No, not now. Just let her say it. Let me hear it o—

Jed awoke.

He did not have time to mourn the loss of that precious encounter. That thunderous ringing was still there, and now that he had returned fully to reality, it was louder than ever.

What in the hell is that? Still frowning, and still holding a single hand against his head, Jed sprang up from his living room couch and rushed over to the window, pulling back the shades hastily.

Chaos greeted him.

Pedestrians crowded the edges of the street, their faces contorted in confusion and fright as they huddled in groups, all of them pointing at the same thing.

A van, non-descript and dark gray in color, was lying in the center of the street, upturned on its side. Flames roared out of the van's split underside, pushing their way through the metal hungrily. The tongues of fire crackled and hissed in the open air and beneath a patch of roadside, which was now charred black. Jed noticed the roof of the van and saw a light attached there which was rapidly blinking red, just like a siren.

Then, Jed saw the bodies.

His breath hitched slightly in his throat as he finally understood the cause of the gathered pedestrians' terror and confusion.

They weren't bodies. Jed took in the horrific scene and saw that they were mannequins—dozens upon dozens of them littered the roadside. They had fallen out of the van's back doors, which now hung open. The mannequins all looked the same: they all had a Caucasian skin tone and were not wearing any clothes. As Jed squinted closely in their direction, his balled fist pressed against the windowpane, he understood why.

Something was written on them.

Even from here, he could see the red paint. The letters were only vague outlines, though. What message they were trying to spell out would only become apparent upon closer inspection.

The door to his apartment flung open as Jed stormed down the stairs, skipping down two steps at a time, and not at all concerned for his safety. He could not quite pinpoint why, but there was suddenly a very nasty feeling in his chest—a dark, constricted feeling, the kind you get when you get a phone call late at night and immediately know it cannot be good news.

The nagging sensation only grew as Jed stepped out onto the sidewalk and began running toward the disaster. He knew he didn't have much time. The police would be here any minute, and the first thing they would do would be to cordon off the area and push away any curious bystanders. That included him. Unfortunately for him, his relationship with the police was no longer like it used to be. He could no longer expect any assistance from them.

The thought pushed Jed to run faster, before the scene was sealed off for good. He knew he had to see it. He couldn't logically explain it, but he just had to. Every instinct within him was driving him forward. This was no mere accident. It was something else.

The heat was the first thing he felt upon nearing the vehicle. Hot gusts of wind whipped against Jed's face and neck as he stepped around the gray van and stared at it.

His eyes scanned the nearby roadside, and his brain automatically formed the connection before he even had a chance to consciously realize it. This was not an automobile accident. It couldn't be. There were no skid marks on the road. Jed's initial thought upon seeing the van was that it must have been going at a tremendous speed before it veered sharply off course to avoid an oncoming collision. But a driver that was smart enough to turn the steering at the last moment was also smart enough to break. Yet, the road ahead and behind the van was unblemished.

Perhaps the van was resting and another vehicle hit it?

Jed dismissed the thought. The road right around him was littered with shattered glass, torn leather, and crumpled pieces of smoking metal. All of them looked to be of the same kind, which meant that they only belonged to this vehicle. Which meant that this couldn't have been an accident because there would have been some damage inflicted upon the other vehicle, as well.

Then what...? An explosion?

That didn't make much sense. Why detonate a bomb inside a van in the middle of an empty street, where there are no people to hurt and no property to damage? What was the point? Unless...

Unless the goal was to send a message.

Slowly, as if on a swivel, Jed's head turned sideways in the direction of the mannequins piled up on the road. With legs that had suddenly turned rubbery, he found himself walking in that direction, knowing deep in his heart of hearts that he would not like what he found.

There were slightly more than two dozen mannequins, all of them scattered at the van's backend. The white, faceless, expressionless puppets lay sprawled on the concrete in different positions, looking uncomfortably humanlike in their postures. It took a moment for his heartbeat to slow down, closer to normal, before he could appreciate the fact that this carnage did not hurt anyone. The pale white bodies reminded Jed of some ancient Victorian painting depicting souls being cast into hell.

But the worst was yet to come.

Jed did not need to step any closer to read the messages that had been scrawled across the mannequins' naked bodies. Or rather, he did not need to step any closer in order to read *the message* which had been painted. Because it was only one message, repeated over and over on each body, like a prisoner in an asylum engraving the walls of his cell with an untiring lunacy. Jed's eyes traveled over the message. Every ounce of blood in his veins froze solid, and he felt his heart come to a jarring, stuttering halt.

Therapy kills.
Therapy kills.
Therapy kills.

A choked grunt tore its way out of Jed's mouth. He took a step backward, as if one of the mannequins had suddenly risen to its feet and he was trying to flee from it. His foot hit a bump in the pavement, and he went sprawling, the remainder of his breath knocked out of him. Breathing harshly, his gaze returned to the mannequins, and he saw that they still lay before him, motionless, except now their faces weren't quite so blank anymore. Jed could swear that they were taunting him, jeering at him for being such a fool.

Did you really think disaster wouldn't come again? One of the faceless mannequins seemed to whisper to him from the ground. *You're a disaster magnet, remember? It was only a matter of time before you brought havoc back into your life… and into the lives of those around you.*

Jed was aware that he was close to hyperventilating. He was also aware that if he didn't get ahold of himself soon, he would lose the chance to critically analyze the scene. The police would arrive, and that would be the end of it. He couldn't let that happen because this entire charade was clearly intended for him. He needed to find out what this mysterious madman wanted, or if he had left any clues leading to his identity.

Taking a deep breath, Jed composed himself and stood back up. Behind him, he could hear an entire crowd murmuring with both unease and fascination. They were all watching him, he knew, and trying to understand why this man was behaving so strangely around a pile of scattered dolls. To his left, the flames in the van roared and flung themselves ever higher, feeding on the air's oxygen and expanding every second. They would escape the van and ignite the surrounding bushes and trees, if the firetrucks didn't arrive soon. But the cavalry was already on its way. Jed could hear the dim sound of sirens in the distance. Whether those sirens belonged to firetrucks or police cars was something he would soon find out. Regardless, there wasn't much time. If he wanted to act, he would have to act now.

"Come on, you can do this," Jed muttered to himself in a hoarse whisper. Then he sucked in a large lungful of air and began walking again to the mannequins. It would be okay. He had already seen everything and, now, just needed to analyze it. Whatever happened, the situation would not get any worse, at least.

But he was wrong again.

The explosion, the fire, and the messages crudely carved on the mannequins' undressed bodies had thrown Jed so much that he had missed a key detail. The mannequins were not naked—not exactly. Jed's eyes fell over this missed detail now, and whereas before his blood had turned to ice, now it turned into a thunder that bellowed through his entire body, making his vision fuzzy. His dream came back to him, then: Christie, smiling at him, her tawny strands glinting like gold in the sun. He looked back at the fallen mannequins and swallowed deeply, unable to remove the heavy lump from his throat.

All the mannequins were female and wearing blonde wigs.

CHAPTER 2

JED SAT AND WAITED. His hands were resting patiently in his lap, and his feet lay motionless on the office's carpeted floor. Through the window situated opposite him, he could see the outside corridor bustling with activity. Uniformed men and women were dashing left and right, some holding clipboards in their hands, others talking urgently into their phones, and a few giving him a passing glance as they disappeared beyond the window.

No one came in, though.

Oh, how the world changes.

Despite the madness he was currently engulfed in, Jed couldn't help but feel a twinge of disappointment. Things had changed so radically and rapidly that he was finding it hard to adjust. How much time had passed? A month-and-a-half? Two? Yes, around that much. Maybe even less. That was all it had taken for him to go from a friend to an utter stranger. From a trusted consultant to an ordinary citizen, made to wait in the office like everyone else. There had been a time when he would walk into these quarters like they were his second office, feeling completely at ease and in his element. Now, everything stared back at him with no recognition, marked by a cold alienness that made him feel like he had, somehow, been betrayed.

It's not like you're blameless, though.

Jed sighed, a soft sound that was amplified to loudness in the office's quiet interior. He drummed his fingers against his thighs, more out of agitation than thought.

It was true. Yes, he was the one responsible for the way he was currently being treated. He was the one who had done the betraying, after all—unintentionally, yes, but still a betrayal. Intentions do not really count when your blunder caused a psychopath to slip through the police's fingers, a psychopath who had caused untold havoc in the city and boasted a list of murders to his name that was getting more expansive by the day. All thanks to the mistake Jed had unknowingly made.

He hissed in a sharp breath as that memory rose within him again, painful as ever. It had been tormenting him every day since the fateful death of their witness had occurred. Part of Jed firmly believed he deserved all the pain. It was his penance for what he had done. If he hadn't been so careless in his conversation with Alexis, perhaps things would have gone very differently. Perhaps today's disaster wouldn't have happened.

"Mr. Gray?"

The voice snapped him out of his dark reverie. Jed looked up to find an officer's head poking through the door, staring at him.

"Sorry, what?" he asked, beginning to get up.

"Are you Mr. Gray?" the officer repeated.

Jed nodded.

"Okay." Jed saw the man wave a hand to usher him back into his chair. "Please remain seated. Our officers will be coming to meet with you any moment."

Disappointed, Jed sagged back into his chair and crossed his legs impatiently. How much longer was this going to take? He had been waiting for forty minutes already. The accident outside his apartment had been such a big one, surely it warranted more attention than what it was c—

The door opened again, cutting off that train of thought. Jed looked up and saw not strangers, but his previous colleagues entering the room. Derek and Graham were in the front, their faces marked by serious lines. They looked down at Jed unsmilingly, as if they were seeing him for the first time in their lives and he was nothing more to them than a witness.

Behind them came Christie.

Everything faded away. Even the horrific explosion that had just occurred left Jed's mind. All he could see was her. *Her*. His partner. His friend. His...

God, she was beautiful. He had always known that, always appreciated it, but seeing her almost daily had taken away some of the shock factor from her appearance. Now, an almost two-month break had left Jed unprepared to see her. It hit him harder than he had been expecting.

Christie's face was far sterner than both Derek and Graham combined, yet her austerity only added to her beauty, gave it that icy elegance which was so good at driving men crazy. Her hair was tied behind her in a tight bun, tawny as ever under the ceiling's yellow lights. Her eyes were wide and dark and unfathomably alluring, caves of endless enchantment that Jed had found himself lost in more than once. Her left hand balanced a file against the crook of her elbow, and her right hand held a Styrofoam coffee cup. Jed knew that it was a cappuccino with exactly two spoonsful of sugar in it. That was what she liked. He knew everything about her. Yet, tragically enough, the woman standing before him was a stranger, nothing more.

"Gray," Christie spoke, and the flatness in her tone made Jed wince inwardly. He was not used to hearing her call his name without some sort of emotional inflection. "Come with me, please."

Without waiting to hear his answer, Christie turned around and walked out of the room. Jed followed behind, trailed wordlessly by Derek and Graham, who he was also seeing for the first time in two months, but who were both acting as if they were seeing him for the first time in their lives—and preferably the last.

Christie led Jed through those snaking corridors he had grown so familiar with. He knew where she was going before they even arrived. A conference room, of course. What else lay beyond the kitchens with the coffeemaker and the mal-functioning vending machine?

Less than a minute later, they had arrived. Christie turned the handle to conference room 10-B and stepped in. Jed followed after her.

The rest were waiting for him inside. Carter, Joseph, and Jason, all of them sitting in their chairs and watching the prodigal son return. Jed locked eyes with each of them re-luctantly. Joseph and Carter gave him blank stares, which were far more painful than if they had actually displayed some anger. Jason regarded him with undisguised hostility and suspicion—and more than a smidgen of satisfaction. That was one reaction Jed was not surprised by. The man had always hated him, and now he had perfect reason for it.

"Take a seat," Christie ordered, gesturing toward a chair on the opposite end of the table. Jed quietly obeyed, watching Graham and Derek sitting down next to their crew. Christie stood at the head of the table, watching everyone ready them-selves. She did not look at Jed. She did not give him any more attention than was needed.

"Let's begin, shall we?" she stated once everyone was set-tled. "So, the mysterious figure we hold to be responsible for the murders of Joel, Ethan, Alex, Carl, and Sheila has returned once again, as expected, after a two-month hiatus." She paused. "And this time, his message is far bolder than ever before. It seems like he's confronting us head-on."

"A confrontation requires you to reveal your identity," Graham muttered sourly. "Not hide in the shadows while doing all your plotting."

Christie nodded in understanding. "Unfortunately, what we have is what we have, and we must work with it." She gestured toward Jed without actually looking at him. "Now, I'm going to be briefing you all on the latest act of mayhem by our mysterious assailant that took place outside Gray's apartment. Listen attentively, take notes if you need to, because this guy's never done something on this scale before."

"One second." Jason's shrill voice broke through the momentary silence, and Jed knew instantly what he was going to talk about. "I have an objection."

Christie paused. Something flitted across her face, briefly visible then gone. "Yes?"

"Why is *he* here?" Jason stabbed a finger in Jed's direction. His face was twisted with fury, his eyes bright pinpricks of hate. "He's already recorded his testimony with an officer, and we have our personnel on the scene anyways, combing it for evidence. Any information we need to find our guy, we already have. Our own resources are more than enough to fill in what's missing." Jason's finger flexed even more, tightening with the force of his animosity. "So, why is this traitor still sitting here? We all know what he did! It's because of him this whole drama is still going on! If he had kept his mouth shut, we would have that psychopath behind bars right now! I want him out!"

Silence. A silence so complete that Jed heard the dim honk of a car outside, far beyond the building. He looked at the officers sitting opposite him, unspeaking and unmoving. What could they have said in defense? Jason was right. Each word he had uttered was the truth. Jed did not belong here anymore—not after what had happened.

"Jason." It was Christie who spoke. Her voice was remarkably devoid of emotion. She seemed to be addressing a technical issue rather than a personal one. Jed turned his gaze toward her in surprise, taking in the carefully blank mask of indifference she had drawn across her features.

"While your concerns regarding Gray are legitimate," Christie acknowledged softly, causing Jed's heart to squeeze with pain. "Jed holds a personal connection with our suspect, and because of that, we cannot keep him out of the loop. We need him with us, on the case, because the man we're trying to catch is only interested in Jed, not us. It is only through Jed that we get a shot at beating him." A pause, and Christie breathed out. That indifferent mask on her face rippled slightly, as if there were something turbulent beneath it, trying to make itself known. But then, Christie recomposed herself, her eyes as hardened as ever. She made her concluding statement.

"Jed stays."

No one else in the room spoke. Jed wondered what his other colleagues thought of his presence here. Were they happy, angry, unbothered? Were they the ones who had secretly chosen Jason as their spokesperson and asked him to communicate their reservations to Christie in the meeting?

"I still don't find this okay," Jason grumbled, his hands fidgeting on the desk. "We're going to be discussing sensitive information in these meetings, information we would normally never share with a civilian. What if Jed 'accidentally'"—he made sarcastic quotation marks with his fingers—"leaks that information again? We're having a hard enough time outsmarting this criminal as it is. I don't know how we can do it with an informant among us."

Informant.

That did it. Jed was a composed man, but even he had his limits of how much nonsense he could tolerate from someone else. Jason had just crossed the line. He felt the anger rising with him, disrupting the rhythm of his steady breaths. A muscle in his lower jaw twitched.

"I get it, Jason," Christie added, shooting Jed a look. Of course, she had sensed instantly that he was getting angry, and it was time to defuse this situation and move onto the case. "But like I said, removing Jed from the equation only makes things harder for us. Remember, Jed knows this man from his past. If we keep him in the loop, giving him our latest intel and updates, who knows? Maybe Jed can figure out who the guy is, and we will have his identity in our hands."

More silence. Jason still didn't look quite pleased with the outcome, but he knew he was at the end of his leash. Christie would tolerate no more protests from him. Her tightly pressed lips were signal enough.

"Fine," Jason muttered, leaning back in his seat. He gave Jed a glowering look. "At the very least, though, I suggest we confiscate Jed's phone during the next meeting we have. We don't want the man who tapped Alexis' phone to fool us again in the same way."

Christie nodded. It was a painful nod. "Fine," she conceded. "We will, uh… confiscate Gray's phone for every meeting." The words fell out of her mouth in awkward and clunky fashion. They filled the room up and created an unease with their presence, as if they didn't belong there.

"Great." Jason said nothing more.

Without a word, Jed stood up and removed his phone from his pocket. He slid it over to where Graham sat. The burly officer picked up the device and walked out of the room with it, returning empty-handed moments later and settling back into his seat. His expression was carefully guarded.

"Okay, then." Christie looked relieved to be done with that conversation. She let out a pent-up breath before returning her focus to her colleagues. "Now, to fill you in on the details regarding today's incident." She reached out and fiddled with her laptop that was set open before her. A moment later, the large screen behind Christie blinked to life. It showed an image of Jed's street, one side of it filled with onlookers and the other with that overturned van and its horrible contents.

"At 6:37 this morning," Christie began, gesturing toward the screen, "this van met with an accident outside Jed's apartment. We don't yet know how the accident occurred, but our collision experts are on it, analyzing the current evidence. What we do know is that there was an explosion, presumably from inside the van. Then, of course, the material inside the van spilled out..." Christie's voice faded. She leaned forward and fiddled some more with her laptop. The image on the screen suddenly zoomed in, clearly showing the van and its displaced contents.

The room stirred uneasily.

"Is that...?" Graham leaned forward, squinting at the screen, his eyes disbelieving.

"Yes," Christie confirmed. "Those are mannequins. More than two dozen of them, as far as I can tell."

"And there's something written on them as well," Carter observed darkly. "Therapy kills." His eyes flitted toward Jed, then sprung away from him again before Jed could spot the emotion lurking within them.

"Shit," Derek whispered. "That's messed up."

Christie's laugh was hollow. "Yeah. Messed up is one way to describe this whole thing, for sure."

"Are there any fingerprints or documents inside the van?" Joseph inquired. "Anything we could use for identification?"

"We don't know yet," Christie told him. "Our team is still on the scene, collecting evidence. But I'd bet my left arm and leg that we won't find anything inside that van. Nothing other than what he wanted us to find. He's too precise, too methodical to make such rookie mistakes."

"You're forgetting the blonde wigs on the mannequins," Jed added quietly.

Everyone in the room turned toward him. It was the first time he had spoken, the first time they had heard his voice in months.

"Yeah, Je—Gray's right," Derek murmured, staring at the screen. "They're all wearing that same golden wig. Huh, weird."

Christie only gave the screen a passing glance before focusing on Jed. Her throat bulged up and down, and she squirmed slightly, as if struggling to get something out.

"Is there an inference you've drawn from those wigs which might prove useful in our investigation?" she asked in a formal tone.

Jed stared straight back at her. "Yeah. The inference is you. You have blonde hair."

Christie was taken aback. She had not been expecting that. Her hand automatically went to touch her hair, and then she turned back to the screen. For a moment, she was silent, struggling with the annoyance surging within her. God, why hadn't she made that connection on her own? It was so obvious!

"He's right," Graham grunted finally, not looking pleased in the slightest. "Goddamn it, those mannequins have hair exactly like yours, Christie."

Christie paused. "But why?" She didn't look at Jed when she spoke, but the question was directed at him, nevertheless. He was the only one here who knew their enemy.

"It's a threat," Jed told them all in a low voice. "That's been his pattern from the start. Hurt the people around me, those I... care about." He swallowed. Christie had turned her face away from everyone in the room and was staring intently at the floor. Her expression was drowned in a puddle of shadows.

"Now, he's escalating," Jed continued in a firmer voice, after getting a grip on his derailing emotions. "He's telling me he might come after Christie next."

"Come after a police officer?" Jason repeated with incredulity. "Ha! I'd like to see him try. I think that's a bit beyond even his abilities."

"Don't be so quick to judge that," Graham commented. "This man has been two steps ahead of us the entire time. We cannot risk underestimating him at all. If he makes a threat, we treat it with the utmost seriousness."

"Right," Carter agreed. "I say we secretly station police officers around Christie wherever she goes to ensure her protection and create a honey trap to lure this guy in. If he does show up, we'll get him."

"Yeah, I concur," Joseph muttered. "Three rotating shifts of undercover officers trailing Christie wherever she goes outside office hours. A shift for her apartment, for her weekend plans with friends and whatever, and to escort her to and from work as well. That would work."

Jed did not say anything. But sitting in that room and hearing the discussion taking place, he felt everything within him settling down peacefully. *This* had been his biggest worry ever since he had seen the blonde wigs on those mannequins. Christie's safety. And he was glad to find out that her colleagues would take good care of her.

Even if he no longer had that privilege.

"Right," Christie rose again from her seat, closing the laptop and signaling the end of the meeting. "Those are all the details we have on this case so far, so I think today's meeting has reached its end. If we find anything from the van or its contents, all of you will be promptly informed. Until then, stay safe and keep working at it." She scooped up the files on the table and walked out. Her colleagues, too, began to rise one-by-one, their faces lost in thought.

Jed quietly rose from his place and left the conference room before he could be accosted by Jason and forced to listen to more of the guy's angry ramblings. He wasn't in the mood right now. His life had become eventful enough as it was.

Jed stepped outside into the corridor and looked around. His phone was lying on a nearby table, in a clear plastic container. He sighed, picked it up. Christie was nowhere to be seen. She had probably hurried back to her office, a place he now had no authority to enter. Their brief reunion for today was over.

Stay safe, Christie. Be as angry as you want with me, but please stay safe.

After sending out that silent plea in the hopes that it would somehow reach her mind and communicate itself to her, Jed began walking down the hallway, back where he had come from.

CHAPTER 3

"YOU'RE NOT MAD, ARE YOU?"

Jed put his drink down in amused exasperation. He smiled at Alexis, a full, uninhibited smile that showed his emotions without concealing anything.

"For the thousandth time, Alexis," he repeated patiently, "I'm not mad at you. Not even a bit."

Alexis still looked skeptical. She also looked sorry, which only made Jed feel worse about his own actions. "You're sure, right? You're not just saying that to make me feel better."

"I swear upon all that is holy and true." Jed leaned forward, that patient amusement still coloring his expressions. "Alexis, how can I be mad when it wasn't your fault at all? Trust me, it really wasn't. You didn't do anything wrong. Whatever blame there is to pin, it should all be pinned on me."

"Don't say that," Alexis complained. "That just makes me feel worse."

Jed raised his hands in defeat. "Okay, you know what? Let's just drop this subject and act like it never happened. There's so many other things to talk about. Such as that new guy you've recently started seeing."

The worry left Alexis's face in an instant. She picked up her drink and took a slow sip, hoping that would conceal her smile. But Jed was too sharp to miss such a thing.

"Interesting how a mere mention of him turns you into a giddy schoolgirl," he teased, noticing the flush creeping up her neck. "If only I had such an effect on women, life would be quite the adventure."

"Stop it," Alexis said, laughing. "Mark and I are still in the early stages of our... friendship. I don't want to get my hopes up in case it leads nowhere."

"Why would you think it'll lead nowhere?" Jed inquired, genuinely curious.

Alexis sighed, and that sigh was enough of answer. But she still spoke. "Because of my ex. The one I had before you."

"Ah," Jed commented, understanding. Before him, Alexis had been with someone else, someone whom she'd had quite a turbulent relationship with. They'd been together for less than a year, and those 10 months had been quite the rocky journey for his friend. She'd been using at that time, so she wasn't in the right frame of mind anyways. Later, she'd found out that the guy she had been dating, and had at one point planned to spend her whole life with, had in actuality been a drug dealer. He'd been arrested by the police and sent to prison. The realization had really thrown Alexis' view of her own judgement into a spin. She'd started doubting everyone, not knowing what secrets they were hiding beneath their smiling exteriors. Dating Jed and finding out that honest men existed, too, did little to alleviate that doubt. Some of it still lingered till today, a remnant of the past that refused to relinquish its grip on her.

"I notice that you never mention his name," Jed observed. "You always refer to him as 'my ex'. Is there a reason for that?"

Alexis shrugged. Her eyebrows pinched together in distaste. "I just don't enjoy bringing up all those memories," she explained. "Referring to him in past tense makes it seem like he no longer matters or has an effect on me. When I say his name, I feel that same old doubt resurfacing. I can almost picture him again as he used to be, clean-shaven and dressed entirely in black, always chewing gum. The images are just too unnerving. I don't want them cluttering my mind."

"Hmmm. Have you considered talking to someone about it?" Jed spread his hands out on the table. "Not therapy, just venting to someone—a close friend maybe. Sometimes, that's all that's needed to let go of a memory for good. You just need to relive it completely one final time, in all its ugly vividness, before you find the strength to move on."

Alexis frowned. She sipped her drink absently. "I think I have moved on," she spoke after a while, "for the most part, at least. It's just that whenever I'm first getting to know someone, my internal radar is on high alert, searching for the slightest sign of suspicious behavior. If I find it, I ghost the guy without a second thought."

"Wow," Jed murmured. "That takes courage."

Alexis shrugged again. "Better to be disappointed earlier than to be hurt later on, you know. That's how I view it."

"And that's not a very unwise view to hold." Jed leaned back momentarily as their waiter arrived with their order, placing the tray of sushi and tuna pizza on the table. "I don't remember you being such a sage when we were dating. The Alexis I recall did all sorts of goofy stuff."

"Oh, I'm still goofy, don't worry." As if to prove her point, Alexis grabbed her chopsticks and plucked from his grasp the California roll that Jed had picked up for himself. She popped it into her mouth and gave him a look of smug satisfaction. Jed shook his head, fighting back a smile.

"Some things never change, I guess."

"You bet. Ahhmm." She swallowed the roll, cleared her throat, and began again. "Speaking of change. How are things between you and… Christie? That's her name, right?"

"Yeah," Jed answered flatly, filling his mouth with some pizza and chewing vigorously so his expressions wouldn't give him away. These days, just a mere mention of her was enough to sour his mood and remind him of what was dearly missing in his life.

"Right, Christie," Alexis mused. She let out a low chuckle. "One hell of a woman, honestly. Scared me that night. She has such delicate, entrancing features, like a renaissance painting, but when she gets angry it's like someone doused that painting in oil and set it on fire."

"Yeah," Jed muttered, taking another large bite of the pizza and stuffing his face to its utmost limit.

Alexis stopped talking and looked at him suspiciously. She could see what he was doing.

"Are you guys still, like, working together?" She asked hesitantly.

Jed nodded once.

"Oh, that's nice." Alexis looked relieved. "Do you meet as often as you used to? I remember you once had to run out midway during one of our meets because she had messaged you."

Jed's morsel had finished by then. He had nothing to hide behind.

"We… don't meet as often as we used to," he confessed, a heaviness in his chest that couldn't have been because of the few bites he had taken. "Things are more professional now."

"Oh, I'm sorry about that." Alexis tried and failed not to look upset. "Is it because of that… because of what happened with my phone?"

Jed cleared his throat. He suddenly wasn't hungry at all anymore. "That does seem to be one of the driving factors," he admitted.

"Oh, God." Alexis shook her head repeatedly. "I can't believe what a big disaster this has been. And I can't believe someone tapped my phone without me even knowing! How is that even possible unless you're some kind of a ninja—or a ghost, maybe?"

Ninja, I don't think so. But ghost is definitely one of his titles.

"You still haven't figured out where it could have happened?" Jed prodded. "Maybe there's a specific place or time in your life when your phone isn't with you? Maybe someone bugged it then?"

Alexis shook her head. "It's always with me," she stated with certainty. "I mean, sometimes I keep it out on the table or around me, but that's when I'm there, too. Otherwise, it stays in my hands or in my pocket. I'm a consultant, remember?" She pursed her lips together. "Most of my work is on my cell and laptop."

Jed nodded and leaned back, forcing away the frustration so it wouldn't spoil his dinner. This was another unsolved mystery, another puzzle their mysterious enemy had left for them to figure out. But they were proving hopelessly inept at it.

"Anyways," Alexis said quickly, diverting the topic to a less irritating one. "Forget that. I'm sure the police will figure it out. Tell me, how's your practice going?"

Jed hesitated, feeling the déjà vu wash over him. He was back in that same situation, where anything he spoke about carelessly might reveal a crucial aspect of the case.

"I'm currently taking a hiatus from work," he said. "Just need to refresh my mind a little, after recent events."

"Oh, makes sense," Alexis answered. "You deserve the rest after everything that happened."

"Yeah," Jed muttered, his mind flashing with an image of his shuttered office and the real reason he had decided to close it temporarily. He could not put any of his clients at risk of this psychopath.

Therapy kills.

They finished the rest of their dinner quickly, talking about everything and nothing but taking care not to let the conversation stray to a sensitive subject. There were so many of them, though, to watch out for. It seemed like life had turned into a cramped maze of cacti. It was necessary to tread very carefully to avoid being pricked by something sharp.

Once they were done, Jed escorted Alexis outside and bid her goodbye before heading for his Jeep. He got inside and turned the ignition, hearing the familiar roar of its awakened engine. The sound was comforting. He didn't have very many familiar things left in his life right now, after that radio silence from Christie and now the closure of his practice, so he was going to seek solace with what he had.

His foot was coming down on the accelerator when his phone vibrated in his pocket, tickling his left thigh in its usual manner. Jed stopped mid-motion and let the car idle in neutral, taking out the flashing device with one hand. It showed that he had just received a text.

From an unknown number.

Jed's pulse sped up. He cast a quick look around him. There were a few pedestrians standing on the sidewalk, but they were all with their families and none of them seemed to be watching him. To his diagonal left, a man was squatting on the curb, trying to wedge his hands through the grill of a sewer lid in order to retrieve something that must have fallen through it. Jed silently wished both that man and himself good luck, then opened his phone and checked the text.

It was a picture.

He nearly dropped the phone upon seeing it. His hands fumbled and caught it mid-fall. He righted the screen again, his heart pummeling the inside his chest with its frenzied beats, hoping that his eyes had been tricked by the light and he hadn't really seen the image that had just filled his vision.

But it was still there. The image in front of him remained unchanged, as if preserved for all time, and he stared back at it. The woman in that picture seemed to be staring right into Jed's soul, her mouth open in an eternally beseeching cry. It was a cry that he could not hear, of course, because this was a picture, not the real thing, and also because there was a white gag stuffed inside the woman's mouth, stifling her screams. Her pleas.

Jed stared. A strange heaving sound filled the car's interior, and he realized moments later that it was his breath whooshing out past his lips in sharp bursts. His hands ached from clenching the phone so tightly. He could feel his seatbelt digging into his abdomen, cutting off the blood flow to the rest of his body.

Gripped by a sudden and excruciating sense of claustrophobia, he opened the Jeep's doors and threw aside his seatbelt before stumbling outside. He put his hands against his knees and bent down, gasping for air. But it just wouldn't come in the amount he needed to steady his manic heart. The phone held in his hands wasn't helping either. Every time Jed's eyes drifted to that grotesque picture glaring from the screen, he winced and looked away, squeezing his eyes shut. It didn't help. That poor woman's frozen look of terror had been seared into his retinas. It would haunt him until the day he died, and maybe even after that, following him into the murky lands of purgatory.

For the next five minutes, he remained standing outside, refusing to look anywhere except at the ground. Once he had calmed down somewhat and gained his composure, Jed straightened up. He sucked in a large lungful of the frosty nighttime air, letting it cleanse his insides. He counted backwards from a hundred, noting his heart steadying itself as he reached zero. Once he had finished, once he was ready to face the world again, he got back inside his vehicle and looked again at the photo.

It had not changed in that tiny interval. The woman's terrified expressions had not lessened by any margin. She was still crying out for help, begging for mercy from an unseen captor or an uncaring God. Or both, maybe.

Pushing aside his emotions, Jed inspected the picture more closely. The woman was in some kind of room with nondescript walls and no windows, seated in a black armchair. A tiny light fixture directly overhead highlighted her anguish in dirty sulfur tones. The ropes binding her arms had once been white but were now smeared to a dull brown with dirt. The gag choking her mouth was equally shabby. There were no other details present, nothing more to see. Just that blank room and its single occupant, staring out at Jed to communicate something he could not figure out, no matter how hard he tried. He forced himself to stare long and hard into the woman's eyes, trying to discern the message she was soundlessly screaming his way. As he did, the hair on the back of his neck suddenly prickled with recognition.

He knew this woman. Christ in heaven, her face was familiar. It had taken him a while to figure it out because the gag and the contorted expressions had really thrown him off. But now that the shock was wearing off, he could see it more clearly. Something about those thin eyebrows and that slanted nose... that tint of brown in otherwise black hair. He had seen it before somewhere.

Oh. Oh, yes.

He remembered.

She was a client.

"Maria?" Jed whispered, as if the woman could hear him and he didn't want to upset her with a loud voice. "Maria Cordoba?"

It couldn't be. It simply couldn't be. Yet it was. Maria Cordoba, a 35-year-old banker suffering from the wounds her alcoholic monster of a father had gifted her adolescent self with before he died, had come to Jed's practice three years ago, seeking help. She'd been in a prestigious position in a finance firm, engaged to a loving man and with a strong circle of friends. Living a good life by anyone's standard. Yet deep within, Maria had been a tormented soul. Nightmares had been plaguing her, making her wake up in a cold sweat with a scream building up inside her. Her heart would begin to palpitate randomly during the day, for no reason at all. And worst of all, Maria had begun to find herself thinking more and more about consuming alcohol to drown her worries, just like her father had done.

Desperate to escape this cycle, she had arrived at Jed's practice one day, a confident, well-dressed young woman whose darting eyes and fidgety fingers revealed the true turmoil unfolding beneath her calm surface. Jed had worked with her extensively for over three months, slowly making her break free from the control her father was exerting over her from beyond his grave. It had been difficult work, but at the end, Maria had left a changed woman. Jed couldn't have been happier for her.

Now, here she was: his old client, one of his success stories, wearing a look so horrified it suggested her father had risen from the grave and must be standing before her, smiling with his tombstone teeth and rotten face.

"Maria," Jed croaked. The phone shook in his hands. Maria's face became mercifully blurry for a few seconds, as Jed fought to control his tremors. When he looked back at her again, no new information greeted him. No new insights.

The picture's purpose remained unknown, as mysterious as the room his old client was being held in.

Jed felt his own scream building in his throat. Why? Why Maria? What did it mean? And what was he supposed to do with this goddamned photograph, which gave no further instructions? Was it a threat? A mockery? Just a reminder that his title as the "Disaster Magnet' still very much applied to him?

In his mix of fury and grief, Jed's hand began shaking again. This time, he was unable to control it. One of his fingers accidentally swiped against the enlarged picture and minimized it, showing the rest of his phone's screen. That was when Jed saw it. Right beneath the picture, something he had never thought about in his charged-up state. It sat there even now, waiting for him.

A message.

CHAPTER 4

"Tell Larry to keep two backup units on standby," Christie spoke urgently into the phone. "We may need them later tonight. Yes, thank you."

They were in the conference room again, all of them, listening to her talk. Jed was on one end, and his former colleagues on the other. No one else was talking. Their eyes were fixed on the large screen in the room, which had been split into two halves, showing two separate images. The first half showed the picture of Maria Cordoba that Jed had set eyes upon earlier that night. Magnified by the screen's huge size, it appeared even grislier than before, as if Maria's predicament had worsened in the time it had taken Jed to contact Christie and rush to the station.

"Okay, police cars are on standby." Christie shut off the phone and took a deep breath. She turned to face the screen. "Jesus Christ, this guy is a nutcase. What is he trying to tell us through this?"

"He wants us to play the game." It was Jed who spoke. His voice was numb. "He wants us to play."

Graham cursed under his breath and stared at the screen. "Can anyone make sense of that message? Is it an instruction, a hint, or is this guy just plain crazy?"

They all gazed in silence at the other half of the bifurcated screen. It showed the message Jed had received along with the picture, a message that had surpassed its visual counterpart in inscrutability. All it said was this:

We hurt without moving.

We poison without touching.

We bear the truth and the lies.

We are not to be judged by our size.

(24 hours remaining)

"Anyone?" Christie offered, throwing up her hands. "Anyone have any guesses?"

"I think this is a riddle," Carter murmured, squinting at the screen. "I think we're supposed to... solve it? And the 24 hours written below... I think that's the time we have?"

Graham snorted. "What happens if we don't answer this stupid riddle on ti—" He came to an abrupt halt, as the answer occurred to him. It was there for everyone to see: Maria's terrified face pleading for help.

"This is madness," Derek whispered. "This is complete madness. What, leaving murders for us to solve wasn't enough for this guy? Now he's making us solve riddles while he holds a victim's life in the balance! As if this is some kind of sick game show? I wi—"

"Words," Jed broke in, interrupting him.

Christie looked at her former colleague and his pale visage. She fought the urge to go over to him and wrap her arms around him. Now was not the time.

"What did you say, Jed?" she asked softly.

Jed looked at her. His eyes were haunted. Christie felt a stab of grief at realizing how long it had been since she had last stared into them, since she had last felt herself drowning in their soulful depths.

"Words," Jed repeated quietly. "That's the answer to the riddle."

Christie jerked her head back toward the TV. Every pair of eyes in the room followed her.

"Hurt without moving," Derek muttered. "Poison without touching….Yeah, Jed's right."

"Not to be judged by our size," Graham grunted. "Great, we've solved the damn thing. Now what?"

They stared silently at the picture, as if expecting it to spring into motion or reveal some new detail now that they had unraveled the first mystery.

"Jed," Christie suggested. "I think we have to text the killer the answer of this riddle."

Jed moved upon hearing her words. His arm reached out robotically for his phone, which the police department had scanned for bugs before returning to him, and he typed in the message, then sent it. He put the phone back down and stared blankly at the table. Everyone in the room noticed. They took in the trancelike look in Jed's eyes and the terrible grayness of his skin.

God, I can't let him go on like this alone. Christie pushed aside all the vows she had made to herself over the past month and hurried toward her partner. She pulled out a chair and sat down next to him before clasping his hands in her own.

"Hey," she whispered, her face inches from his, her eyes trying to draw out his own. "Hey, it'll be okay, Jed. I promise. We will find this woman. At all costs."

Once more, Jed was broken out of his stupor by her voice. He looked up at her, and Christie found her heart shattering into a thousand pieces at the fragility marking him. It was as if, at any moment, at the slightest pressure, he would finally crack and splinter irreparably.

"Jed." She squeezed his hands even tighter and leaned even closer, aware that the others in the room who had been watching them had politely averted their gazes. "Listen to me. It'll be okay. We will find this woman. We will crack this madman's puzzles, no matter how many there are. Don't we always? Don't we always find a way through, despite how dismal things look?"

Jed forced a nod.

"Exactly,' Christie reminded him fervently. "So, we'll do it this time, too. I promise you."

Slowly, some of the color finally seemed to seep back into Jed's skin. His eyes lost their deadened sheen and began to regain that typical alertness which usually marked them. Jed looked around at the room, as if seeing it for the first time. Christie watched his jaw clench with determination and had to hold back a relieved smile.

Her partner was back.

Right at that moment, the phone rang, cutting her celebration short. It was as if their unseen foe was watching them from afar, waiting for Jed to return to normalcy so he could resume his sadistic game. The second round had begun.

For a few seconds, they all stared at it vibrating on the table, crying shrilly. The screen flashed with *Unknown Caller*, the same way Jed had received the message.

"Jed? You should probably answer that," Christie advised.

His arm shot forward, and he answered the call, putting the phone on speaker and placing it in the center of the table.

The whole room held its breath.

Silence.

More silence.

Finally, Jed spoke into the receiver. His voice was remarkably composed considering where they were and what was happening.

"Hello? This is Jed Gray."

No immediate response came, a moment more of that graveyard silence. And then:

"Good evening, Gray. And good evening officers. Especially you, detective Christie. An especially beautiful evening to you." The voice that emerged from the speakers was mechanical, like the masked, modified voice of a human that now resembled a robot's tone but still managed to retain enough of its owner's personality to sound unsettling. To sound mocking.

Jed cleared his throat. He leaned forward. "May I know who I'm speaking to?"

"Don't ask questions you already know the answer to, Gray. It's a waste of my time and a waste of your intelligence. I expect better from you, you know. I've always expected better. And you've always exceeded my expectations."

Jed took a moment to absorb that. He glanced up at the room and found everyone frozen in their places, not moving an inch, their eyes locked on him. Right beneath him, his caller waited for his response.

"Okay," Jed admitted. "How about this, then? I solved your riddle within the timeframe you gave me. So, why don't you let Maria go now? She has nothing to do with this. She's innocent."

What came next from the speakers was a series of bizarre crashing noises, as if giant metallic objects were being crumpled and thrown against one another. It took Jed a few moments to realize that what he was hearing was the voice's distorted, mechanized laughter. The sound chilled him to the bone.

"Innocent?" The voice sounded genuinely surprised. "Wasn't Alex innocent? And Joel? Ethan? And what about Sheila, that poor dancer? But did their innocence stop you from having these people killed? Of course not."

Jed gripped the wooden table with his other hand to steady himself, as if he wasn't inside a building but on the deck of a pitching boat. Christie's hand landed on his back and rubbed it in calming strokes.

"I didn't kill those people," he spoke through gritted teeth. "You did."

"Ah, Jed." Now, the voice had switched in tone to that of a disappointed schoolteacher. "You and I both know the truth. We know who's responsible. Yes, I may have pulled the trigger, in certain cases, but does that really mean the blame doesn't fall all on you? You and your terrible, sinful past? Look deep within yourself, and you will find that evil already resides there. I am merely the one sent to wipe it away."

Silence fell again while they waited for Jed to respond. He took his time, focusing on the warmth of Christie's palm on his neck to anchor himself to the real world and not get swept away by those tidal waves of memory the voice on the phone was unleashing.

"Why don't we cut to the chase?" He asked curtly. "You clearly hate me, and you want me dead. So, why not just make your final move instead of playing these childish games? You and me, face-to-face. No one else present. No outside interference. No police, no family members, no clients of mine, no hired assassins or gang members of yours, just me and you. Finishing this off like men. What do you say? Are you up for it? Or are you the kind of coward who likes to hurt women and hide in the shadows?"

Quiet again. Derek let out a soft hiss and covered his mouth with his fingers. Graham's face was so tense with alertness that his eyelashes trembled minutely. Even Jason appeared shaken.

"I haven't hurt her yet." The voice gave no indication of being offended at Jed's words. On the contrary, it had become even more robotic, even more soulless than before. "But whether that continues to be the case depends on how well you do in your next trial, Jed. I wish you the best of luck. The instructions will be coming to you soon."

"Why are you doing this?" Jed exclaimed. "What's the point? Why not just attack me directly?"

A pause.

"Because I like to watch you dance."

The line disconnected.

"Fucking hell," Carter whispered. He wiped a hand across his forehead, which was shining with perspiration despite the coolness of the room. "What now?"

"Now, we wait." Christie was still holding Jed's hand, letting him lean into her for support. "In the meantime, Graham, talk to Simon and set up call tracing equipment for the next time he calls. Someth—"

She was cut off by that familiar shrill ring, a sound that had now turned traumatizing for Jed. He looked down at his phone and found it blinking with a message. The instructions had arrived.

Jed opened the screen, with Christie peering intently over his shoulder, and read the text.

Once upon a time, there was a nasty young boy named Jed Gray. Jed Gray was so nasty that he liked doing nasty things all the time. As a result, one day his nasty acts got him caught, and Jed was sent to a place where all nasty boys were sent so they could be fixed. While he was stuck there, Jed often spoke to others about the first place he would visit when he got out. Time passed, and eventually nasty little Jed was allowed to leave. But by then, he had forgotten about that place he had spoken of to others and never visited it. But that place never forgot. It still stands today, waiting for nasty little Jed to visit it, like he had always vowed.

Will Jed make good on his promise?

Will he visit that place and turn his lie into a truth?

Before time runs out?

(24 hours)

"Jed," Christie began. "Do you reme—"

"Not yet," Jed answered angrily. "That's the point of this damn game. If it were that easy, he wouldn't have bothered playing it."

"Guys, what is it?" Derek, Joseph and Carter all spoke up at the same time. "What's happening? What message did Jed get?"

Jed slid his phone over to them. He rubbed a hand over his temples. "Okay," he breathed. "I just need to remember one specific thing I accidentally said years ago at a rehab clinic. If I don't, an innocent woman will die. No pressure."

"How can you even know which rehab clinic this text is talking about?" Christie demanded with frustration. "Didn't you go to two?"

"Yes, but it's talking about the first one," Jed answered. "I remember clearly where I went after my second rehab clinic. That was one promise I fulfilled. No, this has to do with the earlier one, the very first rehab of my life."

The others were reading and re-reading the text, their faces twisted into grimaces, as if the callous, awful words were physically hurting their eyes.

"This is clearly something that only Jed can answer," Graham stated, raising his face from the screen. He looked like he had aged several years in the last few minutes. "All we can do is wait and hope his memory works before the time runs out."

"Jed, what do you need?" Christie asked. "Tell me, and I'll arrange it for you."

"Just some rest," Jed replied. "There's no way I can remember anything in my current state. It's hard enough recalling what I had for dinner." He barked an empty laugh before rising from his chair. "I'm going to go to my apartment and get a good night's rest. Then, in the morning, I'll see what I can do with this clue. If anything turns up, I'll let you know."

"Do you want me to drop you?" Christie offered. "I can—it's not a problem. We'll have someone deliver your Jeep at your apartment later tonight."

Jed smiled faintly at her. "No, but thank you, Christie. I'll manage." He seemed about to say more, then realized that this was not the right time. "I'll see you tomorrow."

"Yeah, okay," Christie called out, watching him go. "Take care of yourself, Gray."

Jed nodded at her before turning and stepping out of the conference room.

CHAPTER 5

"*WHAT ABOUT YOU, JED?*"

The young Jed turns around at that voice. His brown hair is long and unruly, falling over his forehead. "What about me?" He asks Dalton, the man who has spoken.

Dalton smiles patiently at him, unbothered by his lack of attention. Surrounding them both, the small circle of men and women all watch Jed intently. Their oversized hospital-issued clothing flutters in the breeze, calling notice to their bony frames. Their skins are waxy, and their eyes have a broken glint to them, one that becomes clearer when they relax and let their guards down. But they have all survived this place. They are surviving, still.

"We were discussing the first place we would all like to visit when we leave here," Dalton explains again. "And I was asking you where you'd like to go."

Jed pauses and thinks. He scratches a needle-mark on his wrist while his mind combs through the many options, trying to pick one that appeals to him the most.

"Uh, I don't know," he says honestly. "I'll just go straight home from here."

A few people in the group chuckle, Dalton among them.

"We will all go home once we get out, Jed," Dalton states in a kind voice. *"But is there a specific place that you're really dying to visit? Like, for instance, Dahlia here just told us that she can't wait to go to the movies again. To just sit in a theater with a bunch of normal people, munching popcorn and watching a movie, doing the most normal shit ever. That's her dream."*

Dahlia smiles at that comment, a smile wide enough to reach her upper cheeks. She's about to be released in two weeks and has already begun searching the cinemas for a movie she wants to watch. It's begun to feel like the biggest event of her life to her. The excitement is palpable, coloring every waking moment—and her dreams, too.

"Come on, Jed," Dalton presses gently. *"Think of something and tell us. We're not moving on until you do."*

Young Jed thinks harder. Where is it he would like to go? It's hard to know, honestly. All he had in his life before rehab were trashy alleyways and dirty basements to get stoned in. Now that he's coming out a changed man—a supposedly changed man—he doesn't know what to do with his life anymore.

Then, it strikes him. A place. A place that's not a bad option to choose. It won't exactly be a lie, either, because he does kind of want to go there.

"Oh, I know!" Jed exclaims, his face lighting up. *"There's this place. It's a..."*

"Ugh, damn it!" Jed slammed a hand down on the coffee table, making the items on it rattle. "Damn, I was so close this time! So close!" He massaged the top of his skull with two fingers, trying to coax that elusive memory out.

Above him, the wall clock chimed, signaling the departure of another hour. It was now close to nine in the evening, and Jed had received the message with the clue at 10:23 PM last night. Which meant he had around an hour-and-a-half to go. An hour-and-a-half to find that memory and yank it out from his mind's archives. He had spent the whole day trying to do just that, mentally wrestling with himself in order to remember the promise he had made as a teen. But it was proving impossible to move beyond this point. Jed could remember his younger self reaching a decision about what place to mention, but he couldn't remember the place itself. His memory banks refused to give him access to that intel. No matter how much he tried, no matter how insistently he beat his mental fists against his mind's barrier, it did not yield. The memory continued to evade him.

On the table, his phone rang.

Jed's first reaction was a gut-clenching sense of dread. He looked down, expecting to see *Unknown Caller*, with that same awfully robotic voice waiting on the other end, ready to bombard him with its harsh metallic laughter and unsolvable clues.

But it was not an unknown caller.

It was Christie.

Jed picked it up in a flash.

'Hello, yes?"

"I'm coming to pick you up in ten," came Christie's prompt reply. "Get ready."

"Christie, I'm trying to rem—"

"I'm going to help you do just that," Christie interrupted. "Sitting at home and worrying yourself about not being able to remember will not help. Your mind will only become more resistant. You need a rest. You need to relax a little and be distracted from your problems."

"How do you plan on doing that?" Jed inquired.

He could feel Christie smiling on the other end. "Trust me, I can be quite the entertainer when I want to be."

She arrived 15 minutes later, shooting him a text to let him know she was waiting outside. Jed stepped out of his apartment dressed in jeans and a t-shirt, something he rarely wore when with Christie. But she had said to relax, and the idea of being encased in a formal clothes just felt too suffocating for him right now.

"Hello," Jed greeted her softly, sliding in the passenger seat. He noticed Christie taking in his casual slacks with a look that bordered on intrigue.

"Wow, I've never seen you dressed so…" Her voice trailed off.

"So casually?" Jed finished. "Well, you're the one who wanted me to relax, so here I am."

"Here you are," Christie agreed, looking him over one final time before returning her attention to the road. "Let's go."

"Where exactly are we going?" Jed asked, as the car began to move forward on the empty road.

"Oh, here and there," Christie answered mysteriously. "Stop worrying about it so much and just chill out. You're with me. I'll protect you if anything goes wrong."

There was a moment's pause before Jed spoke. "That's technically supposed to be my job, but since you're the officer here, I'll let you get away with that one."

"Let me get away with it?" Christie laughed. She turned the steering wheel to the left, and they entered the street flowing with people and vehicles. "What do you mean *let me*? Last I checked, I was the one who saved our asses when we went to inquire about that Alfonso guy at the tattoo shop."

"I was the one who got us out of Alfonso's apartment," Jed countered. "So, best-case scenario, the scores are even."

"No, not even," Christie retorted, grinning. "You wouldn't have made it out of Alfonso's apartment if I hadn't been with you, remember? I was the one who did the shooting and the breaking in."

"Oh, is that how we're playing it now, huh? Counting individual contributions?" Jed tsk-tsked. "Fine. In that case, may I remind you that we wouldn't have made many of our major breakthroughs in our last case had it not been for my deductions. I didn't want to bring this up, but you have forced my hand."

"Oh, yeah?" Christie shot back. Her eyes were shining with a fierce, playful light. "Well, then, may I remind you that all the important deductions you made on the case were because *we*, the police department, gave you special access to the evidence and information. Had it not been for the privileges we bestowed upon you, an ordinary citizen, you would have been in no position to make any breakthroughs. In the end, it all boils down to us."

Jed fell silent. The seconds stretched by, but he said nothing in response.

"What's the matter?" Christie chuckled. "Cat got your t—"

"Wait," Jed whispered. "Wait; I'm almost there."

Christie frowned and gave him a side-glance. Jed was sitting very still in his seat, his hands coiled into fists on his lap.

"Almost where?" she asked him, confused.

"The memory." Jed did not elaborate, as if he feared speaking too much would let his dawning discovery flee from his grasp.

Christie wisely held her tongue. She took an early left onto a street that was relatively more secluded, hoping the quiet would help Jed's memory. He still hadn't moved beside her, nor was he saying anything. To an outsider, Christie thought with amusement, they probably looked like a couple that had just had a fight.

But you need to be a couple first for that to happen, a voice inside Christie whispered. *Forget couple—you've even stopped being friends with him like you used to be.*

It's not my fault! Christie thought helplessly. *Jed made a huge mistake! He betrayed my trust! Telling that stupid Alexis he's so close to the details about our case! How could I not have pulled away?*

"I got it," Jed said. His voice was so simple and straightforward that Christie was initially thrown aback.

"What?" she asked, pushing her mind's annoying voice away. "What did you say?"

"I got it," Jed repeated with that same calmness that showed neither excitement nor fear. "I remember now."

Christie's mouth fell open. "Jed, that's great! What is it?"

"A graffiti street," he told her. "In East Harlem."

Without another word, Christie swung the steering wheel around and revved the engine. Suddenly, they were no longer coasting pleasantly down the road. Now, the Ford had turned into a crazed hellhound racing after its prey, blue lights flashing. Christie picked up her phone and dialed Graham's number.

"Hello, yes, Jed's remembered," she spoke into the receiver. "It's that graffiti place in East Harlem. Yes, we're going there right now." She closed the phone and checked her watch, which showed that it was 15 minutes past nine. There was still close to an hour before their time ran out. Jed had remembered in time, but *barely*.

"Why this place?" she asked abruptly, gunning the pedal and sticking to the empty streets. "I didn't know you were into graffiti."

Jed made a sound that was a mix between a sigh and a laugh. "I used to be, for a while, when I was young. A passing phase, you could call it. You know how edgy and artistic teenagers like to be."

"Uh-huh." Christie could imagine that, but she was having trouble imagining an edgy, artistic teenage Jed. That surely would be something interesting to see—how all that edginess got transformed into the composed, calm man sitting next to her, who always thought twice before sharing his emotions.

They reached their destination 15 minutes later, their sirens cutting harshly through the street's chatter as their car whizzed by the signal that was just about to turn red. Christie parked them on the sidewalk and looked out the window.

The street was teeming with people, both graffiti artists and regular folks just passing by. The graffiti itself was every-where, bright splashes of color and creativity that stood out it in stark contrast to the concrete jungle they had been sprayed onto. Christie could see that the art stretched along both sides of several city blocks. Abstract symbols, ingeniously decorat-ed slogans, caricatures of celebrities, religious paintings, it was all here. Every possible opinion or political stance or religious inclination or philosophy of life you could imagine, they had all been given visual expression in this place. This was the city's drawing board, and it was a chaotically beautiful one at that.

"Jed." She turned toward him. "We seem to have a problem. How are you going to find whatever you need to find here? This place is huge."

Jed grunted, peering past her at the street and its open display of artwork. "It's going to be right around East Harlem," he told her. "That's what I said in that rehab clinic, a lifetime ago. East Harlem. We'll find the answers there."

Christie looked around uncertainly. Even if it was just that neighborhood they had to inspect, it was still a heck of a challenge. The area was huge, and there was graffiti around it everywhere. How were they going to find what they needed in time? More importantly, what the hell were they even looking for?

"Hey." Jed's hand came down on hers, warm and firm. "Come on, let's go. It's going to be near the center. I can feel it."

They left the car together and started walking briskly toward the street, their eyes scanning their surroundings for something of interest. But either everything was of interest, or nothing was. Christie couldn't decide what to give her attention to. They went past a brick wall that had been spray-painted with an illustration of the pope smoking a joint rolled from one of the bible's pages. The pope's eyes were red and glazed, and there was a speech bubble hovering above his head, reading: *This book is fire!*

Christie tore her gaze away and went further, past drawings of political candidates depicted with crocodile teeth and doe eyes, past pithy quotes written in creative, flamboyant style, and past raunchy portraits of female celebrities wearing expressions no decent person would wear in public. She went past it all, her eyes continuously scanning the mad mélange of hues for something that was relevant to them. But nothing seemed to be there; or if there was, it had gotten lost in the chaos.

Two steps ahead of her, Jed strode forth with purpose, his eyes on the street and the walls surrounding it. He knew it was there, whatever it was he was expected to find. He could feel its presence getting stronger the closer he got, almost clouding the air like a pungent odor.

Then, he saw it.

Christie bumped into him from behind because of how abruptly he had come to a halt. Her shoulder struck his back, and she tore her gaze away from the graffiti.

"Jed, wha—" She stopped midway, as Jed simply pointed with his finger. Christie's eyes followed his directions, and she saw what had made him stop. Her heart did a tiny leap inside her chest.

There was a drawing on the brick wall, a drawing as expertly made as all the others, with an equal level of attention given to each detail. The color of the face and body was the perfect shade, an exactly balanced whitish-gray that conveyed utter lifelessness. The eyes were two beady drops of black ink that stared out from the sterile background.

It was a perfectly drawn mannequin, in every regard.

It was wearing a blonde wig.

Jed stared, and the more he stared, the uneasier he got. With every second that passed, he was struck more by the realization of who they were up against and how far his reach went. How obsessed he was with his little games.

"Jed," Christie whispered, nudging him in the ribs, "look at the stomach."

Jed did, and he saw that something had been written inside the painted mannequin's stomach. It was a meaningless string of numbers, digits, and symbols. He knew exactly what he was supposed to do with them, of course.

"I think we need to message that code to him," Christie suggested, but Jed was already on it, his phone in his hands. He typed in the code slowly, making sure no errors were made, and then sent it. His eyes went to the time, and he saw that they had forty-five minutes left.

The answer came back instantly, either set on an automated reply or sent by someone who must have been sitting with their phone in their hand, waiting. Jed looked down at the text. Christie came to him and stared down at it, too, her lips moving soundlessly as she read the words.

Congratulations! You have remembered correctly and acted in time! Your prize is this address:

Warehouse Castala, 2100 E 49th St.

P.S: I would hurry up if I were you. A certain woman is waiting for you there, and she's not in very good shape.

"That's on the other side of the city." Christie swore. "Shit, I—Jed, come with me fast." They began sprinting back to their car, feeling the seconds dripping by like blood leaking from their bodies. Christie's phone was against her ear. She spoke while she ran, her voice coming out in breathless pants.

"Graham, Warehouse Castala, 2100 E 49th St. Get there now." She hung up and resumed her run, catching up with Jed, who was already rounding the car and reaching for the passenger door.

They both got inside and Christie gunned the accelerator without even buckling her seatbelt. There was no time. There was just no time. The Ford's tires screeched and sent a plume of dust everywhere. A few of the pedestrians gave them a passing glance, shaking their heads in disappointment. Jed and Christie left the colorful street behind them and turned onto another road clogged with vehicles.

"Move! Move, goddammit!" The sirens on Christie's cars were blaring, allowing them to carve a path through the trickling river of steel. But there was only so much help they could offer. Eventually, once they had gotten further ahead, there was no space for the cars in front of them to move into. Christie could only press the brakes and grind her teeth and wait.

Time passed by. It was a miracle how fast it seemed to go when you didn't want it to and how infuriatingly slow it trudged by when you were impatient. Almost as if it harbored a personal grudge against humanity and didn't waste any opportunity to show its hate for the species.

They sat in the traffic and waited, the sirens muted for the time being, with their lights still flashing, not letting the cars around them forget that they were in a hurry. Christie turned toward Jed and found him sitting stoically, his hands hanging loose in his lap.

"You okay?" she asked out of habit because, sometimes, with Jed what you saw on the outside was not a good indicator of what was happening on the inside.

Jed turned toward her and smiled. "Yes. Why wouldn't I be?"

"Uh…" Christie couldn't help but glance at his watch.

"We'll make it on time." Jed read her thoughts, gazing out at the red signal with unending patience. "Trust me, we will."

Christie couldn't stop herself from asking. "How do you know?"

"Because I do." He fiddled absently with the dashboard handle. "The main problem was solving the riddle, which we did. We finished the first trial. The only thing I'm worrying about is what comes next."

"I was thinking," Christie began, "and I'm sure you've already thought of this, too. How did this man know that you'd chosen the graffiti street as the place you'd visit when you first got out? How could he have possibly known that, unless he was with you?"

"He was," Jed confirmed. "That much I already know. Out of the two rehab clinics I went to, he was there in one of them."

"No, I'm not just talking about him being in the same clinic as you." Christie shook her head. "He had to have been *with you* when you gave that answer about going there. He had to have been sitting in that same circle of people, possibly right next to you. Am I right?"

Jed nodded. "You are."

"Then," Christie exhaled sharply, "can you not remember his face? If you were able to remember what answer you gave that day, can't you recall the people that had been sitting around you? Their faces, at least, if not their names?"

"I do remember some of the faces, Christie," Jed told her. "It's kind of like a semi-blurry picture that pops up in my mind every time I think about it. Someone's sharp nose, someone else's colorful knitted sweater. But we can't piece together an identity from those disparate pieces. Anyways, as far as I can tell, there were at least eight or nine people in that group that day. Even if I can remember someone's face with perfect accuracy, the chances of him being our suspect are quite low."

"One-in-eight isn't that bad, considering where we are right now," Christie stated softly. "Also, even if you remember someone who doesn't turn out to be our suspect, it's still a big help. We can go and talk to them and ask them to remember that day in the clinic and who else had been with them. Maybe they knew our guy better than you did. Maybe they can even tell us his name."

Jed shifted in his seat, turning his attention to Christie. "You know, that's not such a bad idea," he said slowly. "It never occurred to me. Maybe someone else from that day knows what I don't and can help me out. Can help *us* out."

The signal finally turned green. Christie whipped up the volume for the sirens and made the cars before them part reluctantly, allowing them to speed through the gaps. They raced down the street with the engine roaring and the seconds quietly ticking away inside Christie's head. She tried not to focus on them, tried not to think about the time that was slipping through her fingers like sand. Instead, she clenched her hands on the steering wheel and pushed the Ford even harder, sticking to empty roads and streets as much as she could.

Only a few minutes were left when they finally arrived. The warehouse appeared before them, a rickety wooden structure squatting on an empty plot of land. There were no people around it, not even other police vehicles. Christie's mad driving had made them the first arrivals.

They were out of the car and rushing toward the building within 10 seconds, their clothes flapping in the nighttime wind which howled and moaned and urged them to run faster. Jed took in the warehouse's sorry condition: the moss clinging to its dislodged planks and the jagged bits of glass protruding from its windows like grinning teeth. He could see no lights on inside from here. The whole place looked and felt like it had been abandoned for decades.

Except that it was not.

Someone was inside.

He grabbed the doorknob and turned it, aware of the grease sticking to his palms. A draft of stale air struck him in the face as the door was flung open, revealing an interior riddled with shadows. Something hissed and fluttered in one of the top-right corners, and Jed heard leathery wings preparing themselves for flight. The next moment, he was ducking to the ground as the bats dashed out from over his head, screeching hatefully at the intruders which had invaded their home.

"Move."

Christie gently pushed past him and turned on her flashlight. She held her flashlight and her weapon in her outstretched arms as she surveyed the darkness inside the building. In an instant, the warehouse's threatening interior was turned into a graveyard of junk. Jed saw that everything was falling apart, even the floor. There were large holes in random places all over it where someone had pried the planks out.

But there were no more threats present, thankfully. He could see that now, under Christie's scouring light. She waved the light around, letting them take in the place and its layout. From here, they could see what was presumably a kitchen right in front of them and another segmented space to their right. Both were empty, save for the cobwebs decorating their ceilings. To their left, a small staircase spiraled upward into more darkness.

"I think we have to go up," Christie murmured, not looking pleased at all about it. Aiming her pistol and light toward the stairs, she walked cautiously in that direction. "Get behind me, Jed."

Jed dutifully obeyed. He looked down at his watch. It showed 10:18 PM. They had five minutes left. After that... what? What would happen?

Not keen on finding out, Christie hurried toward the staircase. The floorboards creaked and groaned beneath her feet, creating a terrible ruckus, expressing the warehouse's displeasure at being disturbed from its sleep. The staircase only added to that noise, and for a split-second, Jed heard a sharp crack and thought the wood beneath him had given away. But it held. For all its complaints, it held their weight, and then they were on the second floor, where a chair sat at the very end.

There was someone in it.

"Maria," Jed whispered, rushing forward, ignoring Christie's hiss behind him telling him to stay with her. He couldn't. Maria was here, and it was all his fault that she had been involved in this horrible nightmare. The least he could do was rescue her and apologize for the trauma she had—

Wait.

Something was wrong.

"Maria? Maria?" Jed whispered his client's name harshly, finding it strange upon his tongue after so many years. He was standing right in front of the woman, and his body blocked Christie's flashlight. In the accompanying darkness, Maria was little more than a lumpy outline. But Jed could still tell from that shape that her chin was resting on her chest. Her face was down-turned, and she wasn't responding to his voice. Not a bit.

He began fumbling in his pocket for his phone, to use its flashlight, but by that time Christie had arrived. She shone her flashlight unapologetically in Maria's face, and Jed finally saw his client from up close.

He cried out.

His body was already rearing back, his feet scrambling against the flimsy floorboards in order to create some distance between him and the sight in front of him. He couldn't believe it. He couldn't accept it. Yet it was true, as real as anything he had ever known.

Maria was dead.

CHAPTER 6

"JED! JED, CALM DOWN."

Christie's hands were on his chest, trying to soothe his heart back into its normal rhythm. Her voice was a reassuring murmur in his ear, telling him that it was okay, that it would be okay, that he would be okay.

But nothing was okay. Even once Jed had calmed down somewhat, he knew that and recognized it to be true now and forever. Nothing would ever be okay. Nothing.

"Christie, h—" His voice caught, and he refused to speak further. Instead, still holding Christie's hand, Jed took a hesitant step toward the woman in the chair, as if any quick movements would cause her corpse to erupt into movement. Christie followed beside him, and once they were close enough, she refocused her light onto Maria's face.

Maria was dead. As dead as one could get. Her eyes were glassy and vacant, staring off into nothing. Her lips were parted slightly, her mouth hanging open, but it was a bitterly futile posture to take because no air would ever enter her lungs again.

"Maria," Jed whispered, kneeling in front of his client and cupping her hands in his own. They were still warm but wouldn't be for much longer. The coldness of death would have its way soon enough, and her pale, soft flesh would turn brittle and gray before the sun rose in the sky.

"Maria. Oh, Maria." Jed felt tears prickling the edges of his eyes and blinked them back. He squeezed Maria's hands tighter and leaned against her, whispering into her body. "I'm sorry. I'm so, so sorry."

"Jed, it's not your fault. Stop saying that." Christie was hugging him from behind, her face buried in the crook of his shoulders. Jed could feel her tears wetting his shirt. She was actually crying, shaking softly against him.

They stayed that way for a while, Jed clinging to the dead woman and Christie clinging against him, wiping away her tears with one hand only for more to take their place. It was only when they heard the approaching sirens of other cars that they stood up and composed themselves. Jed still did not move from his place right next to Maria. He couldn't, not until the others had arrived. He didn't want to leave her alone.

Graham was the first through the door, the light from his flashlight arcing across the room, landing turn-by-turn on Jed, Christie, and their deceased companion.

"What in the hell...?" Graham came forward, his voice dying when he saw the dead woman. He looked at her for a few seconds, then stared at Jed and Christie in utter shock.

"What happened?" Graham asked them. "Did you not get here in time?"

Christie shook her head. Her eyes were still slightly red and swollen. "It didn't matter," she told her colleague in a thick voice. "She was already dead when we got here."

"Huh? B—but we had a deadline!" Graham sputtered. "What was the point of giving us one if he wasn't going to stick to it?"

Christie only shook her head again. She seemed incapable of saying anything more.

Derek and Carter came through the door next, trailed by Joseph and Jason. They saw the woman sitting lifelessly in her chair and let out twin noises of surprise, their flashlights waving wildly as they ran forward. A slew of unbelieving voices filled the night.

"What the...?"

"Ho—is she dead?"

"But you guys made it before time ended! Why?"

"So, this was all pointless, then. Motherf—"

"Do we know how she died?"

Jed stood numbly beside the woman and tuned all those voices out. He didn't care. He just didn't care anymore. All he had wanted was to save Maria, and he had failed. There was no point staying here now. This place was not going to give them any more information.

"Guys, I think there's something in her mouth," Derek said, peering closer to the body.

That caught Jed's attention, managed to pierce through the fog of grief he had enveloped himself in. He turned slightly to the right and saw Derek leaning over Maria, pointing with one finger at her parted lips. The rest all focused their flashlights in that direction, and Jed winced as Maria's face was washed in a scouring brightness.

This world won't let her rest even now, after taking her life, Jed thought.

But Derek was right. There was something, something barely visible through the gap in her lips, a sliver of white that the room's darkness had hidden completely and which Jed and Christie, in their shock, had failed to notice.

Carter slowly opened Maria's mouth. Jed wanted to look away. He didn't want to see his client suffer such indignities by officers who had failed to rescue her. But another part of him was helplessly transfixed, desperate to know what new clue their sadistic opponent had left behind. So, he watched with horrified, curious eyes.

As Carter pried open the dead woman's mouth, that sliver of white came fully into view, and they all saw it for what it was: a tiny square of paper that was resting snugly in the middle of Maria's tongue.

"Christ in heaven, save us all from evil," Carter murmured before reaching in with two gloved fingers and plucking the paper. It was slightly wet with saliva but otherwise untainted. The whole room watched Carter unfold it, their phones' beams trained down upon the scene like stadium floodlights.

Silence fell, interrupted only by the polite rustle of paper. Once Carter had fully opened it, he held it out for them to see, and they saw what was written on it. Just one word, in neat, cursive handwriting, the blue-ink slightly smudged. One word, nothing more and nothing less.

Oops.

Jed read the message for a second time and felt a strange sensation building up inside him. His body released the tension with a shiver that ran from the top of his head through the tip of his toes. He inadvertently emitted a low, growling sound.

They all looked silently at him, then back at the paper. They continued looking down at it, hoping that perhaps the combined intensity of their gazes would cause that message to change, would cause it to transform into something less monstrous or something that made sense.

Jed was no longer interested in standing there. He walked out, away from Maria, away from Christie and the others, out into the open. The wind was still howling, and the stars were chips of ice in the sky, glowing feverishly. In some of the nearby trees, owls hooted repeatedly, their calls answered by the chirping of crickets. Everything was as it was, as it should be. A woman was dead, but the world had already moved on. It stopped for no one.

Jed went to the parked Ford Explorer and stood there quietly. Waiting. Wondering. Planning.

He stayed there while the rest of the team continued to survey the scene and waited for forensics to arrive. A long while later, Christie came out looking for him.

"Jed?"

He heard her approaching footsteps and turned around. The shadows masked his face, hid his emotions beneath their inky capes. It was a good thing. He did not want Christie to see what he was going through.

"Jed." She stepped up to him and stopped. "The forensics team is almost here. Why are you stan—"

"I need to go," he interrupted softly. "I'm leaving, Christie."

She blinked at him in surprise. "Leaving? But the for—"

"The forensics team will find nothing," he finished with a small, sad smile. "Like they always find nothing. I think we both know that, don't we?"

She stood and stared at him, her eyes lined with moonlight. "But why are you leaving? Where are you even going?"

Jed shook his head. "I... I'm sorry, I can't tell you yet. All I can say is I need to do this next bit on my own. Things have gotten too far out of hand." He paused, seemed about to say something more, but just sighed instead. "I'm sorry. I'm sorry it all has to come to this. You take care of yourself, Christie." He turned left and saw a cruiser approaching them, its lights flashing.

"That one's for me, I think. I asked Derek to order me a car." Jed began walking away. He did not turn back. He couldn't.

He couldn't face her, or anyone else, after what had happened. He could barely face himself.

Christie watched him leave—a lone, burdened figure trudging through the night, shoulders bent beneath an invisible weight she could not see but could feel very well. If only she could relieve him of it. If only she could take some of the pain away.

But she didn't know how.

CHAPTER 7

CHRISTIE KNOCKED ON THE apartment door twice—two sharp raps to let the person inside know she meant business and wouldn't go away soon. Then, she waited, one hand on her holster and her body alert. Every few seconds, her eyes would quickly survey the street to see if anyone was secretly watching. It was crucial to make sure that she hadn't been followed here. Everything depended on it. Plus, this area was one of the nastier ones of the city, and lone women traveling at night were more prone to be victims of muggings. Especially if those women called attention to themselves by standing outside apartment doors and banging loudly.

But there was no other choice.

Once she was sure that the street was still mostly empty—at least for now—Christie swore under her breath and turned back to the door. It was a bent, corrugated sheet of iron with a tiny peephole in the middle. The walls around it were marked with lewd graffiti and tobacco stains. A perpetual smell of undisposed garbage hung in the air.

"Open up, for God's sake." Christie hammered the door with her fist again. It rattled and shook on its hinges, throwing flecks of rust onto the ground. The peephole stared silently at her. Was there someone on the other side, watching? Waiting for her to go?

"Well, I'm not going," Christie muttered. She fingered her holster for a moment, wondering if shooting the door's lock and barging in would be a good idea. No, it would not, she quickly decided. A gunshot here would call attention to her like honey calling flies. It was the worst thing she could do.

"Ope—" Christie's flattened palm had struck the door once again and was gearing up for its second hit when the door suddenly swung back, leaving her standing awkwardly with her arm in the air.

A man stood in front of her.

Christie took in his appearance. The stubble coating his sharp jaw and cheeks. The hair that hadn't been cut in weeks, which now hung over his forehead in tangled locks. Most noticeable of all, the dark circles beneath his eyes, which somehow stood out in contrast with the eyes themselves because they were bright and alert, their stormy grayness devoid of any exhaustion.

She had finally found him.

"Chri—what?" the man sputtered. "How did you find me?"

Christie smiled at him. "Hello, Jed. You look good."

Jed blinked at her words, confused, and then ran a hand over his stubble. His confusion only deepened further, as if he weren't sure how it had gotten on his face.

"What are you doing here?"

Christie's smile widened. "Can I come in?"

"Oh—" Jed remembered his manners. He turned sideways and gestured for her to enter. "Please, come in."

Christie walked into the apartment. It was small to the point of being claustrophobic, with a cramped living room and two tiny bedrooms and a kitchen. She cast a look around. A low whistle escaped her lips.

"Wow, now I know what you were up to in your month-long disappearance." The frontmost wall in the lounge was barely visible. Pictures and sticky notes and A-4 sheets covered every inch of it, and wherever some empty space had accidentally survived, it had been filled with writing from a red marker. Stacks of printed papers and old photographs piled high on the table. There were notebooks strewn on the coffee table, pages bleeding red with that same handwriting that marked the wall.

"Yeah, I've been doing a bit of work," Jed answered from behind, shutting the door and walking toward her.

Christie turned around to face him. There were two lightbulbs flickering inside the place, and their dim glow fell onto Jed's face. Such a strange sight for someone like Jed, who always kept himself clean and presentable. Christie had rarely ever seen him with more than a hint of stubble, and now he was sporting something that would soon turn into a beard if not dealt with. His hair had gotten longer, too, covering his ears and kissing the nape of his neck. No longer that neatly-combed style Christie had gotten so used to seeing every day, and which she sometimes focused on to calm herself—when Jed wasn't looking.

"Jed," she said to him, feeling her voice rising with each word that left her mouth, "where have you been?"

Jed grinned disarmingly at her. Even now, with his new, untamed look, the grin was charming, perhaps even more so than usual. He spread his hands apart. "Here."

Christie put her hands on her waist. Her eyebrows united in a frown. "But *why?* Why did you move out here into this dismal place, and why haven't you been answering anyone's calls for the past month?"

Jed's smile wavered. He looked toward the small window in the lounge, even though its blinds had been drawn.

"I didn't want him to track me." His voice was low, careful, as if he were discussing someone who could be magically summoned simply upon being mentioned.

"Jed, how would he track you?" Christie threw up her hands in exasperation. "I was the one calling you this past week, remember? Unless you think our guy managed to get my phone tapped as well, you should have picked up the call."

"Christie, we can't put anything past him anymore," Jed answered, and Christie saw the fierceness blazing in his eyes. Her gaze strayed to his balled fists hanging by his sides, and it was then she noticed something else about him that had changed. He had gotten more muscular. Quite a bit. It was hard to tell in the loose-sleeved Henley he was wearing, but when she put her attention to it, she could see the shape of his wide shoulders and bulging arms.

She swallowed.

"What have you been doing?" she asked, trying to keep her eyes on his face.

"Working. Trying to solve this case." Jed pointed at the wall. The half-heartedness of the gesture showed how much progress he had made. "Trying to find out something that'll let us get one step ahead of him, instead of it always being the other way around. I couldn't go to the cabin, in case he summoned me with another deadline."

Squinting, Christie stepped up to the wall. She could make no sense of the pictures and notes that had been pinned everywhere, popping out in a burst of incoherent colors. There were printed photos of different rehab centers, she noticed, as well as some old, faded polaroids of different people—Jed's friends from rehab?—with large red markings made next to them. Most of the markings were question marks. Large, blood-red question marks were slapped everywhere on the wall, next to every potential clue or lead, throwing it all into doubt. Because doubt was their one and only constant in this whole case. Even now, after everything that had transpired, after every death they had witnessed, they did not even know what their enemy looked like.

"Have you made any progress?" Christie was unable to stop herself from asking, despite already knowing the answer.

Jed sighed from behind. She felt him step up to her, until he was right behind her. "Not yet," he answered. "Not yet. But… I'm getting there."

Christie tore her eyes away from that sprawling junkyard of investigative material and turned yet again to face her partner. They were standing right opposite one another now, and she had to tilt her head up slightly to look at him. His presence was imposing from up close, especially in his current state. The gray of his eyes seemed to have turned darker, stormier, from being cooped up in this place all month.

"You haven't been going to your office either," Christie whispered, fighting not to avert her gaze. "I came in to check on you four days ago."

Jed nodded once. "I've closed it up," he told her and suddenly glanced down at the floor—but not before Christie saw a flash of pain brighten the darkness of his pupils. "Since a therapist's job is to help heal his clients, and I seem to be getting mine killed, I thought it would be appropriate to take an early retirement."

"Oh, Jed." She stepped closer to him, so close that if she leaned in any further, she would be able to hear his heart beating against her own. "This is all about Maria, isn't it? I know you're blaming yourself for her death."

Jed laughed. It was a laugh much like the apartment he was staying in: drab and gloomy.

"Shouldn't I blame myself?" he asked Christie, giving her a thin smile. "And what about Ethan? Is there anyone else who's responsible for this madness?"

"How about that psychopath we're both trying to catch?" She raised a hand and placed it on his arm. A momentary surprise seized her. Yes, Jed *had* changed. She had been expecting to feel that familiar hardness which always characterized him from the outside, and she had felt that. But far more than normal. Far more than she was used to. Jed had always been a muscular man, but he seemed to be taking that definition to a different level.

"Have you been working out?" Christie blurted, unable to stop herself.

Jed appeared caught off-guard by that sudden shift in topic. But then, his eyes drifted down to her hand lightly touching his arm, and he smiled again. This time, the smile had a bit more life to it.

"Yes," he told her, absently touching his abdomen. "I... I—uh decided that since I might have to go after this man alone, I'm going to need all the strength I can get. I can't always be relying on you to bail me out of fights, you know?" He chuckled. "So, I've been working out whenever I wasn't pursuing the case. I've upped the intensity, too. At least three-fold. It's going well. A few more weeks, and I wager that I'll be able to kick Jason's butt the next time he makes one of his snarky comments."

Christie laughed. She couldn't help herself. Her hand tightened a fraction on Jed's arm, and she felt the smooth ridges of his triceps flexing beneath her fingers. A sudden thrill shot through her body, one that made her heartbeat flutter up to her throat for a second. She swallowed and quickly withdrew her arm, aware of how close they were standing in a random apartment in the middle of nowhere, with no one watching.

But then, she realized what he had just said.

Jed was watching Christie's flustered expression with some amusement when he saw all that nervousness suddenly turn into anger. It happened so fast he didn't even have time to marvel at it, because the anger was directed at him.

"What did you just say?" Christie asked slowly, narrowing her eyes at him. Her hands went to her waist, and Jed knew he was in trouble. He just didn't know why.

"I—what do you mean?" he asked, raising his arms in a plea of innocence. "Say what?"

"Just now." Christie let out a huff of breath. "What did you say just now?"

"That… I would kick Jason's butt?" Jed frowned. "Are you angry about that? I'm sorry. I know he's your colleague and all, but I was only j—"

"No, not that," Christie interrupted. She rolled her eyes. "You kicking Jason's ass would be a sight the whole police department would pay to watch. But I'm talking about what you said before that."

Now, Jed was really mystified. He opened his mouth but could not think of anything to say. "Christie, I—"

"*Since I might have to go after this man alone*," Christie finished, her voice filled with ice. "That's what you said." She poked him in the chest with a ramrod straight finger. "How dare you, Jed Gray?"

"How dare I what?" Jed answered, taking a step back.

"How dare you think you're in this mess alone!" Christie came toward him with her finger still stretched out, pointing right at his heart. "After everything we've been through together, how dare you decide to finish off the rest of this story alone!" She poked his chest again, with even more force. "You have no right! No right to cut me off like that!"

Silence fell in the wake of Christie's short tirade. It remained for a long while, politely waiting for Jed to break it. In the end, though, he could only manage a whisper that further strengthened the quiet, turning it uncomfortable.

"I'm not the one who cut you off."

The words were spoken softly, in a matter-of-fact way. They slipped from Jed's mouth and cluttered the floor between him and his partner, acting as an obstacle, not allowing them to properly meet. Christie looked at him hard and long, with unblinking eyes. When she finally spoke, her voice matched Jed's. It was a tiny murmur, fluttering past her lips, out into the open, where everyone could see it.

"I had my reasons for doing what I did. You know that."

Jed nodded. He looked tired now, no longer interested in arguing further. "I do, and there's no blame on you for what you did. But I still have to catch this man, Christie."

"*We* still have to catch him," she corrected him, walking forward, stepping over the invisible obstacles that lay between her and her partner. She brushed his loosely hanging hand with her own, fighting the urge to twine her fingers around his. "I propose a deal."

Jed looked down at her. "I'm listening."

Christie took in a breath. "Until this whole case is over, we put the past behind us. Whatever happened, happened. We can't afford to be tiptoeing around each other right now. We can't afford to not have complete trust between us. Our bond was one of our greatest strengths when dealing with this man. It is the only thing that has allowed us to get this far. We can't just throw it away now, when we're in the final round. We need each other more than ever."

Jed studied her face before nodding slowly. "I agree. Working here all alone hasn't been easy. I've become so used to bouncing my ideas off you that when you're not around, it's like part of my thinking abilities are missing."

"Exactly," Christie answered quickly. "Which is why we need to be back on the same page until this is over. No more sneaking around behind the other person's back. No more keeping secrets. Understood?"

"Yeah." Jed gave her a faint half-smile. "Understood, Detective."

Christie returned his smile with a fuller one of her own. "I'm glad I was able to get my point across, Gray. Now, fill me in: where are we on the investigation?"

"Well," Jed sighed. He ran a hand through his hair, combing his locks back, and Christie marveled at their length. It was a strange look for Jed, but it was also... appealing. In its own peculiar way.

"Come, sit," he said, pointing to the sofa near the wall where he had done his brainstorming. "Unfortunately, despite all the work, I haven't made any progress. Our suspect remains as elusive as ever."

Christie took her seat on a ratty sofa in one of the corners. There were bits of trash poking out from underneath the armrests, and a musty smell lingered around the whole thing. Part of the fabric had been torn out from the sides, and the sofa's innards were spilling out.

"Do you want some lemonade?" Jed offered. "Or something to eat, maybe? I have a shawarma in the fridge. I can heat it up for you if you want."

Christie shook her head. This place wasn't exactly doing wonders for her appetite.

"Remind me again how long you're going to stay here for?" she asked him.

Jed shrugged. "As long as it takes. Until the case is over."

"Right." Christie uncrossed her legs. She heard the sofa's springs squealing beneath her weight, threatening to give in. "Um, Jed, I have to ask: is this really necessary?"

As soon as the question had left her mouth, Christie regretted it. She saw Jed's face darken. She saw whatever little playfulness that had been visible there all this while get snuffed out in an instant. His jaw tensed, his lips straightened, and his eyes narrowed into slits.

"She died, Christie," Jed stated softly. "She died because of me. Maria died *because of me.* And don't tell me it's not my fault because we both know it technically is. Maria was my patient. The only reason she's not alive is because we failed to catch the killer before, and that is also on me. I slipped up when speaking to Alexis. I let the killer in on our plan. The result? He took advantage of it and murdered an innocent woman."

"Jed…" Christie began.

Jed shook his head vehemently. "No, don't do that. Don't use your soft eyes and soft voice to lift the blame from my shoulders. It belongs there, Christie. I deserve that blame. I'm going to make damn sure it doesn't happen again." He paused and swallowed, regaining some control over his unfurling emotions. "So, yes. This is necessary. I can't let the killer hurt someone else through me. I have to cut off all ties from my previous life. That includes leaving my practice and my apartment. It also includes sending my mom somewhere she's safe and secure, which I also did before coming here, by the way."

"You sent her away?" Christie asked. "Where?"

84

Jed shook his head and grinned. "Even I don't know. That's the thing. There is no way the killer can access anyone's whereabouts through me. I don't even speak with her on the phone, in case someone's tapped the call." He came forward, his eyes shining with enough excitement to dispel some of the darkness marring his features. "Don't you see, Christie? Don't you see what I've done? I've leveled the playing field!"

"Leveled the playing field... how?" Christie asked. "By staying in this terrible place and abandoning your life?"

Jed shook his head. His grin widened. The stubble on his face seemed to bristle in anticipation. "No. By *becoming a ghost*, Christie. That's how. I am now to my enemy exactly what my enemy is to me. No one. Nowhere." He bit his lower lip and nodded, turning thoughtful. "I'm sure what I've done has thrown him off-guard. He's probably trying to dig me up even now, wondering where I've disappeared off to. But he can't dig me up because the—"

"There's no one in your life you're meeting," Christie finished for him. "There's no one you're meeting and no one who knows your whereabouts."

Jed sucked in a sharp breath. Emotions warred across his features, a strange mix of worry and relief struggling for dominance. "No one but you, Detective. I must admit, I have conflicted feelings about you being here, but now that you are, I'm trusting you'll keep my secret. We're going to need it if we want to win this fight."

Christie nodded. Suddenly, this dismal apartment in the middle of nowhere wasn't looking quite so unappealing anymore. Hidden within its shabby appearance was a big advantage she hadn't noticed before. All that grime encrusting the sofa, the cigarette burn marks on the carpet's edge, the flecks of ugly brown paint splotching the celling, and the urine-yellow light, they were all offering something vital. Something Jed had spotted and taken instantly.

Anonymity.

They were off the radar here. No one could keep tabs on them and predict their next move. Since the very start, when Joel was murdered, their enemy had been a shark in an ink-black ocean, rearing his head when no one was expecting it and disappearing back into the water's lightless depths after making his move. No matter what they did, they were never able to catch even a whiff of him. The ocean of anonymity was too large, too riddled with shadows to search properly.

Except now. Now Jed had done the very same thing. He had plunged into that same ocean, too, right within its hidden heart. Yes, they still had no idea where their enemy was.

But he didn't know where Jed was now either.

"You're going after him," Christie realized aloud. She glanced up at Jed, who was standing before her with his untamed hair, looking like a hunter so obsessed with catching his quarry that he had started living in the jungle to accomplish his goal.

"You're going to catch him," Christie repeated. She stood up, unable to keep herself calm. "You're no longer going to just solve his riddles, are you? No, you're digging him up, searching for a hidden trail that'll lead you to his identity. The moment you find it, he's finished."

"He's finished," Jed whispered in agreement. He rubbed his beard eagerly, a man awaiting a meal that he knows will be served to him soon, no matter what. "I know that my disappearance already has him on edge. He wasn't expecting this. He's used to being in control, to knowing exactly what the opponent will do and then acting accordingly. But now I've messed everything up by moving here. He's going to act rashly. He's going to slip-up. I know it. I can *feel* it."

"Did he contact you on your phone?" Christie asked. "After that day?"

Jed nodded. His eyes lit up with a savage glint. "Yes, he did, as a matter of fact. Here, take a look." He fished out his phone from his pocket and opened the message before handing it over to Christie.

"When?" she asked as she stood and read the message.

My dear partner in crime, my trusted confabulator, where have you disappeared? My heart bemoans your absence. My bones groan with your vanishing. The world feels hollow and cold with you no longer visible in it.

Don't tell me you've taken Maria's departure too strongly. I have to admit, I do feel rather bad about it. I know I should've left her alive for you, considering that you solved the riddle. But what can

I say, my dear friend? I have a bit of a goofy bone in my body. I like to cheat sometimes, when I'm having too much fun.

Sorry. Sorry. My bad. It won't happen again. I promise. (Cross my heart and hope to die, that sort of thing ha ha.). Now, I'm going to need you to return back to the playing field, beloved friend. More riddles await you. More glorious fun awaits us both! Exactly two days from now at midnight, I will be sending you your next challenge. It is going to be much tougher than the first one, let me warn you. But I know that you will solve it. You always do. That's why I like playing with you so much.

Best wishes,

Your friend from the past

XOXO :)

"Something's different," Christie muttered. "His text… he sounds more unhinged than usual."

"Correct," Jed told her. "His texts are usually short and cryptic. He saves the lunacy for when he's actually speaking with me on the phone. But now he's broken his pattern."

"Because you're no longer available like you used to be," Christie stated in understanding, her eyes wide. "He doesn't know what to do with your disappearance, so he's unloading his madness onto the text!"

"If he keeps doing this," Jed said grimly, "if we keep yanking his chain and drawing him out, sooner or later, he'll say or do something that'll be a huge blunder."

"A blunder we'll take advantage of to find out who he is!" Christie exclaimed. Her hands were raised by her sides, coiled into fists. "We might just catch this monster after all!"

"We will catch this monster," Jed corrected her firmly. "He will pay for what he did to Maria. I won't rest until he does."

Christie looked back at the message again. "When did you get this?" she asked Jed, frowning at the screen. "He said he would message you two days later. How much time do we have?"

Jed looked at his watch. "Around two hours."

Christie's jaw fell open. "You got this message two days ago?" she nearly shouted, eyes flashing with that same indignant fire. "Jed, why didn't you tell me? Why would you keep something like this to yourself?"

"Christie, we've already talked about this. I can't afford to let anyone else get hurt because of me." Unable to help himself, Jed felt his eyes straying to Christie's hair. Despite the low-grade lighting in the room, it had still managed to retain its golden sheen and was as lustrous as ever. "Don't forget, the killer's first direct message to me was about *you*. Those mannequins with the blonde wigs? They were a direct threat to you, Christie."

Christie sniffed. "His threats don't scare me one bit. I know how to take care of myself."

"I know that you do." Jed stepped closer to her. "But still, if you were put in danger because of me, if something were to happen to you…." The thought was so awful he couldn't even complete it. Christie saw the anguished look on his face and squeezed his hand in reassurance. Jed felt a sudden urge to pull her forward into his embrace. He was getting tired of these casual hand-squeezes and shoulder-taps and side-hugs. It was frustrating, to be constantly skirting the edges of what his heart really wanted without ever moving further. How much longer would this game of pretend last? How much longer could they act like they were just friends and nothing more, partners and nothing more, colleagues and nothing more?

"Jed." Christie seemed to sense his thoughts, for she squeezed his hand harder and stepped closer to him. Jed felt her thumb rotating soothingly over his skin, driving away his worries. It was a miracle how good she was at doing that.

"You need to stop worrying about me and start worrying about yourself," Christie murmured. "I promise you, I will be fine. Nothing will happen to me. At least, not until…"

When she didn't finish her sentence, Jed looked up at her quizzically. "Until?" he inquired.

Christie's eyelids fluttered nervously. She swallowed. "Until we've had that conversation we were supposed to."

Oh.

Jed had always taken a certain measure of pride in his quick wit and clever tongue, but in that moment both those talents deserted him. He could think of nothing sensible to say. Christie saw that she had whacked him speechless with her words and laughed.

"Wow. The great Jed Gray, master therapist and analyzer of human behavior, clever craftsman of words, left speechless by something I said?" She clucked her tongue chidingly.

Jed did not add to the joke. He didn't feel like it in that moment. They were finally discussing something serious for once, something which had been on their to-do list for a long, long time. He didn't want to sidetrack them again with humor.

"Did you mean what you just said?" he asked Christie.

Christie's smile straightened. The playful light in her eyes winked out. Her grip slackened on Jed's hand, but she did not let go.

"Yes. I mean it." She nodded once, in that same brisk style she used when speaking to someone in her office. "It's time we had that conversation."

"Hmmm." Now that the shock had passed, Jed felt brave—much braver than he had felt in a while with Christie. "How about we have that conversation now, then? Why waste more time?"

Christie laughed and shook her head violently. Her tawny locks swung in the air like frozen sunbeams.

"I'm not discussing our future in this slum," she told him, chuckling. "Absolutely not."

Jed arched an eyebrow. "*Our* future? Wow, you sure do move fast lady. Three weeks ago, we weren't even on proper speaking terms. Now look at us."

A tinge of red began to spread across Christie's cheeks. She felt a spurt of giggles rising within her, triggered by the kind of conversation they were having and the odds at which it stood with their current situation and location.

"Facing bloodthirsty criminals for a living makes you appreciate the time you have," she answered with a smile. "I've realized that I can't keep putting things on delay indefinitely. There will always be another killer to apprehend, another threat lurking around the corner. It's part of my job. But my job is only a part of my life, and I can't neglect the latter."

"Spoken like the wise soul you are," Jed grunted. He glanced again at the clock. "So, we have a few hours until that crazy son of a bitch contacts us again. Since you're not in the mood for any big talks, what else do you fancy doing?"

Christie looked at him sheepishly. "I had an idea, but I don't know if it'll keep our cover or not. I mean, the whole point of you staying here is to lay low, right? Not to be found out."

Jed waved a hand. "New York is a big city, Christie. I'm not trapped indoors. I can go out if I need to. Tell me, what do you want?"

She smiled uncertainly. "Can we get some food?"

Jed felt his own smile creeping back up. "Oh, I thought you'd never ask."

CHAPTER 8

THE PHONE PINGED.

At the center of the coffee table, its screen flashed with color—a single incoming text. Then, it went silent again, turning as black and dead as it had been a moment before.

Jed looked at Christie. She was sitting on the opposite end of the sofa, her hands laced together, her hair tied back. Together, both of them turned to face the clock. They saw its hands standing erect in the same spot, like lovers huddled together.

Midnight.

It was time.

"Pick it up, Jed," Christie spoke softly. She was looking at the phone with a mixture of curiosity and apprehension. Her legs were coiled, ready to spring into action against a threat neither of them could see but knew had finally made its move.

Jed leaned forward and picked up the phone. It felt oddly heavy in his hands, as if burdened by the text it had just received. He swiped a thumb against the screen to unlock it and saw what he had received.

"Is it him?" Christie asked before jumping to her feet without waiting for Jed's answer. Because Jed's frighteningly white face was answer enough. There weren't a lot of people in the world who could have that effect on him.

Jed felt Christie sit down next to him. He felt the comforting warmth of her body pressing into his. He felt her soothing presence trying to calm his mad heart, but it was a fruitless endeavor. Their enemy had struck again, and like always, he knew just the thing to get under Jed's skin and destroy all his composure.

There was another photo.

This time he recognized her instantly because he knew what to look for. Lauren Harding. That was her name. Or at least, it was the name she had given to him when she had first knocked upon his office door over a year ago. Lauren Harding, the pretty redhead. Lauren Harding, the goofy young girl. Most importantly, Lauren Harding, the 23-year-old tech-genius who had created a financial management app that had hit 10 million downloads in six months. She had gone from working as a barista at Starbucks to sipping cocktails in Greece and all the expensive resorts of the world. She had gone from saving up for new sneakers to buying her dad a Mercedes-Benz.

Now, she was here.

Jed could not bring himself to look at the picture. Seeing Maria had been bad enough, but Lauren… Lauren had been a kid when she first came to see Jed. Full of silly jokes and nervous tics. Like a younger sister, if he'd had one.

"Jed?"

Christie's gentle voice snapped Jed out of his haze of anxiety and grief. He looked toward her, if only because it would keep his eyes away from that horrible picture.

"Do you recognize that girl in the photo, Jed?" Christie asked him.

Jed nodded. He couldn't bring himself to speak just yet. His teeth would chatter in his mouth if he loosened it.

"Okay. Okay. There's some kind of a riddle posted beneath that photo. Ca—"

The riddle! Oh yes!

Jed had completely forgotten about that. His head whipped back to the front, back to that awful photo. This time, he was unable to stop his eyes from taking in Lauren's silently pleading image. It was identical in style to the previous photograph. There was a gag in her mouth, she was in that same blank room, and her eyes were open just like Maria's had been. But whereas Maria's eyes had been pleading for help, Lauren's seemed to be burning with accusation.

Are you going to let me die, too? They seemed to ask. *Just like you did with Maria? Is this the kind of therapist you are, taking lives instead of saving them?*

"Jed? Jed?" Christie nudged him in the side, and Jed broke out of his reverie once more. He swallowed and touched a hand to his forehead. It was feverish and slick with sweat.

"Sorry," he muttered. "The riddle, yes."

It was a shorter one than before, only four lines. Jed read each one of them slowly, trying not to let his attention stray to the furious girl staring out at him from his phone's screen.

The maker sells me.

The buyer doesn't use me.

The user doesn't know he's using me.

What am I?

"The user doesn't know he's using me..." Christie murmured thoughtfully. "What kin—"

"A coffin," Jed uttered tiredly. His hands were aching from holding the phone. It was too heavy, far too heavy for him to carry. He just couldn't do it. "It's a coffin."

"Wait, yeah, you're right!" Christie exclaimed. "Wow! That was fast, Jed! Type in the answer and throw it back in his face!"

Jed did. His fingers move lethargically over the screen. He typed in the answer and sent it, then laid his phone back on the table. Christie watched him sag back against the sofa, covering his face with his hands.

"How in the goddamn hell did he get to Lauren?" Jed cursed harshly. "My clients! They're all my past clients! How is he accessing their information? It's not available anywhere except for my laptop!"

"Your laptop?" Christie frowned. "Where is it? Did you lose it?"

"No, it's with me," Jed said. "I had it scanned ages ago for any sort of bugging or spyware. Nothing. Nada." He shook his head in disbelief. "Whoever this guy is, he began drawing up his plans against me a long time ago. He didn't need to burrow into my laptop's personal files. He already knew who he was going after."

Silence hung in the room after that dark revelation. When Christie spoke again, her voice was soft. "Is Lauren the name of the girl in the photo?"

"Yes," Jed said through gritted teeth. He punched the sofa's armrest in fury, relishing the pain which shot through his knuckles as they connected with the toughened slab. "I can't protect them. I can't protect any of them. He's picking them off one-by-one like a sniper, and there's nothing I can do about it."

Christie bit her lower lip. Seeing Jed like this, so utterly helpless, killed her from the inside. But there was nothing she could do. What could anyone do right now?

"Maybe we could station some patrol cars outside your clients' homes," Christie suggested weakly, wringing her hands. "Maybe I can talk with the police department to offer them some kind of protection?"

Jed laughed. It was a high, bitter sound. "I've had dozens upon dozens upon dozens of clients in the last few years, Christie. Are you going to protect all of them? No police department in the world has that kind of manpower. No, there's only one way we can save them. That's by find—"

The phone rang, cutting him off. Its shrill beeps rose into the air and filled the apartment's empty spaces. Jed looked down at it and saw that familiar unknown number flashing on the screen. After taking a second to compose himself, he reached forward and answered the call on speaker.

"Hello?"

A pause.

"Do you think you can escape the past?" The robotic voice crackled through the speakers. It was loud and deep, as if being amplified through a megaphone. *"Do you think running away and hiding in a hole in the ground will make your troubles go away? You think it will stop more people from dying? Most importantly, do you think it will remove the blame from your shoulders?"*

Nerve-wracked, Christie looked at Jed, expecting him to be boiling with fury at the caller's statements. But she saw only calm on his face. Calm and a glint of... was that satisfaction?

Jed cleared his throat softly. He brought the phone closer to himself.

"I am only giving you a taste of your own medicine," he answered in the gentlest of voices. "What's the matter? Do you not like it?"

More silence.

Then they heard those same harsh crashing noises, the sound of metal being crumpled and tortured in imaginative ways. It was their caller's mechanized, disguised laughter, they knew. The eerie cackle of a cyborg from beyond the grave.

"Oh, my dear friend, I liked it very much. It was a brilliant move on your part." The voice paused for a moment before speaking again. *"But now it's time to put the games aside and get to the real fun. I want you back in your regular apartment, working your regular job. I want you back in your old life, with your friends in the police running over to you with every little problem like the incompetent fools they are."* Another brief, metallic chuckle. *"I want this to happen 12 hours from now, before noon tomorrow."*

In the silence that followed, Christie looked at Jed. Jed looked back at her. A silent exchange seemed to pass between them. Jed leaned over the phone and answered in a low, flat voice.

"What if I don't?"

There was a pause that seemed to stretch forever, a deathly silence preceding the announcement of a terrible verdict. When the voice spoke again, it was no longer as loud as it had been before. Instead of a host of cyber-spirits hissing through the speakerphone, now there was just one. One ghost left. The enemy.

"If you fail to comply with the regulations, you shall be immediately disqualified from your second challenge without further notice. Furthermore, the decapitated body of your old client shall be mailed to your residence. Is that what you would like?"

Aghast, Christie let out a pent-up breath. She placed a hand over her mouth. So, it was over. Jed's brief cover had been blown apart, just like that. Now they were ba—

"Go ahead."

Jed spoke the words with that same gentleness into the speakerphone. Christie looked at him in shock and found her shock deepening when she saw not a hint of fear or worry marking his face. He was perfectly calm. Perfectly composed. In control.

More hissing. More squealing, crashing sounds. More ghostly laughter that you could only expect to find echoing in a metal junkyard. Except that this time it was *too* high. Going on for *too* long. Almost as if it were being forced.

"Are you sure, Jed Gray? I would hate to squeeze the life out of this pretty redhead, but if you insist, that is what I will do. Tell me again: was that your request?"

Jed answered again instantly, without any hesitation.

"Yes. Go ahead."

More silence. A confused, uncertain one, where Jed was the only one out of the three participants who seemed entirely devoid of any confusion. He sat over the silent phone looking down at it, waiting for the voice to answer. But the pause continued to stretch on, as if the robotic voice had no answer to Jed's request. Eventually, it was Jed who spoke again.

"Now that you've been shown your place, and where exactly you stand, let me clarify the rules of the game for you a bit." He placed a coiled hand on the table. "*You* are the one who wants me, not the other way around. *You* are the one whose entire life revolves around me, not the other way around. *You* are the one who'll be left without a purpose if I suddenly disappear, not me. So, take this as my first and last warning. If you hurt any of my old clients again, if I find that you've harmed even a hair on Lauren's head, you know what I'll do?"

Jed leaned forward further. Unknowingly, Christie leaned forward, too, spellbound. She had no idea what he was going to say. She had no idea what plan her partner had suddenly hatched inside his mind.

"I'll disappear," Jed hissed. "I'll vanish from the face of the Earth, changing even my phone and contact details, leaving you entirely alone. Then, you can spend the rest of your life searching for me, obsessing about me, hating me. But it'll be to no avail, because you'll never see me again. You'll never find me. That will be my revenge on you, to truly become the ghost in your life, like you pretend to be in mine. So, I tell you again, for the very last time: Do. Not. Touch. A. Hair. On. Lauren's. Head."

Christie fought back the urge to jump to her feet and applaud. A vein was throbbing in the side of Jed's head, his lips were a pale thin line, and his fingers were stiff on the table. But he had given a master performance. He had upturned the tables entirely, shifted all the winning cards to his side. There was no way the voice was going to call his bluff. Not this one. Even Christie wasn't quite sure whether Jed actually meant what he had said or not.

They waited for an answer. Jed leaned back against the sofa, crossing his legs and resting his head back. He closed his eyes.

Waited for the opponent to make his move. Twenty seconds later, he did.

"*Bravo. Bravo, my dear boy.*" Sharp, popping sounds erupted from the speakers, like low-quality fireworks being set off. Christie frowned, not understanding at first. It was only after the seventh pop that she realized what she was hearing. Clapping. Applause.

"*It seems like you've finally learned how to play the game,*" the warbled voice spoke. "*Splendid! Brilliant! Now this will be truly fun. I accept your rules, all of them, with just one condition. I will not harm a hair on Lauren's head… if, and only if, you manage to get to her in time. Your next challenge is on its way, Gray, and it won't be quite so easy as the last one. I wish you the best of fortunes on your journey. May Lauren Harding survive to see many more glorious dawns. Good luck.*"

A click, and the call disconnected.

Christie jumped up from her seat. "Jed, that was amazing!" she cried out. "Brilliant! You really outplayed him this time!" Unable to contain her excitement, she embraced her partner, wrapping her arms around his muscular frame.

"Whoa, whoa, easy," Jed said, laughing. "We haven't solved anything yet. We still have to find Lauren and catch this guy." He could feel Christie's chest against his own, her heart pounding against his. Some of her hair had fallen across him and was tickling the nape of his neck. But Jed didn't mind. He felt like he could stay in this posture forever, with his hands around Christie's back and hers encircling his waist. They were cocooned together, with no troubles allowed to get in the way. Not in this moment.

"What now?" Christie murmured into his shoulder. "Should I call Graham and the rest? In case we need any help for the next riddle or whatever the hell he's going to send?"

Jed shook his head, brushing his chin against Christie's back so she could feel his answer. "No, not yet. I still want to maintain my cover. You saw how agitated he was because of it, right? He knows the cards aren't entirely in his hands. He doesn't hold all the leverage. I want to keep it that way. It's easier if it's just the two of us to ensure that we aren't followed, that we're moving incognito. The moment you involve more people, you add to the game's risk. I can't afford that right now."

"Uh-huh. Okay." Gently, even though she didn't want to, Christie extricated herself from Jed's embrace. She withdrew a little, tucking her hair back into place again and smoothing the wrinkles in her shirt and pants. Then, she looked at the clock.

"God, it's really late. I did—"

"Yeah, you should be getting home now," Jed reminded her. "I think whatever's coming next will come tomorrow, not at this hour. It's best that we get some sleep so we're ready to face it."

"Yeah," Christie nodded, still looking reluctant. "Or, I could…"

Jed raised an eyebrow. "What?"

She shrugged. "You know. Stay here."

"Absolutely not." Jed playfully grabbed her by the shoulders and began to steer her toward the door. "You are not staying in this slum with me. Not a chance. You're going back to your nice apartment."

"Just hear me out for a moment." Christie swiveled around in his grasp. "There's no telling when you get the next message. It could be tomorrow, like you said, or in the middle of the night. There's no telling with this guy. He's insane, remember?"

Jed crossed his arms across his chest. "Your point being?"

"Point being that I don't want you gallivanting all over the city on your own, in case I'm not here." Christie held up a finger. "That's only the first problem. The second problem is your cover. If you want to remain in hiding, you can't have me constantly visiting your place again and again. I took great care today to ensure I wasn't followed, but who's to say it won't happen sooner or later? The only solution is I stay here, at least for now. Until we have a better plan."

Jed did not speak. Christie knew she had him stumped. There was no denying the logic she had presented, and Jed was all for logic and calm reasoning.

"Well, uh—" Jed glanced reluctantly at one of the rooms to the side. It was brimming with shadows. "You can take the spare bedroom, but let me remind you that this is not exactly the Hilton. If you find the odd cockroach or two sharing your bunk with you, don't say I didn't warn you."

Christie sniffed indignantly. "I'm a police officer. Cockroaches don't scare me."

Jed held up his hands in apology. "Okay… okay, as you wish. If you want to stay, you can stay. Just…"

"Just what?" Christie pressed. "What's bothering you? Say it."

Jed's upper lip curled in distaste. "I don't like the idea of making a lady stay in this place. It's rude. It's undignified. Especially a woman as accomplished and brilliant as you. You deserve better, Christie."

Christie laughed. She couldn't help it. Jed could be so adorable sometimes. "We're not on our honeymoon, Jed. We're chasing a mentally ill killer. That requires staying in bad places sometimes. It's okay. Just keep your mind on the case and don't worry about me. I've stayed in worse places in my life, believe me."

Jed still looked skeptical, but he didn't argue any more. He showed Christie to her room, flicking on a single whitish light that drove away the shadows. Christie cast her eyes around. In the corner lay a wooden bed with its paint peeling from the corners and chipped around the headboard. The paint on the walls had also begun to flake. There was ash lining the windowsills, probably centuries old by the looks of it. At least there were no cockroaches, though—or none that could be seen.

"Sweet dreams," Jed said dryly. "If you need anything, feel free to come in and wake me up, no matter what hour it is. If you're having trouble sleeping alone here, my bed is always big enough for two. Just saying." With that, he turned around and walked out of the room, leaving a furiously blushing Christie standing in it.

"Wait!" she called after him. "Hold on."

"What is it?" Jed's head poked through the doorway. He grinned. "Already missing me?"

Christie rolled her eyes. "I—I do—I need something to wear," she stammered, pointing at her jeans and shirt. "I can't sleep in these."

Jed scrunched his eyebrows. "I could give you one of my shirts, if that would work?" he offered.

"A shirt will do perfectly." Christie nodded at him. "I'll just sleep with that on and… the blanket."

A muscle ticked in Jed's lower cheek. His lips quivered slightly, but he did not say anything. He turned around and left the doorway, coming back moments later with a white shirt in his hands, which he flung toward Christie. She caught it in both hands and made a sound of approval, running her fingers over the soft cotton.

"Great, this will do perfectly," she stated with a smile. "Thanks."

"You're most welcome." Jed's eyes went to his shirt and then to Christie. He seemed wanting to say more, to do more. There was a smolder in his eyes, just a tiny pinprick of fire that had overtaken his earlier drowsiness. For a couple of moments, he lingered at the door, gripped by an indecision he couldn't resolve, before Christie finally saw him turn around and leave, closing the door in his wake.

CHAPTER 9

CHRISTIE WOKE TO KNOCKING.

Her eyes opened slowly, one tired blink at a time, and for a frightening moment, she had no idea where she was. Panic gripped her, turning her mind blank, while she looked around at what was surely the interior of some seedy hotel room in the middle of nowhere. How had she gotten here? Had someone drugged her?

There were three more sharp raps. Christie glanced sideways, and that was when the memories came back. She looked at the shut door and remembered Jed standing there, last night, after she had decided to stay with him at his new, off-the-radar place. Yes, that was where she was. Lying in a strange bed wearing a man's soft shirt and nothing more substantial.

Two more raps, insistent and unrelenting.

"Coming!" Christie called out, jumping to her feet. She found her pants and tugged them on in a hurry, checking her phone while she did so. It was 3:24 AM. Why was Jed up at this hour? Had something happened?

When she finally opened the door, dressed in yesterday's clothes, she saw her grim-faced partner standing outside, dark rings of exhaustion circling his eyes.

"Sorry to disturb you from your sleep," Jed said, "but you were right. He decided to schedule his craziness at the worst possible time." He held up his phone toward her. Christie's heart sank as she saw the new text Jed had received.

"Oh, God," she muttered. "What is it now? Show me." She took the phone from his hands and read the message.

WAKE UP! WAKE UP! WAKE UP!

21st Street Sycamore Avenue.

A crime is about to happen.

Two adorable lovebirds are in danger.

Can you save them in time?

A clue awaits you if you do.

XOXO :)

"Christ, let's go," Christie was already moving ahead, patting her pants for her car keys. "Jed hurry up, I parked my car some distance away from here so no one would notice it. We're going to have to run."

They went together to the door, and Christie threw it open. Jed felt the chill of the night snake its way in and scurry up his spine. He exhaled through his nostrils, seeing his breath fogging in the dim yellow light.

Outside, everything lay dead and quiet and dark. The night was a tapestry of stars, but even their light wasn't enough to drive away the shadows in this place. They were everywhere, infesting every corner, lurking in every hiding spot and bend, watching Jed and Christie with patient, malignant eyes.

"Wait, hold up." Jed fumbled with his phone and turned on the flashlight. He pointed it straight ahead, cutting a path through the blackness. They began to run forward, the noise of their feet hitting the asphalt uncomfortably loud in the night's quiet. Christie led Jed on a winding path past his building and two others that were clustered nearby. Beyond all three, on an abandoned corner where even the street lamp had stopped working, stood Christie's car. It resembled a hellhound from the distance; a huge, hulking shape crouched on all fours. Christie pressed a button on her key, and the car's headlights flashed, showing them the way.

A minute later, they were inside with their seatbelts fastened. Christie turned the ignition and started them on their journey. They coasted forward on the dark street, the Ford's headlights set at maximum brightness, the heater working extra hard to keep the cold away at this late hour.

Jed cast his eyes around. He could barely make out anything, let alone anyone. But he knew they were there, sprawled in the innermost recesses of the shadows. All the city's human refuse that it had no idea what to do with. It all ended up flushed here. The homeless, the addicts who couldn't afford rehab or had failed too many times to try again, the HIV patients, the prostitutes barely managing to scrape out a living. Desperate, dangerous people, clinging onto life by the very tips of their fingernails. Desperate enough to do crazy things if the opportunity arose. Christie's big, shiny car was drawing all that attention right to them, trying to provoke the hyenas out of their lair.

"Christie, hurry up," Jed whispered. "People are watching. They're taking note of this car and us in it. I don't want someone recognizing me when I step outside my apartment."

Christie gunned the accelerator in response. The Ford surged forward, speeding past the slummy residences and shops, past all those dead, crooked streetlamps that stood like wizened men bending over, and past the mounds of trash flanking alleyway entrances and covering the sidewalks in generous servings. The Ford Explorer went past it all, its engine groaning with effort, as if trying to outrace the crumbling decay of this place.

Two minutes later, they turned right and entered the main road, back into the city's functioning orange lights. There was no trash here, no sense of unseen threats hiding in the corners. Just an endless strip of concrete stretching into the horizon, unpopulated by any vehicles at this hour. Jed's head pressed against his seat as Christie pushed the car even faster, her hands clenching the steering wheel.

"Sometimes, I think about getting you a gun," Christie muttered. "We keep storming into dangerous situations unarmed and without backup. It's stupid."

Jed did not respond. Yet his silence was answer enough. Having spent enough time around him, Christie had learned to decode it. After a few seconds, she glanced at him sharply, her eyes unbelieving.

"You didn't," she said in a warning voice. "Tell me you didn't."

Jed pursed his lips sheepishly. He still did not speak, further confirming Christie's initial guess.

"You did!" She gasped. "You actually went ahead and bought a firearm for yourself! Jed, what's wrong with you?"

Now that the secret was out, Jed found his tongue. "I had to, Christie," he explained to his partner. "I was planning on facing this guy on my own, remember? I can't always be counting on you to rescue me from disaster. No, it was time I picked up a few skills of my own."

"Jed, why didn't you talk to me before doing something so reckless?" Christie was close to fuming. She was finding it hard to keep staring ahead at the road. This current revelation had rocked her badly. "Do you know what the stats on firearms suggest? You're more likely to die if you walk into a situation *with* a gun than without one! Because now the other person also knows you're armed, and they won't take a chance. They'll just shoot you!"

"Not if I shoot them first," Jed answered in a voice filled with false bravado, infuriating Christie even more. She turned her face to frown at him again, hoping the road ahead remained empty.

"This is not funny," Christie snapped. "This is not funny at all. You're doing things that are putting your life at risk. Can you not understand that? I'm worried about you, Jed!"

"Don't be," Jed answered simply. "I can handle myself. Haven't I proven that again and again around you guys? So, what's the big deal with getting a gun? It's only until this crisis is resolved, I promise."

Christie did not say anything, but displeasure radiated from her in palpable waves. Her eyes strayed once again to Jed, this time drifting down to his waist. He was wearing that same loose, somewhat oversized Henley over blue jeans.

"Do you have it with you now?" she asked in a low voice. "Where is it? Tucked into your waistband?"

Jed paused. "Yeah," he answered reluctantly.

Christie shook her head in disapproval. Things were getting out of hand. It was hard enough protecting Jed when he was behind the action; her mind worried for him even then. Now, he had brought his own weapon and was planning on diving headfirst into battle with her. That would do wonders for her nerves.

"Do you know how to use it?" she asked. "A gun has a recoil, you know, a pretty strong one. Then, there's the sound of the shot. It's loud enough to make you shake. These are things you have to know. You can't just buy a gun like you're buying candy and decide t—"

"I've practiced, Christie," Jed interrupted. He touched her hand on the steering wheel in reassurance. "I've been going to a gun range for this whole month and shooting rounds for an hour every day."

It seemed like there was no end to the surprising revelations tonight. "A gun range?" Christie repeated. "Practice? Then, you must know how difficult it is to use a firearm. You don't just point and shoot and expect the bad guy at the other end to fall down, like it happens in the movies."

"I know," Jed said softly. "But my aim isn't too bad. I'd say I can manage to hit a vital organ in every four out of five shots."

"Oh, Jesus Christ," Christie muttered. "My peaceful, soft-spoken partner who used to be a therapist is turning into a gun-wielding maniac. How did you even get such good aim in the first place? You told me you've never dealt with weapons in your life."

"I haven't," Jed confirmed.

"Then how come you've become Mr. Deadshot, huh? Explain that."

Jed grinned. "I just imagine our mysterious enemy's face in place of all the targets."

"You don't know what he looks like."

"Exactly, which gives me the liberty to create any face I want for him. Let me tell you, I've managed to think up some God-awful ugly designs."

The laughter bubbled out of Christie despite her efforts to contain it. She cracked a half-smile, loosening her fingers on the wheel. They were almost there now.

"Okay, since you've already decided on carrying a weapon," she relented, "I won't push it too much. For now. But you still have to follow the rules I lay down. All of them. And for God's sake, don't shoot me!"

"Of course," Jed agreed quickly. "I nev—"

"Which means that you stay in the car," Christie told him sternly. "That's the first rule. I don't care how good your aim is. I don't even care if you can shoot a flying frisbee in the night. There is no chance in hell I am letting you accompany me into a gunfight, if things ever escalate to that level. Do you understand?"

"Yeah," Jed agreed again, somewhat reluctantly. "Whatever you say, Detective."

Christie breathed out in relief. "Good. That's settled, then. Now, where is that place mentioned in the text? I think we've arrived."

"Two lefts from here," Jed told her. He unbuckled his seatbelt and straightened up in his seat.

Christie noticed. "What are you doing?"

Jed placed one hand on the door handle. "Readying myself for all eventualities. We might need to jump out of the car and start shooting; who knows? I can't waste time then, fiddling with my seatbelt."

"Jed, I just told you you're not joining the fight if there is one!" Christie exclaimed, exasperated.

"Yes, yes, I'm not," Jed explained quickly. "This is just *in case.* You never know what fix you might find your—wait, what is that?"

"What?" Something in Jed's voice made Christie slow down the car. She turned sideways and found her partner craning his head back. "What is it?"

"Park the car to the side," Jed told her urgently, in a low voice. "I think we've arrived."

"Here?" Christie glanced at the empty street they were coasting on. There was no one present, and the shops were all shuttered. "There's no—"

"No, not here," Jed spoke, his head still craned backward. His body was tense. "Behind, on one of the smaller streets joined to this one. I think I saw something... someone in trouble."

That was all the information Christie needed. She pushed the brakes and parked the Ford next to the curb.

"Okay," she breathed, unbuckling her own seatbelt before taking her weapon out from her holster. She held it up in her hands. The Glock 17 caught the street's orangey light and gleamed, as if a match had been struck deep within its tarry depths. Christie checked its chamber, rechecked it, did the same with the ammo, then re-holstered it. She turned to her partner.

"Get in the driver's seat after I get out, okay?" she instructed him. "Keep the engine on and the doors locked. Most importantly, *do not get out of the car* unless I tell you to."

Jed nodded. His face was a mask of seriousness. His eyes were continuously shifting between the empty sidewalks and the car's rearview mirror.

"Be careful," he told Christie. "Call if you need help."

"I will." Christie was suddenly overcome with an urge to embrace him, but she fought it off. Instead, she gave his hand a final squeeze before stepping out of the car. The wind's cold, groping fingers immediately seized her, wrapping around the nape of her neck and trying to worm their way inside her spine. She shivered, partly from the cold and partly from something else. Her weapon out and held in her left hand, Christie began walking backward, toward the adjoining street they had just passed. It was only a dozen meters away from her.

Silence reigned.

When she had gotten to the corner, she peeked past a comic book store's red-bricked wall to see what had caught Jed's attention. In the middle of the street, she spotted it. It was the only thing there, sticking out like a neon-board. The rest of the area lay quiet and empty.

A car. That was what Christie saw first. A sky-blue Cadillac, very old by the looks of it, standing unmoving in the middle of the road. The reason for the car's lack of motion was obvious. Something surrounded the car on all four sides.

Skinheads. There were skinheads everywhere, forming a circle around the vehicle. A constantly revolving circle because they were prowling the boundaries of the Cadillac like a pack of hyenas circling a trapped wildebeest. Their skulls shone brightly, reflecting the streetlamp's glare. Their heavy black boots struck the cement with loud thwacks as they moved. In their hands, they swung machetes and hatchets. Two of them were wielding pistols, Christie saw. One was standing right in front of the Cadillac, pointing his weapon at the windshield, and the other was bent over next to the driver's side, his gun's muzzle pressed against the window.

The promise of violence scented the air.

The night held its breath, waiting for carnage.

Christie squinted at the people inside the Cadillac. There were only two of them. A couple. She could not see much of their faces from here, due to the skinheads' ever-shifting bodies obstructing her view. But she saw enough to notice the terrorized looks the couple inside the vehicle were wearing. They were sitting frozen in their seats, helplessly watching the herd moving around them. It was a ghastly sight. Christie's stomach turned when the wind brought her the skinheads' occasional hoots and giggles. They were trying their best to keep their voices down, but their excitement wasn't letting them. They were giddy with the prospect of hurting these innocent folks, high as kites on their victims' terror.

Christie brought her weapon up.

She considered. Should she step out into the open, display her badge and weapon, and hope for the animals to run off? Or should she pull the trigger and take them down? It was a tough choice. Part of her wanted to blow them apart for doing what they were doing, but another, more sensible part of her advised her to act according to protocol. The protocol demanded that she call backup and have these criminals behind bars for good.

Except there was no time left.

Christie could sense it in the very air around her. A taut anticipation, a sense of something terrible to come. She looked back at the skinheads and saw their impatience, their inhuman energy. They were prancing around the car now, knocking on the windows with their weapons, urging the couple to come out. Only their two gunmen were standing frozen in position, their weapons aimed inside the car in case the couple decided to suddenly drive off.

She was short on time. Christie was certain of it. Any moment, something was going to change. This teasing game would conclude, and the herd would descend on its prey, ravenous, no longer able to control its appetite. Something needed to be done *now*.

She thought it over one final time before making her decision. Once she had made it, she turned that part of her mind off. There could be no more indecision now, no hesitation or doubt slowing her movements. It was time to move.

The night's brittle silence was blown apart by a deafening gunshot. It was the gunman at the very head of the vehicle who went down first. One moment, he was standing with his pistol raised smugly in front of him, and the next he lay on the ground, unmoving.

The rest of the skinheads screeched and scattered, not knowing what was happening, or where the fire had come from. Since the street was deserted, half of them sought cover behind the car, disappearing beneath its blue exterior. A few were driven to panic by their terror and started madly pulling the doorhandle, trying to get inside even though the vehicle was locked.

From the shadows of the corner building, Christie emerged into the light, her face set in a snarl, her eyes blazing with a terrifying light. She lowered her weapon and shot out the kneecaps of the two targets who were closest to her, frantically yanking on the Cadillac's door. They screamed and collapsed, clutching their knees, their weapons thrown to the sides.

At that point, things took a dangerous turn. One skinhead was dead, two were wailing helplessly on the road, and one had fled away into the night. There were just two left, both of them taking cover behind the Cadillac. As Christie approached the car, her weapon still raised, she heard the roar of a gunshot even though neither of the skinheads had risen from their cover. Something whooshed past her ankles, making her pants ripple with the speed of its passing.

Shit! He's shooting from beneath the car!

Christie broke into a run, a wild, erratic run that left no room for anyone to predict where her next step would land. She raced toward the Cadillac in this bizarre, circuitous path, sometimes leaping to the left and then abruptly shifting right.

Two more explosions ripped apart the air, and she felt those invisible projectiles hurtling between her legs, missing her flesh by mere inches. She kept up her run, heading straight for the car's hood, and once she was there, she leaped over it in one fluid motion, sliding across the smooth metal with all the momentum her run had built up for her. Her gun rose to the left, and she saw the skinhead crouching behind the car finally rising to his feet, his own weapon turning to meet her. But she was faster, and she already had him in her sights.

Christie pressed down on the trigger. There were two more bursts of gunfire. The skinhead who had been trying to aim for her legs was thrown backwards, bright red flowers blossoming on his white vest. He hit the ground with a thud and lay still, head tilted oddly to the left.

But her momentum would not stop so soon. She had shot the man midway through her slide across the bonnet, and now Christie's feet met the tarmac. There was still a lot of pent-up motion left in them, however, and she continued staggering forward on the street for a few more steps, finally coming to a halt some distance ahead of the dead skinhead. Breathing hard, her neck slick with sweat, Christie put a hand on her knees to steady herself.

Someone approached from behind her.

She had forgotten about the last one. In her haste to take out the second gunman, she had lost count of the fact that there had been six skinheads. Five of them had been successfully taken care of, but one still remained.

Christie whirled around at the sound of the rushing footsteps, her weapon rising once more, readying to strike for the f—

The skinhead crashed into her, stopping her halfway, his crazed screams filling her ears and reverberating inside her skull. She stumbled backward and slipped, striking the ground hard. A lance of pain shot through her lower back as it met the tarmac. Her hand hit the ground with equal force, and the gun in it was sent skittering away. Hissing with pain, Christie looked up just in time to see the skinhead falling on top of her.

He was a young, wiry man. Young enough to be a college student, if perhaps he had made some different choices in life. His eyebrows were studded with rings, and his face looked barely human. Grunting and snorting savagely, he grabbed both of Christie's hands and pinned them against the ground, positioning himself on top of her to immobilize her completely.

"Bitch!" he snarled, his face inches from hers. "Fucking interfering bi—"

Christie head-butted him. Hard. Her forehead struck the man's nose, and she heard something crack or give way. The skinhead screamed, jerking his head to the side, letting out a string of obscene curses. Blood streamed from his nose, smearing his upper lips and making its way down to his chin.

But his grip on Christie's hands hadn't loosened even a little. It was surprising, the enormous strength he had despite being so skinny. Christie felt like her hands had been locked in iron manacles. She heaved and struggled, yet the man's grip did not loosen.

"Bitch!" he screamed, turning toward her once again, his face a grisly mask of pain and fury. "You'll pay for this! Tommy will make you pay for this!"

Christie tried to headbutt him again when he brought his face close to hers, but the skinhead dodged her movements. Blood was still oozing from his nose in steady streams. A single fat droplet landed on Christie's cheek. She cursed and turned her head to the side, straining with all her might to free her arms from her assailant's bony grip. He only grunted and pressed her more tightly against the ground, bringing his face right before hers.

"Damn interfering bitch," he hissed. His breath smelled of rotten eggs and alcohol. "I'll make you pay for this. Tommy will make sure you never interfere in other's people's business again."

The skinhead's body suddenly lifted from Christie's. She saw him rise up partially, bring his knee into the air with him, before driving it down straight into her lower abdomen.

Pain. Pain like she had never known. So bright and blinding Christie's vision went black for a few seconds. She came back to consciousness gasping, her lungs struggling to scrape in some air from her swimming surroundings. The man was still on top of her, and he had taken advantage of her momentary lapse in consciousness by shifting his grip on her. Now both of Christie's hands were pinned right above her, with just one of the man's arms. His other arm was free, free to do whatever he had intended for it.

"I hope you enjoy this," the skinhead hissed, grinning. The sight of his mangled nose and bloodied teeth looming above Christie were a horror. She did not want that to be the last thing she saw in her life.

"Aghhh!" A cry ripped out of her throat, and she writhed in the man's grip, using every fiber of strength in her body to get free. Her legs spasmed and her torso shook and her hands wriggled and shivered like caged birds driven mad with their imprisonment. Christie jerked her head forward once again, hoping to catch the skinhead off-guard and further redesign his nose, but he was smart to her movements. He dodged sideways, laughing, relishing her struggle. Another drop of blood fell from his nose onto her lips. A sour metal taste filled her mouth, and she gagged.

"Ha!" The man's laugh was a weird, broken sound. "I hope you're having fun, bitch! Well, now the fun is over. It's time for Tommy to get his revenge."

Without any further talk, the man brought his free hand over Christie's throat. He wrapped his bony fingers around her skin, his face filled with determination.

Then, he squeezed.

Whatever meagre air Christie had been getting was cut off. Her protests died in her mouth, turning into a choked cry. She knew she had only seconds left, mere seconds. She would not die of asphyxiation. No, this animal was going to crush her trachea with his inhuman strength.

"What's the matter? Can't breathe?" the skinhead taunted. His face hovered above Christie, filling her vision. As the pressure increased, as more and more air was driven from her lungs, her vision turned distorted, blurred. All she could make out was a crimson smile and pitch-black eyes staring down at her from the sky. A demon god taunting her before the smiting.

"What's the matter, huh, bitch?" That voice gloated. Christie's fading consciousness was barely able to make sense of it. "Cat got your tongue? No more smart-ass things to s—"

The pressure suddenly lifted. For a terrible moment, it felt like it was too late, that Christie's throat would never again know the sweetness of breathing, but then her cramped muscles loosened, and the oxygen flooded in. She gasped, her chest convulsing on the ground, her eyes flying open. It was like a rebirth, like someone had taken her dying soul and stuffed it back inside her body.

The skinhead was gone. Or rather, he was not on top of her anymore. He was lying to her side, a nasty welt on the back of his head, his face mercifully hidden from view.

Christie looked up into the face of her partner kneeling before her. He was holding his own weapon in one hand, a Heckler and Koch with a textured brown barrel. His eyes were soft, warm and concerned and everything her savage assailant's eyes hadn't been.

"Christie?" Jed asked, and Christie almost broke down at the softness in his voice. The humanness. It was so different from what she had heard in the last five minutes. There was no venom in it, no hate, no *madness.*

"I—I'm okay," she rasped, gingerly touching her throat, tracing her swollen skin with a finger. "If you had been a little later, though, I don't know…"

She felt Jed's hands caressing her throat. She felt his fingers moving over her skin. Her eyes closed. Just the tenderness of his touch was enough to begin the healing process, enough to make her believe everything would be okay.

"Are you sure you're, okay?" Jed asked. "Your throat is red. Too red."

"It's fine." Christie shook her head with some effort. There was a dull ache in her neck when she moved it from side to side. "Just swelling, I think. I can breathe properly, so—"

"Hello? Excuse me?"

They both jumped to their feet at that voice. Or rather, Jed jumped up, his gun already pointing ahead. Christie tried to jump up, but ended up falling back on her butt again, still too disoriented to make such quick moves. She peered past Jed's shoulder.

A young man and a woman stood facing them, looking afraid and uncertain. They were the people from the Cadillac, Christie realized. The boy was the same age as the skinhead, with the only difference being that he wasn't tattooed and looked human. He had a round face and neatly trimmed blonde hair. The girl next to him was his age, her eyes alternating fretfully between Jed and Christie, her hands clasped in front of her skirt.

"Hey, are you okay?" the young boy asked Christie. "Thank you for saving us. I—I'm sorry I just didn't know what to do, when I saw you and that guy fighting… I should have come out sooner. I'm sorry."

Christie rubber her throat again. She managed a weak smile.

"You don't have to apologize," she told the young man. "Dealing with such people isn't your job. It's mine. I'm a police officer."

The girl's eyes widened when she heard that. She took a step forward, emboldened by this knew knowledge.

"You're NYPD?" the girl asked. "Oh, thank God. Sam and I would have… something terrible would have happened if it wasn't for you. Those tattooed guys looked like they were insane."

"Yeah, they were," Christie grunted. Slowly, with great care, she rose to her feet. "What's your name?" she asked the girl.

"Samantha," she answered instantly.

Christie smiled despite the situation. Sam and Samantha. How appropriate.

"Well, Samantha and—both of you." She took out her phone from her pocket and was surprised to find it had remained uncrushed in all the struggle. "I know it's late and you both need to get home, but first we're going to need to get a statement from you at the station."

The young duo exchanged looks.

"Statement?" Sam asked, confused. "Of what? We're not in trouble, are we?"

It was Jed who spoke then, Jed who had been standing quietly, unable to take his worrying attention off of Christie.

"You're not in trouble, no," he told them. "But I have a feeling you both being here at this hour wasn't a mere coincidence, was it?"

The duo exchanged looks again. It was enough for Jed to figure out that he was right.

"Exactly," he said. "We need to have a little chat about that, find out just what happened here tonight. Christie, I think you should call backup, no?" He pointed at the unconscious skinhead he had struck with the butt of his gun. "We can't carry him alone."

"Yeah, I know." Christie dialed the number in her phone. It was answered after three rings.

"Hello?" Graham's sleepy voice spoke.

"Graham," Christie began, absently rubbing her throat again. "Sorry to disturb you from your wonderful dreams, but we need some help."

CHAPTER 10

THE COUPLE WERE SITTING in Christie's office, opposite her desk, on two chairs she had brought in for them. They were both nursing cups of steaming coffee in their hands. Seated next to Christie on a similar chair, Jed watched them both, wondering what role they played in this whole drama. The girl was majoring in architecture studies at NYU, he had found out. And the boy worked with his dad in his automobile rental business. Two ordinary folks, by any measure. Yet he was sure the story they were about to narrate was entirely unordinary.

"So," Christie finally began, once she saw the two were comfortable enough. "Tell us, what happened? Or rather, as Jed asked earlier, how did you both end up on that street in the dead of night?"

The girl looked embarrassed. The boy, Sam, cast his eyes down uncomfortably toward the carpet.

"It's okay," Jed reassured them. "Whatever your story, you won't get in trouble for it, I promise. We just need all the details because it relates to another investigation of ours. So, don't leave anything out, even if you think it isn't important."

He gave them one of his faint, disarming smiles that almost always worked.

Samantha stared at Jed and seemed to be calmed somewhat by his demeanor. She flexed her fingers around her mug of coffee, staring at the curlicues of steam rising from it, building up the courage to speak. Jed stared at her patiently.

"It happened two weeks ago," she began, her eyes still locked on her mug. "Uh—Sam and I, we received something. A gift. From a stranger."

"A gift?" Christie repeated. "What kind of gift?"

Samantha bit her lower lip. She gave Sam a quick, questioning look. He nodded slightly.

"Five hundred dollars," she stated. "That was the gift. Given in cash in a plain pink envelope."

Jed whistled. That was a lot of money for college students. "Who gave you the money?" he asked. "Was the sender's name attached?"

Samantha shook her head. Her hand shook with it, and the coffee in the mug stirred slightly, waves of disturbance rippling across its tranquil surface.

"No details," she told them. "Just a—just a note. A message, for us."

Christie gave Jed a look, but Jed was looking intently at the girl. He leaned forward, placing his hands on the table.

"What did the note say, Samantha?"

Samantha paused, remembering. "I—basically that we had a secret admirer," she answered. "He said that he wanted to send us additional gifts, but it would be more fun if we made it into a game. A game only the three of us knew about."

"Uh-huh." Jed's eyes narrowed. "What did this game entail, exactly?"

Samantha swallowed. She glanced at Sam again, who was sitting quietly with his face bent downward.

"The game was that we had to go to different places to collect the other gifts," she continued. "Like, for instance, a bench at a park, or inside a particular trashcan, or even stuffed in the chair cushions of certain restaurants..."

"Wait." Jed held up a hand. "How much money did this admirer give you?"

The hesitation now bloomed on Samantha's face. Her index finger twitched against the mug's handle. Jed knew in an instant that she was considering lying. He had dealt with enough clients in his practice to become familiar with those common tells.

"Samantha," Jed repeated gently, "we're not here for the money. We're here to catch the guy who you thought was giving it to you out of the goodness of his heart. Trust me, the lives of other people depend on it. You two aren't the only ones he's been playing these strange games with. It's what he does. He enjoys causing chaos."

Samantha looked intently into Jed's eyes. She seemed to see something there, perhaps some trace of the chaos he was speaking of. The hesitation left her face promptly.

"Close to a thousand," she answered. "He gave Sam and me close to a thousand dollars."

Jed and Christie exchanged looks.

"Okay, go on," Jed urged the girl. "What happened next? Did his demands change?"

Samantha shook her head. "Uh, not really. One day we just got a message from him telling us that he had a huge payment ready for us, one that would change our lives. But it couldn't just be given to us in broad daylight. It would cause too much suspicion."

"So, he asked you to visit that street we found you on," Jed finished. "After midnight. When no one else would be there."

Samantha paused. Her lower lip trembled minutely. She fought to regain control over her emotions. "That's what we had thought," she answered in a shaky voice, "that no one else would be there. That the street would be empty at night." Another pause. Her hands clenched her skirt, grabbing a fistful of fabric. "But it wasn't. It wasn't. *They* were there."

"The skinheads," Christie murmured. She frowned at the desk thoughtfully. "Let's go back a little, Samantha. Exactly how long had you been receiving messages from this man before tonight's events?"

Samantha looked quizzical for a moment. She glanced at Sam, trying to confirm. "I think two—"

"Yeah, two weeks," Sam confirmed.

"How many different messages did you receive from this man during that time?" Christie asked.

Samantha sniffed. "About eight. One every other day or so."

Christie nodded slowly. "Eight. Got it. Well, we're going to need all those messages, Samantha. I'm assuming you haven't thrown them away?"

"I haven't." Samantha shook her head. "They're in my room, stuffed beneath my mattress."

"You can give them to the officer that takes you home." Christie let out a long breath. "I think that's it for now." She glanced at her partner. "Do you have any other questions, Jed?"

Jed shook his head. "No. I think we're done, at least for now." He smiled at the young couple. "Thank you both for being so cooperative. And brave, too, considering what you've just gone through." He looked at his partner. "I think the police will be stationing a car outside your homes for a couple of weeks. To ensure there's no danger to you."

Christie nodded in affirmation. "We will be. I don't want either of you to worry—in my estimation, this is the end of your role in our suspect's game. But still, just to be sure, we'll provide you with a rotating team of officers for your safety."

"Thank you," the couple said in unison, their faces flushed with relief. Sam began to get up from his chair but then stopped halfway, looking uncertainly at the two adults seated opposite him.

"Yes, you can leave," Christie confirmed with a smile. "If we need anything else, we'll contact you."

That was all the incentive the couple needed. Tired after a night that could have turned out far worse than it had, they rose to their feet and began walking out of the room. But not before Jed saw the girl, Samantha, pause a few feet away from the door and swivel around to regard him once again.

"I really hope you catch this guy," she said to Jed, her fingers laced together awkwardly in front of her. "Luring us in with money, then trapping us like that and turning it into a game..." She shuddered, tightening her arms across her chest. "I'm not an expert, but I don't think ordinary criminals do that. You'd have to be really messed up in the head to come up with such plans."

Jed stared at the girl for a while. "You're right," he told her. "More messed up than you can imagine. But he won't be hurting any more people, Samantha. Don't you worry about that. His streak has come to an end."

There was something in Jed's tone which caused even Sam to peer at him over his partner's shoulder. Something sharp and electric, like the pungent whiff of ozone coloring the air before a storm.

Samantha bid Jed and Christie goodbye one last time before leaving with Sam. The office door shut in her wake, encasing them both in silence. Christie glanced at Jed.

"Good kids, huh?" She commented.

Jed nodded. "Yeah. Innocent, the way kids usually are. If we had been any later and something had happened..." He sucked in air through his teeth.

"But we weren't late," Christie's comforting voice reached his ears. "We were on time. Thanks to us, they're safe and sound. Why worry about things that didn't happen?"

"Hmm, you're right." Jed tapped the desk rhythmically with his right knuckle. "We got them out unharmed. That's that. Only thing we need to focus on now is Lauren. She's still with him. Still not safe."

"Since we completed the first part of his game," Christie mused, "I imagine there's another riddle we're about to get soon. Instructions for step two, I suppose."

Jed shook his head. "Whatever they are, I hope they don't come until the morning. I'm too tired to think straight right now."

Christie barked out a laugh. "Yeah, you and me both, pal. That bed in your new place feels more like a slat of wood than foam. I only slept for a few hours, but it was enough to make my back sore."

Jed turned towards Christie, immediately looking apologetic. "I'm sorry," he answered with such sincerity that Christie mentally chastised herself for complaining. "I'm sorry. I warned you the place is a dump. You should've just come to my room. My bed is softer. Not amazing by any standards, but at least better than what you got."

"Right." Christie tried to pass off the remark casually, tried not to act like her insides had been inflamed at the prospect of them sleeping together. "Next time, then."

The edges of Jed's lips twitched. He seemed to be holding back a smile.

"Next time, Detective," he answered with a grunt, rising to his feet and pushing in his chair. "In the meantime, I'll take my leave. If any more hints come my way, you will be the first person to be informed, rest assured."

"Wait, how are you going home?" Christie stood up, too, grabbing her keys from the table's corner. "I'll drop you."

Jed only shook his head with a faint smile. "No can do, Detective. I'm trying to stay undercover, remember? A police vehicle escorting me to my premises will be the biggest neon-sign in the world."

"But how will you find a cab at this hour?" Christie tapped her watch as if to emphasize the point. "Don't be silly, Jed. Let me drop you. There's no way you can get to your place alone right now."

Jed only shook his head again. His quirking lips widened into a grin. "You don't know New York like I do. This city always takes care of those who know its ways. I'll be fine, I promise. See you tomorrow."

Hushing Christie's protests with a raised hand and a calming grin, Jed left the office, shutting the door behind him and letting the quiet resume its rightful reign.

CHAPTER 11

"HEYO, MAX HERE. WHO'S dialing?"

Jed fought back a chuckle. "What's the matter, Max? Don't recognize your old therapist's voice?"

A pause. A long, unbelieving pause. "Mr. G? Whoa!" Max's voice rose rapidly, turning shrill with excitement. "Where you been, Mr. G? Were you lost? I thought you done got yourself kidnapped by pirates or something! You disappeared from the face of the earth!"

Jed finally allowed himself to chuckle. It felt good hearing Max's voice again, brimming with all its usual street charm and endearing roughness. "Yes, that was by design, Max. Certain, ah, situations, forced me to lay low for a while."

Another pause. This one quieter, more delicate. "Mr. G, you okay?" Max's voice had lowered below its normal pitch, as if he were handling a situation so brittle it would shatter if spoken of too loudly. "Is everything okay? You tell me if you need Max to cover yo ba—"

"I'm fine, Max," Jed assured him. "Promise. Thank you for the offer of help, though. I don't need it at the moment, but I will let you know if things change."

"Yea, I hear you, Mr. G." Max coughed. Jed heard the sound of a table being pushed back. "Why you dialing me from this rando number? What happened to your usual line? I called you so many times, but you ain't never pick up!"

"Yes, unfortunately I won't be able to answer calls from my usual phone any time soon. Sorry for the inconvenience," Jed apologized. "Until this mess gets resolved, it's best I stay off the map and away from the people I care about."

"Mr. G..." Max trailed off. Jed heard his heavy breathing on the other end. "You're scarin' me with all this layin' low crap. What you got yourself into? Some bad shit? Like, seriously bad shit?"

Jed laughed. "Yes, buddy. You could call it that. Why else would I be contacting you through a burner phone? It's not just for my safety. It's for yours, too."

"Oh, man." The dismay in Max's tone pinched Jed's heart. He had forgotten how close he and the young man had come to be, how much Jed had gotten him to open up.

"Now, forget about me, Max," Jed continued on quickly. "That's not why I called, you know. I called because it's been a while since I've caught up with what's happening in your life. Tell me the updates: what's new?"

"Mr. G, I really don't think you should be worrying about me right now," Max stated. "If you're down so bad, you need to put that damn sharp mind of yours on your own problems, not mine."

Jed chuckled. "What do you think I'm doing right now? I'm rebooting, Max. This is how I return to normal. This is how I get my brain operating at full capacity again. By listening to other people's issues instead of mine. You can think of it as the only way for me to recharge my brain."

"Aww, Mr. G, that's a helluva weird thing to say, you know that?" A dull rapping sound from the other end, as if Max was hitting his knuckles against something hard. "My life... well, there's a buncha stuff that's happened. Where do I start?"

Jed leaned back on the shabby sofa of his apartment, closed his eyes, and pretended he was back in his office, with everything in his life perfectly normal. "From where you always do, Max. From the start."

"Uh-huh... okay..." Hesitation still filled Max's voice. The surprise was too much and too sudden for him. "Well... uh, you know that gig I was doin' in that burger joint? Well, I quit last week."

Jed's eyes shot open. "What? Why?"

"Uh..." There came the sound of Max smacking his lips together. "Mr. G, well you know how it is, huh..."

"No Max, I don't." Jed switched the phone to his other hand and crossed his legs. This was serious. For the first time in their work together, Max had finally struck gold: he had found both his passion as well as something he was good at and could get paid for. Not everyone was that lucky. It didn't make sense to abandon such good fortune.

Jed spoke lightly. "Leaving that burger joint… if I remember correctly, weren't you having a great time there? I also recall you telling me that the chef there gave you a raise for your excelling performance."

"He did." A note of pride entered Max's voice. "Twice. Even though official policy says employees only get annual raises."

"That's exactly my point." Jed said. "Why leave, then, if you were doing so wonderfully?"

"Uh—see," Max cleared his throat. Jed heard some more rustling and shifting sounds from the other end, as if the boy were interested in doing everything except for answering the question. "Mr. G, you know I don't like hiding the truth from ya. Never did. So, Imma just give it to you straight. What do you say?"

"I say go for it." Jed grinned. "I'm pretty interested to hear what you're going to say."

"Uh-huh." Max cleared his throat some more. He scratched his chin. He rubbed his feet against a suspiciously-sounding linoleum floor. Jed listened to it all patiently, waiting for his client's deflections to come to an end so he could get to the actual issue.

"Okay," Max finally stated, when he seemed to realize that there was no escaping from this. "I—uh, I quit that gig because, be—uh, because I've decided to, you know, start a thing of my own."

"Wait, what?" Wrinkles creased Jed's forehead. He leaned forward on the sofa. Somewhere within that convoluted tangle of ahhs and umms, Max had dropped a bombshell. "Max, could you say that again?"

"Yeah, uh…" He was speaking like a man addressing a crowd, expecting it to burst into cruel laughter at any moment. "Mr. G, I've decided I'm gonna start my own lil thing now. My own food… thing."

There was silence on the other end. For the first time in a long time, Jed had been left speechless by one of his clients.

"Your own thing?" Jed repeated slowly, rolling the words around on his tongue and feeling their strangeness. "Wow, that's… doesn't that require a lot of capital? Have you somehow managed to draw in an angel investor with your charm, Max?"

Max did not say anything, but Jed felt him shaking his head on the other end. "Nah, Mr. G," he answered. "Not my own thing like, a restaurant or anything. At least, not now. I've decided Imma kick up a small stall at first. Nothing fancy, just me and some simple ingredients, cooking up some delicious stuff for this city's people. It's time Max took his talents public, ya know?"

Again, Jed found himself struggling to find an appropriate response. This news was so unexpected, so… *out of the blue*… it had even overtaken the surprise of his own that he had given Max.

"Max… that's a really brave step to take," Jed finally answered. "I have to say, most people don't leave the comfort of a stable job so quickly and readily, especially when they're making their way up the corporate ladder. Or the culinary ladder, rather, in your case."

"Yeah," Max drawled. "I just felt like it was time, ya know? If you have a gift, ya better be sure to make good use of it before the world sucks it all out of you. I mean, sure, the restaurant was payin' me decent and all, but I felt like I could do more, ya know? I felt like I was finally in a good enough place to run after my dreams. All my life, I been runnin' from my nightmares, and with your help, Mr. G, I finally got away. I finally managed to escape from them. Now that I'm a free man, why not go after the good stuff? Heck, why not go after the great stuff? The sky should be the ceiling, ya know?"

Jed found himself smiling with an openness he hadn't displayed in a long, long time. "Max, if for some reason you don't manage to make it in the culinary world, I want you to know that you have a great aptitude for being a motivational speaker. The speech you just gave was so moving, even I'm thinking of reopening my office and resuming my sessions!"

Max laughed, a laugh that was cut short. "Why don't ya go ahead and do just that, Mr. G? I'd sure love to meet ya in your office again sometime."

Jed sighed, looking at his phone's screen, which had just lit up with an incoming message. "Soon, Max, once this problem is over. Speaking of, I'm afraid I have to go now. Duty calls."

"Aight, Mr. G, no pressure." Max paused. "Ya let me know if ya need anything, aight? Anything at all, Max is here for you."

"Got it, Max, I'll be sure to remember you when I need some valuable street cred. You take care of yourself in the meantime. Speak to you soon." Jed cut the call and sighed. He had wanted to speak more to Max. He had wanted to hear about his new business plan and how the boy planned on carrying it out. He had wanted to have this meeting happen in his office, where he could see his client face-to-face, like normal therapists did. Like he had once done.

Unfortunately, normal had long ago been flung out the window. During the call, for a sweet moment, Jed had forgotten that, but now reality rushed back at him. He looked around at the abysmal, alien interior of the place he was staying in. He looked at the sofas fraying from their seams, at the stains on the carpet he was afraid to inspect too closely, at the heavy, ugly burner phone he was holding in his hands, and at the sickly light washing the walls and floor, giving it a jaundiced patient's complexion. Finally, he looked at his phone with Christie's message blinking on it, the only ray of brightness in this place, and picked it up.

Found the next clue. Coming to you in ten. Don't worry, will take care not to get followed.

Jed read the message before rising to his feet. He stood there for a moment or two, indecisive, then sat back down again with a sigh. What was the point? Christie was coming over and he had reflexively risen to clean up the place and make it more presentable. Except there was only so much you could do in a place like this. There were no dirty dishes, no weeks'-old socks lying around, no undone piles of laundry cluttering the place. But he still felt uncomfortable meeting with his partner in this apartment. Jed couldn't understand where this unease was coming from, but it seemed to be very deep-rooted in him. Maybe he was just traditional by nature. He had always been taught that women were supposed to be pampered a bit in the way you treated them and not given the same roughness that men usually reserved for other men.

The time passed quickly. Jed sat and stared at the wall he had subjected to his brainstorming, hoping to come across an insight or link he hadn't noticed before. His eyes slowly roamed over the pictures he had pinned there and the messages he had scrawled with a red marker. He thought back to the few times he had spoken on the phone with his mysterious enemy. Who could he be? How did he fit into Jed's past? Most importantly, what did he want with Jed? Why was he so hellbent on ruining his life?

When the knock came at the door, Jed had made no significant progress. He jumped to his feet, feeling happy despite his reluctance to have Christie here. It would be good to not be alone for a while.

She was dressed in a white shirt and black pants when he opened the door. Her hair was tied into a tight bun, and she had sunglasses covering her eyes. In her hands, she held a small white box of what suspiciously looked like food—and delicious food by the smell of it.

"Come in, mademoiselle," Jed announced with comical soberness, opening the door and stepping aside for her to enter. Playing along, Christie offered a small curtsy before walking in. Jed glanced behind her and saw the immediate area around them mostly empty. There were a few people loitering on the sidewalk, but they seemed oblivious of Jed and Christie.

"So," Jed stepped back into his living room to find Christie comfortably sprawled on the sofa, as if she had been coming here all her life and had become best friends with the mildew poking out from the corners. "What clue did you manage to find on your own, without your dear partner's help?"

Christie reached into her pocket and drew out a tiny, folded slip of pink paper. She placed it on the table, next to the box of food, and gestured for Jed to sit down.

"I didn't find it," she answered. "It was left for us, on purpose. Remember Sam and Samantha and the money they were getting from that mystery man, with the notes attached? Well, one of the notes was meant for us. Clearly, this guy plans everything weeks in advance. He knew we were going to save the kids and interview them. He had meant for us to find the note."

Jed found himself not surprised in the slightest by this information. In fact, he was only surprised at the fact that he hadn't predicted it himself. He reached forward for the pink slip on the table and picked it up, unfolding it with wary fingers, as if any manner of unholy terror might be lying in hiding with it.

Christie did not say anything. She sat and watched Jed read the note. His eyebrows puckered in that usual look of distaste, and his lips pressed into each other, as if he had tasted something sour. His eyes moved rapidly over the paper, reading the small paragraph which had been scrawled there.

Here's your next bundle of joy, Sam and Samantha. Spend it however you like, or don't spend it at all. It's all fine by me. I don't judge people, you know? To each their own, as I like to say.

On second thought, might I give a suggestion? If I were you, I'd spend the money on buying a ticket to Rome and seeing its beautiful cathedrals. They really make your spirit soar, you know? Marvelous feats of human engineering. Or maybe I would just rent a Bentley for one night and go cruising around the city. Or maybe... maybe I would visit a place. That place. A very special place. Anyways, I'm rambling, sorry. Choice is yours. Do what you like with the money. You deserve it.

Much love,

XOXX

Your secret admirer

After reading through the note twice, Jed placed it back down on the table. His face was still half-confused, half in deep thought. Absently, without even realizing what he was doing, he reached for the box of food and opened its lid, revealing a messy mountain of cheese and jalapeno fries lying within.

"I take it that note means something to you," Christie observed, watching him closely.

Jed picked up a fry and chewed it slowly, as if pondering some great dilemma. Finally, he looked up at Christie and nodded.

"It does. But how did you guess that?"

Christie shrugged. "The rest of the notes were all boring. This one looked bizarre enough to warrant closer inspection, so I brought it you."

"You did the right thing." One hand cupping his forehead, Jed picked up another fry and began to eat it with that same slow deliberation.

When he did not seem to read her mind and anticipate her unspoken question, Christie voiced it.

"Well, are you going to bring me in on the secret or not? Because I have no idea what's happening."

Jed took his time responding. He was retreating back into his shell, Christie saw—that same dark shell of the past where his face turned curiously vacant and he spoke very little, as if sitting all alone.

"This… is another memory from rehab," he answered finally, giving her a brief glance before letting his gaze drift away to nothing. "Amongst the many games we played during our free time, most of them were games of what-ifs. What would we do if this happened or that happened. Kind of like wishful thinking, you know. It's hard for a rehab patient to ever imagine their life returning to normal. Normal seems too far away, too out of reach. So, they start treating it as a game instead. That way, it sounds more believable. That way, they don't have to get their hopes up and open themselves up to a world of pain later, when things don't work out or when their addiction returns with a vengeance. That way, they can start dreaming, too, without forgetting that the nightmare isn't far behind them and will catch up of they're not careful."

"I understand," Christie spoke softly.

Jed stirred at her voice. He smiled faintly. "I don't think you do, but I appreciate the gesture. Anyways, one of the games you already know about. Our last puzzle was based on it."

"Where would you go when you got out," Christie finished.

Jed nodded. "Correct. But that wasn't the only one we played, you know? There were many others, far too many to count." He chuckled. It was a harsh sound, full of sharp edges and an inexpressible bittersweetness. "We had a what-if for every damn thing we imagined our healthy selves doing. A game to dream up a whole life where our addiction wasn't standing behind like a tyrannical master wielding a whip. A life of freedom. A life of, dare I say it, happiness."

This time, Christie held her silence. She let the words flow out of Jed. He spoke of his old life so rarely that whenever the topic did come up, it was best not to interrupt his stream of thought.

"So, anyway," Jed continued, staring at a blank space on the wall, "one of our what-if games involved money, of course. How could it not? We were all addicts sent to a government-funded rehab clinic. Whatever money we had acquired in our lives had been wasted away to fuel our habit. We weren't exactly dripping wealth is what I'm saying. So, when the time to dream came up, we let our imaginations fly wild. Nothing could restrict us, not the sickness in our bodies, not the empty spaces in our wallets." He chuckled again, but this time, the sound was softer, more amused. "You should've seen the lot of us. Such mad ambitions. Such sky-high desires. As if we weren't societies muck but part of its topmost cream."

"I'm guessing that the idea to visit the roman cathedrals was yours," Christie commented.

Jed looked at her in surprise. "Yes. How did you know that?"

Christie splayed her hands. "You said you were interested in graffiti. Not very hard to make the leap from there."

"Ah." Jed nodded in understanding. His eyes twinkled as he appraised his partner. "You're becoming more perceptive. Could it be happening because of—dare I say it—the time you're spending in my company?"

Christie cracked a half-smile. "Perhaps. Continue with your story."

Jed spread his hands on his lap as well, to match her earlier gesture. "There's nothing more to tell. That game is what this note is about. It's what our next clue is."

Christie looked back at the pink slip lying on the table, a tiny splash of brightness against the room's drab colors. "Well, the clue mentions some kind of place. A special place. Do you know where that is?"

Jed smiled sadly. "Wouldn't be much of a challenge if I already knew it beforehand, now, would it?" He paused to snatch another cheese-smeared fry from the box and popped it in his mouth. "No, I need some time to think. Hopefully, the answer will come to me before our enemy decides to do something drastic."

"I have no doubt it will." Christie leaned back against the sofa. She ran her hands over her knees, looking around, eyeing the remaining bits of daylight puddled around the closed blinds. Then, she looked at the clock and noted the time. Close to six-thirty.

"Anything on your mind, Detective?" Jed's voice pulled her back to the present. She found him staring at her, an inscrutable expression on his face.

"Penny for your thoughts," he added, his eyes never leaving hers. Christie met his gaze squarely, without blinking.

"You already know what I'm thinking," she answered without much surprise. "So, why don't *you* tell me?"

Jed grinned. "You're thinking that you want to stay here tonight as well," he stated in a voice bordering on slyness, "but you don't know how to approach the subject because you know I'll resist. At the same time, you don't want to leave me alone either, in case our enemy sends us another midnight excursion to embark on. Tssk, choices, choices." He twiddled his thumbs in his lap, his grin turning teasing. "Am I right, or am I right?"

Christie smiled sweetly at him. "Perfectly right. Now would you mind if I guess what *you're* thinking?"

Jed blinked. He hadn't been expecting that. "Sure. Go ahead."

Christie leaned forward until her knees were touching the table's legs, until it looked like Jed was having the most intense therapy session of his life with a client.

"You're thinking about how you can dissuade me from staying here tonight." She held up a finger in front of her. "But you're also trying to simultaneously make up a reason to let me stay here, something that'll ease your heart and take away the guilt. It's a tough conundrum." She raised her middle finger to join her index one, held them together tightly. "On one hand, you want my safety above all else. On the other hand, you want me with you as well because of how much you enjoy my scintillating company." She grinned briefly, before turning serious once again. "Finally, even if you somehow did find a way to get me to stay here, part of you will still be reluctant because the idea of opening up to someone you care about is frightening."

Jed opened his mouth. Only after opening it did he seem to realize that there were no words in it, so he closed it again. He blinked multiple times at Christie, as if she were suddenly an apparition that had appeared in the room and he had no idea what to do with her.

"Tskk, decisions, decisions." Christie plucked a fry from the box and ate it whole. She smacked her lips contentedly. "Am I right, or am I right?"

It took a good ten seconds for Jed's speech to return to him. When it did, he spoke slowly, haltingly, a newfound respect marking his voice.

"Well done, Detective. I have to say, you have taken this round entirely. I've been swept off my feet."

"Thank you, thank you, I try when I can." Christie picked up another fry and looked at the thin curtain of cheese hanging from its lower end. She swallowed it whole, curtain and all, and had to resist the urge to lick her greasy fingers. It seemed like staying in grubby places made you want to pick up grubby habits.

"I see that you're really enjoying staying here," Jed noted dryly, "so we can cut to the end. Let's skip all the arguing and convincing one another. If you want, you can stay tonight as well. I won't try and stop you. God knows part of me wants to, but as you rightly said earlier, part of me also wants you to stay. In the end, the choice is yours."

Christie eyed the box of fries, stopping herself from eating more with visible effort.

"As long as this case continues," she told her partner, "and as long as our enemy is still at large, I'm afraid you won't be able to get me out of your hair. No matter how much you plead and insist, I'm not letting you face this challenge alone. No chance."

Jed bowed his head as if tired, although he just didn't want his partner to see how grateful he was. The sudden surge of emotion was making him uncomfortable. He wasn't used to being so open in front of others.

Seeming to guess his intentions, Christie rose from the sofa, wiping her hands together. "I'll let you sit here and absorb my decision," she said to him, walking across the room. "I need to use the restroom."

Jed let her go without another word. He did not raise his head from his lap, but if Christie had knelt down to get a closer look at him, she would have seen a smile of relief marking his features.

CHAPTER 12

CHRISTIE WOKE UP TO an intruder.

At first, her mind was too webbed over with sleep to understand what was happening. She blinked in the room's darkness, wading through the fog of her drowsiness to reach clearer grounds. Right in front of her, there was something in the darkness, something disrupting its uniformity. A smudge. A small, irregular blob a few meters from her face.

It seemed to be moving.

Still waist-deep in the dream she had just been having, Christie's hand reached reflexively for her phone. Her fingers fumbled beneath the pillow, making contact with the cool metal surface and pulling it free. Frowning to herself, trying to prevent her dream from dissipating, she searched for the phone's side button and pressed it with her thumb.

Light flooded the room, cutting through its swathes of blackness to bring Christie's cramped quarters back into view. There wasn't a lot to see, and none of it pretty. Still, she trained her phone in the smudge's direction, absently wondering who it was that was kneeling by her bedside, body half-hidden from view. As she brought the phone down, its light fell on the smudge and brought it into gruesome clarity.

Christie screamed.

On the other end of the corridor, in the apartment's only remaining bedroom, Jed woke up instantly. Unlike Christie, his mind was clear, alert. His feet leaped off the bed and hit the rooms' dusty carpet. Half-a-second later, he was running toward his partner, his heart hammering in his chest, the gun which he kept on his side table held in his hands and pointed at the ground.

Jed kicked the door open and barged inside, expecting anything, everything. A whole army of skinheads waiting inside to ambush him. Jack Stanley's ghost clinging to the ceiling, smiling a deathlike smile with a sniper rifle cradled in his hands. Heck, part of his mind even anticipated his father crouching in the shadows, face contorted with that inhuman fury Jed had seen in their last encounter.

But he saw none of these things. What he saw instead was Christie, her scream already dying in her mouth, her expressions beginning to turn normal. She did not pay Jed any heed when he entered because her focus was right in front of her, in the corner of the room opposite her bed—where an uninvited guest was scurrying to and fro, trying to find an escape.

Jed stared at the rat half-hidden in the darkness and did not quite know what to feel. Amusement began to bubble up within him, mixing with the terror that Christie's scream had dredged up, creating a confusing concoction where part of him wanted to laugh and another part of him wanted to sigh in exasperation.

"Don't say 'I told you so'," Christie warned him, raising a finger. "I was caught off-guard; that's the only reason I screamed. It's not like I'm afraid of rats or anything."

"Uh-huh." Jed's scratched his tousled hair before swiping it away from his forehead. "Not to beat a dead horse, Christie, but I did tell you so."

Christie rolled her eyes. She pulled up her blanket closer to her neck. It was then that Jed realized she looked quite different from how he was used to seeing her. None of that iron-pressed, authoritative law enforcement energy radiated from her. She was just a girl right now, a pretty, blue-eyed girl with messy blond locks covering half her face, hiding the cobwebs of sleep still present in her eyes.

"Sorry to wake you," Christie grumbled, settling back down on the bed. "You can go back to sleep now." Jed noticed half her attention was still on that corner in the other end, where the rat was no longer visible, but they could hear the faint rustling of its feet like a book's pages being flipped.

For a moment, Jed did not move, not sure how to handle this perplexing situation. It was a first for him, after all. He wasn't used to sharing seedy apartments with beautiful women whom he had a complicated relationship with. There was no manual or guidebook he could refer to right now, telling him what to do. Like all the other bizarreness characterizing his life, this was just the newest addition.

"Come on," Jed finally said, gesturing with one hand. "I promise, there's no creepy crawlies on my bed. You can bring your blanket and pillow with you, if you want."

Christie stared up at him silently, her eyes so very large and nervous in the darkness. They blinked at him, taking in his request.

"Err, no need, really," she answered awkwardly, pulling the blanket up even higher toward her chin. "I'll be fine here. The rat won't bother me. Looks like it prefers the floor over my bed."

Jed rolled his eyes. "Christie, I've already compromised all my rules of chivalry and manhood by letting you stay here. If you think that now I'll actually allow you to sleep in a room infested with rats, you're out of your mind. Pick up your blanket and come."

For a moment, it looked like Christie would argue further, but something in Jed's voice made her pause at the last minute. There was a note of finality in it, a steely authority which she knew wouldn't bend no matter how much she tried.

"Okay," Christie murmured. She shifted beneath the blanket but made no move to get up. "I'll be there in a few minutes."

Satisfied, Jed nodded. "Good, I'll be waiting for you. Don't keep me waiting too long." He turned around and left the room, not bothering to close the door.

Christie took in a deep breath.

Here it was. The embarrassment. The consequences of her actions. The risk factor of staying over at his place. She had made a gamble. Now, it was time to pay the price. And the price was sheer awkwardness; the embarrassment of intruding on someone's personal space, knowing they were only offering out of politeness because there was no other choice.

Jed was waiting for her when she came in, her head bent low, her blanket trailing behind her, her footsteps slow and shuffling like a sulking child sentenced to punishment. The room was slightly larger than hers had been, and although little of it was visible in the dimness, Christie could sense its cleanliness. She could sense Jed's discipline at work in this place, keeping the decay at bay. The faint scent of air freshener lingered in the air. Overhead, a wooden fan whirled slowly, producing more sound than air. Best of all, there were no uninvited guests hiding in the corners or scuttling across the floors. The room was empty. Safe.

Despite herself, Christie breathed in a sigh of relief as she put down her blanket and pillow on the bed, before sliding beneath them. She had not been lying when she had told Jed that she wasn't afraid of rats. But just because she wasn't afraid of them didn't mean she wasn't disgusted by them. Repulsed. When she had woken up and seen her new companion perched on the edge of her bed, watching her curiously with its beady black eyes, Christie had almost gagged. The scream had erupted from her mouth afterwards, and it had brought

Jed with it. Now, she was feeling more and more grateful that it had, despite her embarrassment. The idea of staying all alone in that other room wasn't looking very appealing anymore.

"Comfortable?" Jed asked her from the other side, his self a wide outline in the shadows. "Need anything?"

Christie shook her head. "I'm fine, thank you. And—uh thank you also, for letting me... you know, shift here."

"Don't be silly," she heard Jed answer, followed by the sound of a rustling sheet and a pair of feet hitting the floorboard. She turned sideways and found her partner standing by the bedside with his pillow in his hand, his forehead a mess of puffed-up hair.

"Where are you going?" Christie asked, confused. A strange thought entered her mind and she giggled. "Don't tell me you're going to fight the rat."

Jed laughed. "No, I'm already in a fight that's taking up most of my attention. Can't afford any others." He began walking out.

"Wait." Christie sat up straighter in bed. She saw Jed turn around at her words. "Where are you going, then? Like, seriously."

In the silence, she felt Jed's confusion thickening the air, a confusion that was as obvious as the answer she seemed to be missing.

"I'm... going outside to sleep," he answered slowly, in puzzled fashion, pointing toward the lounge to further illustrate his words. "You didn't think… you didn't think I was going to sleep here *with you*, did you?"

Christie was grateful for the dark because it hid the redness rapidly rushing up to her neck and cheeks.

"That's exactly what I was expecting," she responded, keeping her voice even. "That's exactly what you will do."

Jed's outline stared at her for a moment before scratching its head idly. "Christie…"

"Jed, listen," she interrupted, sitting fully upright now in the hopes that it would get her message across. "I've already caused you enough trouble tonight. I'm staying at your place, I woke you up from your sleep, and now I've taken over you room! No, there's no way you're sleeping on that decrepit couch. No way at all. I'm not letting myself fall so far."

"Christie…" Jed began in a voice indicating he planned on arguing with her.

"If you won't do it for yourself," she cut him off, "then just do it for me. Think of it as you saving me from a ton of embarrassment and awkwardness. I'll feel really bad if I'm responsible for evicting you from your own personal space. Please, Jed. It's just one night. Besides," she turned sideways and patted the mattress with one hand, hoping her gesture would come across as funny rather than lewd. "Say what you want about this place, but there's enough space on this bed for a whole football team. Surely you and I can spend one night on it without bumping into each other."

Jed's outline stood unmoving by the bed, his expressions hidden from her. Christie stared at him, waiting for him to decide. She had already made up her mind that if he insisted further, she would continue to argue with him. She would argue until he relented. Some things simply couldn't be allowed. They violated her code of ethics.

In the end, Christie had to argue no further. After a few more seconds of indecision, Jed's shoulders slumped. The pillow dangled in his grip, and he made his way back to the bed, uncertainty present in every bit of his movement. Still, it was better than nothing.

Silence returned to the apartment completely, as the two colleagues took their places on that single shared bed and tried to sleep. Between them lay around a foot of empty space, nothing more, yet that one foot was stretched out into a vast gulf by all those words they held for each other but refused to speak. Even now, as they lay together, nestled in darkness, their unvoiced thoughts clamored in their heads, demanding to be let out. Just as the room sat draped in darkness, so did the truth of their relationship sit between them, covered up. Neither of the two had the courage to pull that cover off to reveal what lay beneath. Instead, they turned to their sides, closed their eyes, and waited for sleep to find them. Eventually, despite their abnormal pulse and arrhythmic hearts, it did, and they drifted off into the land of oblivion.

Or at least, one of them did.

CHAPTER 13

JED IS BACK IN *the past.*

He is in the rehab cafeteria now, sitting with a group of people, most of whose faces have become familiar to him in the many weeks he has been here. Right in front of him lies a paper plate with a sad-looking sandwich on it. The lettuce poking out from the sandwich's sides appears more gray than green, more plastic than organic matter. He touches it listlessly with one finger, trying to work his appetite up. He must eat it because the detox process requires a daily minimum dosage of nutrients to work. If you skip out on meals you start fainting and puking at random times during the day, alongside experiencing painful ringing headaches.

Or at least, that's what the doctors have told them.

"Jeez, can't they put a little bit of effort into making this stuff? I know it's supposed to be super healthy and all, which is why they don't focus on taste, but still."

The voice is low. Jed raises his head up and finds that it belongs to another patient, a reedy little fellow with long black hair and almond eyes. He's sitting across from Jed and one seat to the right, picking at a bowl of what should be pasta but bears a closer kinship to toxic sludge. His fork draws slow circles in the sloppy meal, *lifting up chunks of meat and then letting them sink down again. After a few moments, his eyes rise and meet Jed's. They are bright and wiry, full of unbridled energy. Jed remembers his name is Ansel. He is still a boy, about Jed's age or perhaps a bit older. One of his many friends from rehab. A friend he lost touch with after leaving and never managed to find again.*

"You know what," another gruff voice says from right beside Jed. This is Dalton, Jed knows. One of the older boys from the clinic. Kind of like a big brother to him, strangely enough.

"You know what," Dalton repeats again, louder so that he has the table's attention, "if, by some miraculous stroke of luck, I ever managed to come across a million dollars or some other ungodly sum of money, the first thing I'd do is change my diet."

There are murmurs of agreement from all around, and also a few chuckles, as people look down at their plates with renewed distaste, Ansel digs his fork deep into his porridge-like dish and plucks out a piece of meat that is over cooked and stringy. He makes a face and lets it drop back down onto the plate with a wet plop. Jed finds the remainder of his appetite deserting him and knows he won't be eating anything until tomorrow.

"The first thing I'd eat is steak," Dalton remarks, staring up at the ceiling wistfully. "A huge, juicy-as-hell ribeye slow cooked to medium rare, served with a side of mashed potatoes and chimichurri sauce."

More ahhs of approval follow, with additional sounds of cutlery being put down as people resort to filling their stomachs with

Dalton's delicious description rather than the actual meal in front of them.

"And a tall glass of cider afterward to wash down that steak," Dalton continues, getting into the spirit of the game now, enjoying himself. "Maybe some crusty apple pie, too, in case my sweet tooth starts acting up again. Serve it warm and fresh from the oven, with a big scoop of vanilla ice-cream on top, and you have a meal fit for kings."

They're all talking amongst themselves now, unable to hold back their excitement. Jed finds his own stomach rumbling like a throaty tractor engine, even though his appetite had fled just moments ago. It has returned with a vengeance now, lured back by Dalton's words. Unknown to Jed, this is that pivotal moment of his life when his passion for food will sprout fully. The seed has always been within him, but Dalton's inflamed speech has given it life. This is when Jed the foodie finally takes on full form.

"What about you guys?" Dalton asks, pushing his plate away with a sour look. "Come on, let's do this. What would you do if you suddenly got rich?"

A flurry of different answers surge up at once, cuisines from all over the world clashing into one another, entrees and desserts fighting for dominance. Someone abandons the food idea and mentions buying a Bentley. Jed is asked for his opinion and mentions wanting to visit the cathedrals in Rome. Some people nod appreciatively at that answer, while others look disinterested. They move on from him, continuing their game. In that hodgepodge of voices, there arrives another voice, a softer one, more sullen, saying something…

Jed feels a pinch of fear.

His enemy is at the table.

He wants to look up, look around, search for that one particular face which has been the cause of so much sorrow in his life. But he cannot because this is not the present. It is the past, a recording of events having already taken place. In this recording, young Jed is staring down hard into the steel face of the table, thinking of what else he would do with the money. Somewhere around him, a madman lurks, watching discreetly, perhaps already planning the sick games he will play later on. Jed, though, is completely unaware. He's in a world of his own—a world where his biggest worry is getting out of this place a changed man. In the end, he will be successful in his mission, but something from the center will latch onto him. A remnant of his dark past, maybe, given human form and destined to hound him forever. His own personal enemy, which he will have to struggle against. An addiction given physical form.

"Jed? Jed? Hey, lost young man!" Jed looks up, blinking back the images of bacon and cheese and fish fingers crowding his mind. He finds Ansel and Dalton staring at him.

"What will you have, Jed?" Ansel prompts, fork still held in one hand although he hasn't eaten anything. "What's the first thing you'll have once you get out? Apart from your big trip, I mean. What food will you have?"

Jed purses his lips. Screws up his eyes. Thinks really, really hard, like he has always done all his life for the simplest of questions.

"Eggs for breakfast," he answers, "sunny side up. With the yolk extra soft and melted."

Ansel's face twists with disappointment. "After all that thinking, you come up with an answer so boring?" He grins at Dalton. "Dalton, I think you should take Jed with you for your steak. Maybe give him a bit of the leftover mashed potatoes. It'll sure as hell be better than some lame-ass eggs."

"Don't tease the boy for his honesty," Dalton chastises Ansel lightly. "Food is an art, like music or movies. We're allowed to have different tastes." He pauses for a second before grinning wolfishly. "Although eggs do sound a bit too boring, Jed. You wanna change your answer?"

Jed bows his head to come up with something better. He wants to name a food that will impress Dalton, will make him respect Jed even more, but he just can't think of anything. Prior to rehab, he's spent most of his life doing drugs, then cramming his stomach with cheap junk food when the munchies hit him. Caviar and steak tartare and other such delicacies have always remained alien to him, relics from a different life that different people live.

But now, Jed is thinking. He's thinking really hard. His sharp intellect is combing through every past memory of his, searching for that perfect right answer which will make Dalton proud. Jed wants that more than anything else. The void that his father left within him, he feels he can fill with Dalton's approval. If only he can manage to find the right answer...

Something...

Anything...

Wait.

"Found it!" Jed exclaims triumphantly, a bit too loudly, his fists hitting the table. He looks at Dalton and Ansel with shining eyes. "I know what I want!"

Ansel leans forward, intrigued. "Do enlighten us, then. This better be good, considering the hype you're creating."

Jed beams confidently. He turns toward Dalton, opens his mouth, and—

"… delivers it through mail. Yes, he delivers it through mail," Christie spoke. "No, the postman didn't know who it was, Graham. He only found the mail that had been left for him to deliver to Sam and Samantha. Yeah, there's no point investigating that avenue. It's a dead end. Yeah, okay. Let me know if you have any other updates for me. Bye."

What? What's happening?

Jed rolled over in bed, his vision still struggling to adjust against the room's brightness. What he saw there utterly confounded him for the first second—and also simultaneously made his heart leap with joy.

Christie was sitting up in bed, in *his* bed, right next to him, dressed in his shirt, with her blanket covering her legs. She was typing furiously into her phone, her face still lined with sleep, her hair adorably puffed up to one side.

"Christie?" Jed mumbled, unmindful of the dream that was slipping from his grasp as he spoke, taking its vital bits of information with it.

Christie looked sideways upon hearing Jed's voice. She smiled, and Jed found that he could now die a happy man after seeing this sight. His partner and friend in his bed right next to him, framed by the early morning light, her unkempt hair shimmering like sifted gold, her smile more radiant than anything he had ever seen in his life.

"Good morning," Christie said softly. "Did I wake you? I'm sorry—Graham called me, and I just picked up the phone reflexively. Forgot where I was."

It was then that Jed remembered the dream he had been having and the crucial moment at which it had ended. A tiny pinprick of frustration momentarily seized him, but he found himself unbothered by it entirely. How could he possibly be bothered in a situation like this? They were in an anonymous apartment in the derelict corners of the city, being hunted by and trying to hunt down a crazed killer, yet Christie was here and everything was fine. She was still smiling at him, her dimple accentuated by the golden light, the flecks of blue in her eyes sparkling like quartz.

"What are you looking at?" she asked Jed, frowning. "Do you not remember how I ended up here?"

Jed found himself shaking his head, lips parting into a sardonic grin. "No, but I hope the details are spicy."

His partner bristled next to him, and he enjoyed seeing the red staining her neck and cheeks.

"Jed!" Christie huffed, blowing a strand of hair away from her eyes. "Behave!"

Jed raised his hands, laughing. "Okay, okay. All I'm saying is, if a guy wakes up in the morning and finds a beautiful girl next to him in his bed, smiling down at him, naturally, he's going to think that, you know… something…"

"Jed!" Christie exclaimed, her complexion turning from crimson to beetroot. "I'll have you know that the spicy details you're asking for involve me shifting to your room because of a rat the size of small cat living in mine! Nothing more than that!"

Jed paused and pretended to remember. "Hmm. That does ring a bell. Are you sure there was no—"

"Positive," Christie answered quickly. "Now, since you're up, shall we go back to solving our case, which is the whole reason I'm here?'"

"Arghh, that's exactly what I was doing." Jed ran a hand through his hair to smooth it. "Until you woke me up, that is."

Christie frowned. "What do you mean?"

Jed looked at her. "I was dreaming about it. I had almost reached the answer when your sweet, angelic voice pulled me out of my past and back into the present."

Christie just stared at him, as if she couldn't tell whether he was joking or not. "Are you serious?" she finally asked. "Were you actually having some kind of a dream or—"

"I was," Jed answered. "It's kind of like a science, although the evidence to back this up is still being gathered. You feed the brain only one kind of information throughout the day, make it focus on only one problem, and when you go to sleep, your subconscious continues working, with far greater efficiency than you can consciously manage. If you get good at this technique, you'll usually wake up with answers to really tough puzzles, or simply realize them in a dream."

Christie's jaw dropped. "Wow? Is that how you solve all your cases, make all those crazy deductions?"

"Some of them," Jed grunted. "The ones my conscious mind can't solve, I leave to the unconscious. The rest require hard work. There are no shortcuts."

"Uh-huh." Christie played with her blanket's edge, looking interested. "So, what were you just dreaming about when I woke you?"

"The game," Jed answered, idly wondering if he could go back to sleep right now and resume the dream from where he had left off. No, that wouldn't be possible. The sight of Christie next to him had made him too excited. There was no question of drifting off now.

"Maybe you should try going back to sleep," Christie suggested, voicing his thoughts. "Who knows? Maybe the dream will start playing from where you paused it."

"That actually is possible," yawning and stretching his hands upward and cracking his knuckles. "The problem is I'm not sleepy anymore." He picked up his blanket and swung it off his legs before sitting upright. "Don't worry, though. The answer will most probably come to me during the day, at some random point. All I have to do is wait and not worry too much."

"In that case, let me help you out." Christie rose as well, suddenly looking shy, uncertain. A bit awkward. "I have a surprise for you."

"A surprise?" Jed echoed. "Pray tell, what might that be? Is it another rat?"

Christie rolled her eyes. "Very funny. Get dressed and come out. Then, I'll show you."

Jed felt his curiosity stirring. "But can you give me a hint at—"

"Nope." Christie shook her head. "You're too good at deciphering clues. I don't want my surprise getting ruined. Go brush your teeth and shower and whatever, then you can see for yourself."

"Okay, ma'am, as you command." Jed started making his way to the washroom. "I'll take a nice long shower, in case you need more time."

"Don't take too long, though. I don't want your surprise getting... fizzling out."

Jed nodded at her a final time before slipping inside the washroom and closing the door. The usual 15 minutes it took for him to get ready, he stretched out to 30, standing under the piping hot water and letting it soak his pores. While the steam rose around him and misted over the glass, he wondered what surprise Christie could have thought of in such a place. Had she figured out a clue or something? What else could it be?

There were sounds coming from the lounge when Jed stepped out—sounds of tinkling plates and padding feet on the carpet. Unable to contain his curiosity any longer, with his hair still dripping wet, Jed pulled on a beige sweater and went out to see what the fuss was about.

Christie stood waiting for him. She had placed something on the coffee table. Something perfectly round and melted and the color of a dipping sun.

"What..." Squinting, Jed moved forward. The item on the table became clearer, clear beyond any doubt. He stared at it for a few more seconds, then looked up at Christie, who was standing behind her surprise, smiling at Jed.

"Christie..." Jed was too confused to speak. He took another step forward, taking in the perfect colors of the food on the table. "What is this?"

Christie clasped her hands together. "Eggs. Sunny side up. I made them myself. Like my mom taught me, one of my favorites. I, uh..." Now she looked a bit nervous, a bit uncomfortable, just a tad bit uncertain. "I... well, you were talking in your sleep, Jed. I heard you. You were having some sort of conversation about favorite foods, and you mentioned eggs. So, I just thought, why not surprise you, since you're letting me stay over at your place?"

"Wow." Jed hoped his voice didn't reveal too much of the emotion he felt. He knew that his facial muscles were twitching, eager to convey to Christie what he thought of this surprise, but he held them in place. He didn't want to overwhelm her with his gratitude right now. It could make things strange.

"Go on," Christie urged him, taking a step back. "Have a bite. Tell me how they are."

Jed obliged. He knelt down beside the coffee table and picked up a fork lying next to the plate. He cut out a hearty portion of the egg, noticing the way the yolk split and oozed outward, exactly how he had liked it as a child. Jed raised the forkful of egg to his nose and inhaled, closing his eyes and getting lost in the fragrance of childhood. His mother near the kitchen counter, busily clanging pots and pans and opening cabinet doors, pausing every-so-often to check on the progress of a bunch of dishes cooking simultaneously on the stove. Doing all this whilst little Jed sat on the dining room chair, waiting for his breakfast, waiting for those runny, yolky eggs to be served to him so he could wolf them down.

"Well?" Christie asked, interrupting his trip down memory lane. "What do you think?"

Jed chewed. Chewed some more. Swallowed. Smacked his lips once. "Amazing," he told his partner, his voice sincere. "They're delicious, Christie. Just like my mom used to make them when I was a child."

Christie clapped her hands together and did a small jump "Yay! I'm glad you like them!"

"I love them," Jed corrected her, stuffing his mouth with another forkful of melted, buttery, heavenly egg. "You've even peppered them just the way my mom did. It's uncanny, how identical they are to the ones I used to eat as a child. Almost makes me wonder if you called my mom and asked her for the recipe."

"I did," Christie answered softly, then laughed at seeing Jed's shocked expression. "I joke. I joke with you. I did not. Your mom and I are both good cooks, I guess. Lucky for you. Surrounded by such amazing women in your life."

"Of that, there is no doubt," Jed mumbled, licking his lips. "I remember; on special occasions, like weekend holidays or Christmas or the likes, my mom would add a special touch to the dish. Instead of using normal eggs, she'd go and buy poached bird eggs. They tasted ten t—" He stopped abruptly, and his fork clattered from his hand back onto the plate.

"Jed?" Christie came forward. "What is it? What's wrong?"

Jed looked at her with wide-open eyes. He blinked like someone being brought out of a trance.

"Poached bird eggs," he whispered. "Birds' eggs." A pause. "*Birds.*"

Christie came even closer. There was something in Jed's voice, something telling her that they were no longer just discussing food or past memories. "Jed?"

Jed had risen to his feet. He seemed to be searching for something, looking around the room every which way, even up at the ceiling, his hands clenched by his sides.

"Jed?" Christie repeated, stepping up to him. She tapped his shoulder lightly, and Jed turned to her. He blinked rapidly again, taking in the sight of her.

"Birds, Christie," Jed whispered. A spasm seemed to cross his face, throwing his expression into disarray, squeezing his eyes into slits. When he opened them again a few seconds later, they shone with a new light.

"Bird's nest soup," Jed whispered, in a voice that was almost awed. "Bird's nest soup. That was it. That was the dish."

Christie had been with him long enough to catch up quickly. "The dish you mentioned in that game of yours!" she exclaimed, excited. "Jed, are you sure?"

Jed nodded. "I can remember it now, every bit of it. That's the answer I gave them because I wanted to look cool and unique. I'd heard about bird's nest soup in some TV show at home, and the idea had stuck with me. I had found it amusing, actually, that people would pay money to eat frozen saliva. But that's the world for you. Getting crazier by the day."

Christie shook her head. "Okay, but do you know the place where you said you'd go? I'm sure there's not just one in this city which is serving your bird sa—that nest thing, or whatever."

Jed nodded again with a smile. "I remember. The TV program had mentioned it. A place called Golden Unicorn. I never actually went there after leaving rehab, so I don't know if it's even open or not."

"Oh, it's open," Christie answered confidently. "We wouldn't have received our riddle if it had shut down. Our mysterious enemy is very meticulous with his planning."

Mention of their enemy quickly wiped the nostalgia from Jed's face. His jaw muscle flexed.

"You're right," he told Christie with a frown. "Let's go finish this challenge. Let's go rescue Lauren."

Christie picked up her keys from the table and jangled them. "Let's go."

CHAPTER 14

THE GOLDEN UNICORN LOOKED more like a low-grade gambling den than a restaurant. It had red carpets covering its ground and second floor, and the walls were all unsurprisingly painted golden. As Jed stepped in with Christie, he almost expected to see slot machines lining the corner past the host's stand. But there weren't any, just glass tables and wooden chairs with guests, mostly Asian folk, seated on them.

A man in a bowtie sporting gelled black hair came to greet them.

"Table for two, sir?" he asked in a heavy Thai accent.

Jed nodded slowly, casting his eyes around the place. He didn't know what it was they were supposed to find here. Some other clue? Was this even the right place? He had been so sure before, but now a bit of doubt was starting to creep in.

"Follow me sir, madame." The man turned around, and they followed after him. He led them up a wooden staircase onto the second floor, where Jed spotted a table lying empty right opposite the glass window that overlooked the street.

"Over here, sir." The man pulled out a chair for Christie, who sat down quietly, her eyes scanning the place. Jed took his place opposite her, picked up the menu, and pretended to scan it until their escort went away.

"Well, now what?" Christie asked, leaning forward with both elbows on the table. "I don't see anything suspicious here. Well—I mean, apart from the whole place itself. It has a strange vibe."

Jed nodded, considering. "I think... we should order."

A single eyebrow stood up on Christie's face. "Bird's nest soup? Thanks for the offer, Jed, but I'm not a big fan of animal saliva."

"We don't have to actually eat it," Jed answered, already going through the options in the menu. He couldn't make sense of most of them; they involved strange names and even stranger ingredients. "But we do have to order. One, because we can't stay here unless we do. Two, because I have a feeling that it's part of solving this puzzle."

Christie looked skeptical but said nothing. Jed motioned to the waiter with one hand. He was a young Asian lad with a curiously thin face that seemed to taper off toward his chin.

Jed looked down at the options once more and haltingly pronounced a kind of bird's nest soup featured on the menu. The waiter took their order, bowed, and left. Jed rapped his knuckles against the glass table and looked out at the overcast day.

"Lauren," Christie suddenly said, "she was a client of yours, right?"

Jed nodded.

"Hmmm." Christie played with her napkin. "What—what exactly did she come to you for, if you don't mind me asking?"

"Imposter syndrome," Jed answered with a faint smile. "She was a kid who had earned millions even before graduating from college. And she hadn't earned it through luck, by winning the lottery or buying the right NFT. She had earned it by creating an app that tapped into an unrealized gap in the market, a gap that turned into an unending flood of revenue when the customers finally began to flow in."

"Wow," Christie murmured. "That's really impressive."

"It is," Jed agreed. "The whole world thought so. The whole world... except for Lauren." He pressed his finger against the napkin lying before him, trying to smooth a wrinkle that kept popping back up in different places. "When she came to me, she was very conflicted. Eaten up with self-doubt. Said to me that she constantly wondered whether her success had been anything more than a fluke. Said she didn't deserve the praise people constantly heaped upon her."

"How did you help her?" Christie asked, listening intently.

Jed shrugged. "I tried a different approach with her. Told her that imposter syndrome isn't technically real, since everyone owes their success to luck—even those who work hard."

Christie frowned. "I don't follow."

"Well," Jed cleared his throat. "I told Lauren that success is determined by outside circumstances and the effort you put in. The outside circumstances are determined by luck, which everyone knows, but even the internal circumstances are almost entirely based on the same principle of chance." He paused to make sure Christie was following. "Your genetics determine, to a large degree, how disciplined you will be, how hard you will work. Since genetics are also something you can't control, we can factor them in with luck as well."

"How did this help Lauren?" Christie asked.

Jed smiled again. "Normally, when you're dealing with imposter syndrome, the correct course of treatment is to constantly remind the person of their achievement and make them feel valued. Prove to them through facts and statistics that they are deserving of their success. Make them celebrate every win, no matter how small it is, so the idea really sinks into their brain. But," he paused for a moment, "with Lauren, I tried a different approach because the conventional one hadn't worked for her."

Intrigued, Christie leaned forward further. "Which was?"

Jed pressed his lips together. "I used the syndrome against itself as a weapon. I accepted what it was making her think. I accepted her claims that success was dependent on luck, that there was no reason to feel good about yourself since you had just happened to be at the right place at the right time."

"Huh?" Christie's brows furrowed. "How is that supposed to help?"

Jed raised his hands like a magician readying an audience before the final big reveal. "Because there was one important condition, one rule she had to accept. If this random, arbitrary system of luck applied to her, then it applied to *everyone else*, too."

Jed waited while Christie took in that statement and tried to wrap her head around it.

"Oh," she said finally, after a long pause. "Oh, now I get it."

Jed nodded his head in acknowledgement. "Things were pretty easy to handle after that. Lauren really only had two options to choose from: either success in this world is dependent on hard work, in which case she deserved all the praise that was coming her way. Or success is based entirely on luck and can never be attributed to the person in question, in which case, every successful person is lucky. So, Lauren had no reason to feel bad. No reason to feel like she didn't deserve her status, since no one else deserved theirs either. It was all just a game of chance. Why worry so much about a game? I told her to go and live her life and stop worrying so much."

Christie was looking at Jed with a glint in her eyes, a glint of fascination. She had always assumed that she had a decent enough idea of what went on in that profession, but today he had given her a practical example. Christie realized she had grossly underestimated the difficulty and the value of therapy. It was a daunting task, fixing so many broken people, each uniquely damaged in their own way. A lot of them weren't even capable of fully expressing their problems. You had to find out what was hurting them, then devise a workable solution they would accept, without any resistance.

Damn, and here I was thinking my job is hard.

Now that she considered it, Christie's own position as a police officer in this city seemed, if not easier, definitely more simplistic to her. You didn't have to think so much when implementing the law. Either the violator saw your badge and obeyed, in which case the situation had been handled, or they decided to fight you back, in which case you put to use all those years of training from the academy. Almost all situations in her career had been handled in one of those two ways. But with Jed's role as a therapist, each client was a puzzle entirely different from the others, which you had to learn to decode without any outside help—and sometimes with the puzzle itself fighting you back.

No wonder he's so good at solving clues.

"What are you thinking?" Jed asked, snapping Christie out of her reverie. "You looked so far away for a minute."

Christie shook her head, smiling. "Just about how tough your job is. At least as tough as mine, if not more. But because yours doesn't involve any shooting and fighting, people generally assume it's a walk in the park."

Jed grinned. "It's more like a walk through the gates of purgatory, but it's fully worth it in the end. When you see your client sitting before you, radiant and happy, a transformed version of themselves, you don't mind all those exhausting hours one bit. You would do it all over again, if you could.

In fact, I actu—" He broke off midway as the waiter arrived with their order, carrying a white porcelain cup on a wooden tray. He set it down before them before turning around and practically running away, without saying a word.

"Jeez," Christie muttered. "I know we're kind of like foreigners here, but is that any way to treat a c—"

"What is that?" Jed asked.

Christie blinked. "What?" She saw his eyes looking down at the bowl and followed their direction. She did a double-take when she saw what was there, straightening up in her chair.

"Yeah, what is that?"

There was something white peeking out from beneath the bowl. A folded strip of paper without any creases other than the one dividing it in half. Tiny, by the looks of it. Too tiny to be a bill.

"Did the waiter leave his number or something?" Jed joked, leaning forward. He lifted the bowl and plucked the paper from beneath it. "Christie, I think you may have been hit on."

Frowning, Christie looked at the paper. It didn't look like it contained something as harmless as a phone number. She was beginning to get a bad feeling about this.

"What is it?" she asked Jed, watching him unfold the slip and read it. There couldn't have been much written there, considering its size, but Jed still took his time staring at the thing. Christie saw his pupils swiveling left and right, reading and rereading and re-rereading.

"Jed, what is it?" she pressed.

Jed opened his mouth but did not say anything. There was still a slight frown on his face, and his other hand was reaching for his phone.

"It's... gibberish," he answered finally, holding his phone with one hand. "Contains a random series of numbers and letters. I don't know what it means." He handed over the slip to Christie. She took it from him and looked at the message.

AJM?CDR327?456

"This... definitely looks like gibberish," she concluded quickly, then added, "but it definitely isn't. I think we know that. I think this is a message?"

Jed was scrolling through his phone, squinting at the screen.

"I'm seeing if something in any of his previous messages will allow me to decode this one," he muttered, his thumb swiping fast. "Maybe he left a hint for me somewhere, some clue to get to the bottom of this..."

Christie looked back down at the message, trying to understand what it could possibly mean. After a minute of frustrated concentration, she gave up and glanced sideways, searching for the waiter, that young boy who had served them their meal with this secret message in it. Her eyes scanned the tables and the spaces between them, trying to spot that familiar narrow face, but it was nowhere to be seen. There were three other waiters present at the moment, all of them older men who bore no resemblance to the one she wanted. The boy had disappeared, it seemed, vanished without a trace. Christie turned her focus to the kitchen door diagonally across from her and saw it swing open. An additional trio of waiters stepped out, but they were also new faces, sporting beards and wrinkles and balancing loaded trays in their hands. As one, they headed down the stairs in single file to serve the guests seated on the ground floor. Christie watched them go, mouth silently moving to voice her confusion.

Where is the boy?

There was no answer, and it didn't seem like she would be getting one anytime soon. Christie turned back to the task at hand, returning her gaze to the slip of paper. That was when it happened.

She almost heard the click inside her head as it all fell into place. Her eyes took in the seemingly random string of letters and numbers, and Christie dimly recognized the pattern present there—the way one flying in a helicopter looks down at the land and spots the structure of neighborhoods.

"Jed. Jed." She reached forward and nudged her partner with one hand. "Jed, I see something."

"What?" Jed looked up from his phone. "What is it?"

Christie swallowed. "These look like they are… acronyms for all the people he's killed so far, with the numbers being the order in which they were killed."

Jed's face darkened. "Show me that paper." He took it from her hands and frowned down at it. His lips moved silently. A single vein pulsed in his forehead.

"A for Alex," Christie spoke softly. "C for Carl, Jameson's brother. M for Maria. And J for Joel, of course."

Jed nodded slowly, his face darkening with every passing second. The gray from his eyes seemed to be leeching into his skin, turning him into a figurine of ash. "There are question marks, too," he mumbled.

"Those are the gaps we're supposed to fill in," Christie guessed. "That's the puzzle, I think. We fill those in and send them to him. Text him with the answer, I suppose.

"There are two question marks," Jed grunted. "One in the letter sequence and one in the number sequence. That means he's telling us there's someone else he's killed… someone we know."

"We need to guess his order as well," Christie said grimly. "Christ, this is sick. This is so sick."

"It's sick, but it's also the only way we can prevent the list from having more letters added to it." Jed clucked his tongue. "Okay, let's put it into chronological order. First was Joel."

Feeling bile rising in her throat, Christie joined in the game. "Second was Alex. Anne-Marie's husband, Dave. Wait, no, before him was Carl—"

"Rosa, the masseuse witness," Jed finished. He felt a familiar twinge in his heart as he spoke the woman's name, knowing what a grievous mistake her death had been. "And finally, Maria."

"There is no 'L' for Lauren, which is hopeful. Not that we can trust anything from this psychopath," Christie commented, then added hastily, "not that I think she's dead. I didn't mean that. I'm sor—"

"It's fine, don't worry about it." Jed seemed too engrossed in decoding the message to have properly heard what Christie said. "Okay, so we have a list of kills. We have to find out the missing link, as well as its order. Who could it be?"

Christie screwed up her face. "I... that's a hard one, since I'm a police officer. It's my job to deal with homicides on a daily basis. There have been so many since this lunatic entered our lives. How do we find out which one he's responsible for?"

Jed breathed slowly through his nose, thinking. "It can't just be any homicide. No, that's not his style. In some way, shape, or form, it has to turn back to me. It has to be related to me. Everything this guy has done has been a knife aimed at my heart. So, who could it po—" He froze, suddenly, as it hit him. An answer. A potential answer to this riddle. Too awful if it were true.

"Jed?" Christie asked tentatively. She touched his arm lightly with one hand. "You okay?"

The sculpture of ice that had seconds ago been Jed Gray looked at her. Only its eyes moved, the face utterly immobilized. Christie saw the darkness pooling there, with the fury bubbling beneath it like magma, threatening to erupt forth.

"Ethan," Jed muttered, looking down at the table, through the table, into the past.

Christie waited for Jed to finish before adding gently. "Do you think it could be him?"

Jed gritted his teeth. "It's possible. I've always believed Ethan was murdered—murdered in a way to make it look like an overdose. Now it's looking even more likely. It's practically our enemy's MO. He dresses his crime scenes up as accidents, suicides, even frames others for the murders he commits. Ethan's death falls perfectly within that category."

Christie nodded, pursing her lips. "Then... is that the answer?"

Jed sighed. "I don't know, Christie. It seems to be the best one we've got. Should I send it? I don't even know if there are going to be any... repercussions... for wrong answers."

"Send it," Christie told him. "Don't forget you have the edge over him right now. He doesn't want you to disappear forever. That means he won't risk upsetting you over such minor things. Text him Ethan's answer."

Jed nodded. He copied the code that had been written on the paper before pasting it in the message bar. Then, he deleted the question marks and replaced them with his answers. An E for Ethan in the alphabet series, and a 1 to indicate the order in which he had been killed. Jed pressed the send button, feeling a strange jitter in his stomach as the text was sent. He hoped his hunch had been right.

"I think we should go back to the car," Christie suggested. "We might need to move quickly after this. Plus, I think the restaurant's served its purpose. We've already received t—" She was cut off by the sound of Jed's phone ringing on the table. They both looked down at it and saw *Unknown Caller* flashing eagerly, almost hungrily on the screen, daring Jed to answer it.

"You're right." Jed stood up in a hurry, throwing open his wallet and flinging some cash onto the table. He and Christie dashed down the stairs, out of the restaurant's revolving doors, where Jed answered the call while getting back inside the Ford and locking its doors.

"Hello?" Jed spoke into the receiver.

A taut second of silence.

"How was the bird's nest soup?"

Jed bit back a curse. "Quit with the games. We answered your riddle. Now, let Lauren go. Enough's enough."

"You should've seen the way you both ran," the mechanical voice continued, ignoring what Jed had said. *"I mean, the way you threw back your chair, Gray, and then flung that money on the table. It was really something to see."*

Freezing water sluiced Jed's bones. The phone almost dropped from his hands with the force of the surprise. He turned toward Christie, eyes wide, jaw hanging, unable to speak what he had just realized.

Their enemy was in the restaurant.

"Ah, Ah," that robotic voice cackled as soon as Jed's hand violently pulled on the Ford's door handle. *"Stay where you are, Jed. You missed your shot. You won't find me in that restaurant anymore, I'm afraid."*

But Jed was no longer listening. His pulse roared in his ears. His lips were drawn back in a feral snarl. He jumped out of the Ford and sprinted back inside the Golden Unicorn, ignoring the strange looks passersby gave him. Once inside, he ran up the stairs, leaping three steps at a time, his heartbeat threatening to push its way out of his chest.

There were several people seated on the first floor. Eight of them were in either pairs or triplets, busy wolfing down the strange-looking dishes they had been served. Only one man sat alone, but he was an old Latino dude, with a wispy beard drooping down from his chin and a laptop lying in front of him, on which he was working studiously.

There was no one else there.

No. No. This can't be. Not now. Not after I got so close—

Jed turned and ran back down, almost bumping into Christie, who had followed after him. He didn't pay her any attention. There was no time for that. His enemy had finally appeared, and Jed had missed the opportunity. Missed the one chance to end this madness once and for all.

The ground floor was much the same. There were only families seated there, with fathers trying to control their unruly toddlers or arguing with their spouses about what to order. Jed took in the scene for a few moments before stomping out. As he did, he noticed that the restaurant had two entrances: one in the front, which they had used, and one directly opposite it.

Of course.

He did not bother checking that second entrance. He knew it would lead nowhere. Their enemy had already disappeared, slipped back into the city's torrential flow of people and vehicles. For a moment, though, he had stepped out on the banks. He had stepped out to see Jed, to stand just a few feet away from him, but Jed had been too preoccupied to notice.

This is the second time now I've let him get away, Jed thought bitterly to himself. *Still, I should be celebrating because at least this time my foolishness didn't get anyone killed.*

There was no time for indulging in self-pity, though. The phone was still in his hand, and he could see the call still connected, waiting for him to resume. The self-blame and anger would have to wait for later, after Lauren had been taken to safety.

Jed made his way back to the car. Christie caught up with him, sliding into the driver's seat without a word. They locked their doors once again, and Jed unmuted the call.

"Hello?"

Laughter greeted him, that strange metallic crumpling and twisting steel. It went on for a long while, filling the car's interior.

"Satisfied, Gray?" the warbled voice asked. *"I told you, you wouldn't find me. You missed the chance when I gave it to you, unfortunately."*

Jed squeezed the receiver. "Why did you come here? What was the point? Where's Lauren?"

"I came because I missed you," the voice answered, injecting a tone of artificial sadness into its distorted depths. *"You've disappeared entirely, Gray. I have no idea what you're up to these days. That's why I came, to see my dear friend's pretty face again. Might I say, I'm loving the new beard. It suits you very well."*

"Where's Lauren?" Jed repeated impatiently. "We've solved a bunch of your riddles now. Let her go. Stick to your word. Remember, I warned you not to hurt her. Other—"

"Easy there, tiger." Another mechanized burst of laughter. *"Lauren's safe. For now. You're almost at the end of this level, Gray. Just one more challenge remains. If you can succeed in completing it in time, your client will be given a new life. If not…"*

Jed fought back the urge to drive his fist into the dashboard. "What is it? What do you want now?"

The voice tittered. Amplified and distorted, it sounded like metal pins raining from the sky. *"Why, I want you to go back to the basics once again. I want you to do what you're so good at, and what the police department is so hopelessly inept at. I want you to solve a murder."*

Jed's eyes widened. In the very edge of his periphery, he glimpsed Christie cursing silently.

"You've killed someone else?" he exclaimed. "I warned you. I warned you if you did something like that, it would be the end of our—"

"Relax, my jumped-up little hophead friend. This one's not mine." Through the convoluted mesh of distortion, Jed caught something else. Something he hadn't heard before. A note of admiration tinging the voice's inhuman depths.

"Not yours?" Jed repeated. "Then whose?"

"What does it matter?" The voice tittered again. *"The only thing I want to know is how it was done. You, my dear friend, will find that out for me. In 24 hours."* A pause. *"Starting now."*

"Wai—" Jed began, but the call had already been disconnected. He raised his head from the phone to look at Christie, who was staring at him with an expression of disbelief and anger.

"I can't believe he was here," she whispered, turning toward the restaurant. "He was actually sitting in the same room as us, but we still missed him…" Her voice trailed off, and she turned back to Jed, a glint of hope in her eyes. "Did we, Jed? Did we miss him?"

Jed was looking down at the car's floor mat when Christie spoke to him. There was a strange look on his face, a look Christie couldn't decipher. He seemed neither angry nor worried, nor did he appear particularly calm. His lips were slightly parted, and his eyes were glazed over.

"Jed?" Christie repeated, a bit more loudly, and Jed seemed to stir, as if in a dream. He raised his head slowly and turned to her, confused.

"Sorry, what?" he asked.

Christie paused. "What is going through your mind?"

"Uh…" Jed frowned, casting his gaze down again. He rubbed a hand against his brows. "Nothing. I… uh, nothing. What were you saying just now?"

Strange. What is he thinking about?

Christie bit her lower lip. "I was asking you if we missed him. The man. Our target. When he was sitting in the restaurant with us, God-only-knows how many seats away."

Jed frowned again, as if Christie had asked a silly question. But that was not it, Christie realized. She knew what was happening to him right then, why he looked so frazzled. His brain had picked up on something, something of vital importance, and it was currently using most of its power to analyze that information. This confused, uncomprehending Jed sitting before her was just a tiny remainder of that energy, not really there with her but pretending to be.

"Jed, that's not what I meant." She waved a hand before his face, trying to draw more of him out. "I meant whether or not you remember anyone suspicious-looking from the restaurant when we were there. Our target would have been alone." She paused, unable to stop the hope from creeping into her voice and heart. "Did you see anyone like that? Someone sitting alone, giving off the wrong vibe? Even if you just have a blurry snapshot of his face, it's okay. We can get a sketch artist to—"

Jed was already shaking his head. That absent look still clouded his features, but it was decreasing by the second. "I didn't, Christie," he answered. "There's no one like that I can recall. Just families or people in twos and threes, too bothered with their own lives to pay us any attention."

"But how can that be?" Christie burst out, unable to contain herself any longer. "He was right there! He was right with us! If only we'd turned around and… and…" She fisted her palm angrily, her breath coming out in harsh spurts. "If only we'd been more attentive."

"It doesn't matter." Jed laid a hand against her arm. "We're here, and like he said, the final part of this sick game could be coming any second. There's no time fo—"

The phone's beep cut him off. It was an eerie moment, almost as if their enemy had been spying on them and waiting for the perfect moment to interject. As Jed's phone's screen lit up and the shrill sound of an incoming message filled the car's interior, both he and Christie felt the hair on their necks rising. Right then, it wasn't just the two of them in that car. There was someone else present there, some*thing* else, hovering between them and all around them in incorporeal form, yet weighing down upon their shoulders with a force far greater than physical matter could exert. Jed had never been particularly interested in the supernatural, but in that moment, the only term he could think of to describe their predicament was *haunted.*

Afterward, the device lay dark and silent in his lap, waiting for him to pick it up. He took his time, giving both himself and Christie a final few moments of respite before they plunged back into action. Once that respite was over, once they could no longer avoid the unavoidable, a sigh escaped his lips, and he picked up the device, swiping its screen.

"Let's get to it, then, shall we?"

CHAPTER 15

"OKAY, LET'S GO OVER this one more time."

Christie pressed a hand against her temples and tried to squeeze back an oncoming headache. It worked, but barely. She could still feel that dull throbbing spreading to the edges of her skull, making her feel like she'd just stepped out of a particularly brutal boxing match.

"We've already gone over it six times," she said, hating the whining tone in her voice but unable to keep it back. "How much more? This case is unsolvable."

Jed grinned. The sparse daylight filtering in through the half-closed blinds caught his teeth and turned them gleaming white. He looked like a jacked, crazed version of Sherlock Holmes, Christie thought absently.

And a sexier one, too.

She pushed that thought away with some mixture of irritation and nervousness. It had been happening more and more recently. This prolonged contact with Jed had cracked open some wall deep within her, and now strange thoughts were rising to the surface—thoughts she usually kept hidden from everyone, even herself. They were all related to Jed's physical characteristics, the contrast between his imposing hulk and the disarming softness of his eyes. How his stubble had grown increasingly thick and untamed, yet how his voice still retained its velvety tone. She realized that focusing on the impossible case at hand was becoming increasingly challenging for her. Jed just kept getting in the way.

"There's no such thing as unsolvable, Christie," he told her now, the grin still plastered to his face, driving part of Christie mad. "Only *unsolved*. As of yet." He ran a hand through his hair and pushed a tangle of locks back from his forehead. Christie swallowed and averted her eyes, choosing instead to look at the large whiteboard they had erected in the living room on a wooden tripod stand. Much like Jed's brainstorming wall, the whiteboard was cluttered with writing, images, and a random peppering of question marks, none of it coming together in any way that made sense.

"Okay, so…" Jed snapped his fingers to draw Christie's focus to him. "Let's go through this again. What is our case? Come on, summarize the crux of the issue for me."

Christie rubbed one eye wearily. "A death," she began. "A death inside a freezer room."

Jed raised an eyebrow. "A death?"

Christie paused. "A murder. Sorry, a murder. A murder which was committed without a weapon."

Jed raised a hand. "Let's not jump right to the end. It's better if we take this step-by-step. First: who was murdered?"

"Sean Linehan," Christie answered instantly, the name familiar on her tongue after so many repetitions. "A 33-year-old Irish man. He worked as a butcher in a meat shop that served as a front for the cartel."

Jed beamed. "Excellent. That already gives us enough information to assume that this couldn't just be a mere freak accident. We are dealing with the world of criminals, after all."

Christie nodded. "You're right. It was probably a hit from another mob or something, considering that Linehan used to be the enforcer in the cartel's gang before he switched from cutting up humans to cutting up meat. A rival gang probably killed him for revenge. It's the most likely explanation."

"Exactly!" Jed cheered her on. "See? We've already solved half the case!"

Christie snorted. "Yeah, right! We both know that none of this information matters; it is all speculation. The only thing we were tasked with finding out was *how* Linehan was killed, not why or where or when, or even by whom."

"I know. We'll get there, too." Jed tapped a finger against his chin, affecting the air of one in deep thought. The look was so comical that Christie couldn't help cracking a smile. All her partner needed now was a fedora and a pipe, and he would be the ultimate sleuth detective of the 21st century.

"How was Linehan killed?" Jed mused out loud, feigning great mystique, acting as if they hadn't gone over this whole spiel multiple times in the last two hours, all to no avail.

Christie snickered. "Maybe a ghost killed him."

"Even ghosts leave some kind of evidence behind," Jed muttered. "But in this case, there's nothing at all. Nothing we can look to. Hmmm."

Not having anything worthwhile to contribute to the discussion, Christie remained silent. She glanced sideways at the whiteboard and took in the largest photo that had been stuck there with tape. It showed a sprawling maze of a freezer room where giant refrigerators loomed like walls, and meat hooks wreathed in mist dangled from the ceiling, their misshapen silhouettes suggestive not of ghosts but of ghouls arrived from some dark alternate reality.

"One locked room," Jed muttered, pacing the space between the sofas and rubbing his chin as he did. "One room and no murder weapon. How? How could it have happened?"

'Maybe it was an invisible murder weapon," Christie chimed in, only half-joking. "Like a light saber or some other form of sophisticated technology. Maybe, after using it, the killer turned it back into a pen or something and put it in his pocket before leaving. It's possible, no?"

If Jed had actually taken Christie's input seriously, he didn't seem too convinced by it. His pacing turned quicker around the room, and his eyes furrowed even deeper.

"We're dealing with the mob here," he seemed to speak to himself. "They're not exactly technological geniuses. No, something else happened here… something we just haven't seen yet. Clever but simple."

Christie bit back her frustration and glanced again at the picture on the whiteboard. What could it be? The case was so simple, so open-and-shut, that she was having a hard time believing another explanation existed.

"At 7:35 PM, six months ago," Jed began, coming to a stop right in front of Christie, "one of the refrigerators in The Wallace Meat Shop freezer room malfunctioned."

Christie nodded. Maybe Jed was right. Maybe going over everything again and again would eventually unearth some helpful detail.

"The malfunctioning refrigerator was one of the largest in the freezer room," Jed continued, absorbing each word as he uttered it and reflecting on it. "Something must have happened to the machinery, I guess, because apart from leaking water, which always formed a puddle beneath it, the thing also began releasing a mixture of mist and Freon gas into the room."

"Which obscured the place entirely and made the surveillance cameras useless," Christie added. "In summary, we have no way of witnessing what occurred at the scene of the crime."

"Correct." Jed nodded. "Now, on the day of his tragic demise, our victim, Sean Linehan, was in the freezer room, still working—at its other end, where the gas and the mist didn't fully reach. The maintenance staff in the meat shop had gotten the refrigerator fixed multiple times, of course, but it was a stubborn little thing. Started acting up again a few weeks after every patch-up.

"Eventually, the staff just learned to work around it instead of constantly wasting money on it," Christie finished.

"Indeed." Jed clasped his hands together. He frowned down at the carpet. "Linehan is in the room at around 7:35 PM. Most of the room is filled with mist and Freon gas, which obscures visibility. The camera footage does not show Sean or anyone else. Finally, at around 8:15 PM, the gas begins to dissipate from the room. The refrigerator's tantrums for the day are over. As visibility returns, what is the first thing the security man sees?"

"Linehan lying dead on the floor," Christie answered quietly. She paused for a moment, then spoke again. "He had a stab wound in the side of his neck."

Jed let out his breath in a slow whistle. "Yes, but this is where things get confusing. Everyone thought Linehan had been stabbed, except…"

"Except there was no murder weapon." Christie sighed. "None of the butcher's knives or any other sharp implements, like the meat hooks, inside that freezer room came even close to matching the puncture wound. It was small and very, very sharp."

"Exactly. This led the initial investigating authorities to only one conclusion." Jed flopped down on a sofa opposite Christie. He crossed his legs and waited for her to pitch in.

"That the killer had brought his own weapon with him," Christie obliged.

Jed smiled weakly. "Now, we come to the rub." He tapped his fingers on the sofa's armrest. "There was no way the killer or anyone else could have brought any weapon within the building's premises. Even a pocketknife was out of the question. Why?"

"Because the meat shop was secretly run by the Cartel," Christie murmured. She glanced at the fading twilight glow dripping in through the blinds, waning with every passing second, as if someone were sucking the evening's brightness out with a straw.

"Three security checkpoints before you get to access the back of the meat shop, where the freezers are next to the meeting room," Jed muttered. He rubbed his forehead wearily. "Three different armed guards checking you for any sort of hidden weapon you might be trying to sneak inside."

"Thus, we arrive at the core of our problem. It wasn't possible for the killer to have been armed," Christie concluded. She let out an exasperated sigh, sagging back against the sofa. "Then, how was Sean killed? What was the murder weapon? He needed to use a weapon that was already there… and then, somehow, it disappeared?"

"Most importantly," Jed continued, raising a finger, "even if the killer did manage to get his hands on a weapon of some kind, what did he do with it once he had used it? How did he sneak it out? Because there was an additional security checkpoint placed before the exit, as well!"

"Maybe he stashed it somewhere in the building before fleeing," Christie wondered out loud. The idea didn't make much sense to her, but it wasn't like their desk was overflowing with plausible theories.

"Really?" Jed raised an eyebrow. "I doubt that. The police turned the whole damn place upside down when combing for clues, remember? They even checked the clogged toilet lines in case the killer had tried to flush the evidence of his dirty deed away. But they found nothing. Nothing at all. Nada."

"An invisible weapon, or have we entered into some black magic realm?" Christie whispered. She shivered suddenly, feeling an inexplicable pinch of vulnerability. First was their enemy, an invisible, ghost-like nemesis. Now, this case, with an equally non-existent murder weapon that had taken someone's life. What was happening? She was a police officer, for Christ's sake. She was supposed to deal with real problems, not crazy supernatural stuff. When had her life changed from NYPD to *The Twilight Zone?*

"Penny for your thoughts."

Christie started out of her worrying thoughts as Jed sat down beside her. He placed a hand on her knee, turning to look at her intently. She stared into his eyes. Christie could swear that their grayness had begun to vary depending upon the time of day and Jed's mood. Right now, their color was comparatively lighter, like a scrim of clouds draped over bright skies.

"I'm just thinking… that we should probably get a priest into our team as well." Christie chuckled, brief and hollow. "Invisible men and disappearing murder weapons. These kinds of things, well, they fall a bit outside my jurisdiction, you know?"

Jed cracked a smile. His eyes crinkled, and the grayness within them seemed to turn even brighter. His hand on Christie's leg tightened just a notch, and Christie squirmed within herself. She could feel Jed's individual fingers against her flesh, light yet unyielding, firm but pliant. A contradictory mess, just like their relationship, she supposed. The thought was enough to make her grin.

"What?" Jed asked, staring at her. "What's so funny? Share the joke with me, too, please."

Christie shook her head. "Nothing. It's nothing. Just what we're doing here right now—if you think about it, it's pretty ridiculous." Another chuckle bubbled up and out of her throat. "I mean, where are all the regular criminals who leave clues and go into hiding after committing a crime? Where are the criminals who are supposed to be terrified of cops, who start sweating if they so much as hear a siren in the distance? Where are the solvable murders, the ones with easy motives and obvious suspects?" She shook her head again, massaging her temples slowly with one hand. "When did we get thrown into an episode of *The X-Files*? I just want to know."

Jed was silent for a long time. His hand remained on Christie's leg, slowly firming up with every passing second, which she found both exciting and terrifying in equal measure. It was hard to think straight when her thigh was tingling under his grip.

"You're getting too overwhelmed with all this," Jed finally said, his voice soft and relaxed in the way that it always was, infecting the other person with its calmness. "Take it easy. One simple detail at a time. One case at a time. There are no ghosts, no demons, nothing supernatural. Just clever people trying to deceive the world so they can get away with their crimes. That's all there is to it. They may be a lot smarter than we could have thought, but there's nothing otherworldly or mysterious about that. If you want, you can think about it as receiving a promotion at work."

Christie stopped massaging her head and gazed at her partner through her fingers.

"Promotion?" she echoed.

Jed nodded, smiled faintly. "A promotion, yes. What happens when you're performing exceedingly well at your job? You get promoted, of course. And what inevitably accompanies a promotion, especially a big one?" He paused. "Much more challenging work. Sometimes, the work is so challenging, you begin to feel like you've switched jobs altogether. But you haven't. You've just gotten so good at what you used to do that the game's difficulty level has been upped. Don't think of it as a burden. Think of it as a compliment. No one else was capable of handling a mess of such epic proportions, which is why it came to you."

Christie stared at Jed in mute surprise. "Wow," she murmured, unable to suppress her awe. "Wow, I never thought of it like that. A promotion, a new challenge..."

"Most problems in life are nothing but a framing issue," Jed said quietly. "If you can fix the lens through which you're viewing them, you'll see the problem transform into a possibility on its own. It'll change into a boon. It was never a burden to begin with, actually; you were just making it into one."

"Whoa." Christie let out a low whistle. She couldn't help herself. "Damn, you're good at this, Gray! You're really good! I feel better already!"

Jed laughed. He rolled up his sleeves in comical, exaggerated fashion. "Well, they don't call me the best therapist in the city for nothing, Detective," he drawled in a deep voice, causing Christie to break into hysterics. She leaned forward against his shoulder, laughing into the cottony fabric of his Henley.

"Oh, that's a good way of putting it," she muttered, sighing. "A new challenge because I was too good for the old ones. A promotion at work for my excellent performance, but without the pay raise." She chuckled.

"Yep," Jed agreed. He tapped Christie's head affectionately. She was still leaning against him, the lower half of her face buried in the crook of his elbow. "A terribly difficult puzzle for a terribly brilliant police officer, the most brilliant one I have had the pleasure of coming across in my life."

She said nothing in response, only placed her hand on top of his. They stayed that way for a long, long time, leaning against one another in the cramped, ratty apartment in some neglected corner of the city, surrounded by the details of a grisly, seemingly unsolvable murder. Surrounded by difficulty on all sides, enclosed by danger and uncertainty, and being hounded by a crazed killer who wanted nothing more than to see them suffer. Yet right then, in that moment, everything was okay for Jed and Christie. Everything felt right.

For they were together.

CHAPTER 16

"HELLO, BROTHER."

Jed turns around at those words. He already knows who he'll see facing him. Not because he's recognized the voice, or because the words could have only been spoken by one of two people, but because of where he's standing. If dreams could hold nostalgia, then the one he's currently in would definitely be dripping it.

A dead city surrounds him. As dead as when he last saw it, its silence unbroken, its stillness uninterrupted. The grayness of the asphalt and the skyscrapers and the roads and the overcast sky presses in on him from all sides, perhaps trying to infect him with its lifelessness. There are no birds soaring above him, no wind caressing his face, no honking cars, or hurried footsteps. Just a deathlike emptiness.

And two people.

Jed sees him standing a few feet away, wearing a nondescript gray blazer that is as limp and lifeless as the rest of the city. His face is waxy, his hair covering his forehead. His eyes are fixed on Jed, brimming with a blank kind of intensity.

"Hello, Alex," Jed greets his stepbrother softly. He looks down at Alex's hands and is somewhat relieved to find no coffee cup present

there. His last few encounters with his deceased stepbrother weren't very pleasant, to say the least.

"How are you?" Jed asks Alex, feeling the strangeness of the question as it rolls off his tongue. Still better than being a statue, though, he realizes with relief. At least this is a dream where he isn't a frozen witness, helpless to do anything except watch.

"I'm okay," Alex shrugs, as if the whole of the afterlife is nothing more than a dull stay in some dental office's waiting room. "How are you doing?"

Jed pauses. "I'm okay, too," he answers, stuffing his hands into his pockets. The silence is overbearing, uncomfortable. So absolute in its nature that Jed can almost sense physical fingers digging into his ears, rubbing harshly against his skin.

"Are you, though?" Alex smiles. Not a mocking smile, but not a very friendly one either. "I've been told that you're in some trouble."

"Well…" Jed doesn't know what to say until he realizes where he is, and his hesitation deserts him. This is a dream, after all. A play projected by his subconscious mind. What does he have to hide from his own self?

"I am in trouble," Jed admits, freed by the knowledge that none of this is real. He takes a step toward Alex. Alex doesn't move, doesn't even budge, as if he's only a human figurine and someone stuck him onto this fake city's set with adhesive.

"Quite a bit of trouble," Jed continues, facing his step-brother. "I—the uh, the person responsible for taking your life, he's still at large. And coming after us."

Alex nods seriously. He brushes a lock of raven hair from his face. "But you caught the one who pulled the trigger," he says flatly. "Right?"

Jed nods. "Yes, but Jack—that man was just a puppet. We still haven't caught the puppet master yet."

Alex nods again, then frowns and looks around, observing the city. Jed watches him in silence, waiting for him to say something, anything. Although he knows this is all just a dream, part of him is still hoping for his brother to say something supportive. To tell him everything will be okay. His entire life, Jed has yearned to hear that from a family member apart from his mother. That's all he wants, someone speaking a few kind words to him. Just once. Even if only in a dream.

But Alex says no such thing. When he turns back to Jed, his face is serious, his eyes misty and bleak.

"You need to up your game," he tells Jed. "This man you're fighting against, he's dangerous. Far more dangerous than you or anyone else you know can realize. If you want a shot at winning, you'll have to out think him."

"I know that," Jed answers, stung. "I'm trying." He hates the sourness inflecting his voice, the whiff of petulance marking it. "I'm doing my best."

"Do better." Alex takes in a deep breath. "This current challenge you're facing is only one on an endless list. If you keep playing this madman's games, they will lead you nowhere except toward insanity's doorstep. You have to do more. You have to change the rules of the game."

Jed grits his teeth. "I know that. But how?"

Alex regards him for a moment, a shadow passing over his curt expression. "You know the answer to that. You just received a tiny piece of it not too long ago."

Jed throws his head back and laughs. "Great, seems like I already know everything, then. What's the point of you being here? Just to add some life to this dead city?"

At that, Jed sees his brother smile. Alex's thin white lips curve upward, and his eyes give Jed a chiding look.

"I'm here to tell you that you've already solved your current riddle. The answer is inside you, slowly making its way to the top of your mind, where you'll finally be able to see it. But until that happens, you can't waste any more time. You need to act."

Jed frowns. "Act?"

Alex nods and looks around in a way that makes Jed shiver. He sees his stepbrother's eyes flitting around the empty landscape, almost as if he's expecting someone to arrive any moment.

"I don't have a lot of time left," Alex whispers, drawing his coat tighter around him. "You need to act, Jed. You know what you need to do. You already know all of it. I'm just here to tell you to get to it."

"Okay," Jed answers slowly. "Okay, I think I know what you're talking about. I'll get started on it when I wake up from this d—when this conversation is over."

"Good," Alex looks pleased at having been understood. He jams his hands into his blazer's pockets and wraps it even tighter around

him, until his bony frame is accentuated by the thick fabric. "We're at the very end now, it seems. God, I hate this part."

Jed frowns. "What part? What are you talking about?"

Alex doesn't say anything, only appears deeply irritated. He opens his mouth and sucks in a huge breath, surprising Jed, who was almost beginning to think that there was no air at all in this soundless place.

"Listen to me carefully," Alex says, speaking quickly now, urgency scrawled across his face. "This is the last dream you'll have of me, the last time we'll be together in this place. There's barely any time, but I need to show you something before I go. Something important."

"What?" Jed takes another step forward. "What is it?"

Alex appears pained. "You won't like it, but it's necessary. It'll help the answer float up quicker, so you can solve the puzzle in time. Look at me now, and don't avert your gaze."

Filled with foreboding, Jed gazes at his stepbrother, his heart beginning to speed up inside him. At first, nothing happens. He and Alex just continue to stand face-to-face, unmoving, unspeaking. Two stubborn brothers locked in a staring contest, both refusing to grant the other one the satisfaction of a victory.

And then, Alex begins to change.

Jed notices it near his left cheek first. A kind of swirling darkness, like freshly spilled ink, darting to and fro beneath Alex's pale skin. As if there's something inside him, searching for a way out. Its movements pick up speed fast, turning frenetic, expanding into Alex's other cheek, rushing up to his forehead and neck, giving him an odd monochrome hue. Once it has filled the insides of Alex's face completely, it presses against his skin, finally revealing its true color.

Red.

Blood red.

Jed realizes the truth too late. By the time his mind joins the dots, there is no time to turn away. He watches helplessly as Alex's mouth opens again, just like it did in all those other disturbing dreams. This time, however, the blood doesn't pour out. It falls out. Chunks upon jagged chunks of frozen blood make their way out and hit the pavement with the sound of shattering glass. Accompanying them is a white mist, thick as fog, belching out in quick spurts from Alex's nostrils, surrounding his neck and shoulders like some strange spectral scarf.

It goes on for a long time.

Horrified, hypnotized, unable to look away, Jed watches. The city's graveyard silence is broken by the sound of ice fragmenting against the hard pavement. Piece after piece. Each flurry followed by streams of white mist that continue to coalesce around his stepbrother's neck, hiding it from view.

Finally, it ends. There are no more pieces left to come out, and Jed's heart is in his throat, making his lungs squeeze with effort for each breath. He looks at his brother and is surprised to notice the clarity and peace marking Alex's face. For the first time, Alex actually looks like Alex and not a corpse reanimated. His mouth slowly closes again. He gulps once, perhaps swallowing the remaining dredges of his frozen blood, before turning to Jed. His eyes are clear. Alive. Intelligent. Another chill races down Jed's spine, and he wonders fleetingly if this really is a dream after all.

"I wish we could've known each other better in the time we had," Alex says to him. That's all he says, the last thing he says. Nothing more beyond that.

Then, he collapses.

With him, the dead city collapses, too.

CHAPTER 17

"WHOA, WHOA, EASY. YOU'RE okay, you're okay."

Jed was aware that he was wheezing, his hands flailing in the air for purchase against something that did not exist. His eyes opened, and at first, the world was nothing more than a melting pot of bright, seething, incoherent colors. But then slowly, as he watched, the colors solidified into shape, and the apartment returned once again. He saw the mottled ceiling staring down at him impassively, and just beneath it hovered Christie's concerned face, her eyes blue saucers in the morning light.

"You're okay, Jed. You're okay. You just had an intense dream."

Jed felt himself calming down. He sucked in a deep breath, and the air flung itself into his lungs eagerly. His hands and legs ceased struggling, and he eased back down into the softness of his pill—no, not his pillow. Whatever he was on felt far too soft for that. Wrenching his eyes sideways, he saw that Christie was cradling his head in her lap, her other hand patting his chest soothingly.

Jed let out another pent-up breath. "Sorry about that," he muttered, wiping one hand across his forehead and finding it beaded with sweat. "I had a weird dream. But I think it was the last one for now. I'm okay."

Christie raised her arms from around him and let him sit up. Picking up the water bottle lying on the table to his left, Jed took a big swig, then another one for good measure. He stared into the bottle's watery depths and tried not to remember the frozen blood and those awful tinkling sounds it had made as it splintered.

"You okay?" Christie asked, rubbing his back. "You were... I didn't mean to pry, but you were muttering your stepbrother's name in your sleep. You sounded worried."

Jed rubbed a hand across his face. "There's no time to be worried," he told his partner, beginning to get to his feet even though his knees still felt shaky. "Come on, get up. We have some work to do today."

Christie looked at him from her place on the couch. "Really? Have you solved the murder? Do you know how it happened?"

Jed shook his head. "Not consciously. Until that happens, until the answer comes to me, there's something else we need to do. Something important."

"What?" Christie asked.

Jed did not turn around. "I'll tell you on the way. Get dressed."

"Take a left from here," Jed instructed Christie, pointing forward with one hand. "Where that big, gray van is heading."

"Can you tell me where we're going now?" Christie asked for what she felt was the tenth time. "I still have no idea what plan you hatched in your sleep."

"We are going," Jed told her, redialing the number on his phone and hoping the third time was the charm, "to see my old friend, Jeff. My rehab buddy."

"Your rehab buddy? Oh." Christie paused, thinking. "What exactly do you plan to ask him?"

"About a little slip-up our enemy made during his last call," Jed said. "He called me a hophead, remember? That's not a term everybody uses."

"Really? Huh." Christie muttered. She honked at a gray Chevrolet that was turning left without flashing its turn signal. "I remember him calling you something weird during the call. At the time, I didn't know what it meant, and once the call ended, in the chaos of everything that happened, I forgot to ask."

"Hophead means druggie," Jed replied cheerily. "An addict. Junkie. Dopehead. Stoner. There are many names for it, but hophead is one of the stranger ones. Most people don't use it."

"And you think you can use that to pinpoint your caller's identity?" Christie asked.

Jed pressed his lips together. "Hopefully, I can make some progress on that front, if nothing else. Now, if only Jeff would just pick up my ca—" His phone rang in his hand right at that second, startling him. Once again, the very first emotion Jed felt upon hearing the sound was an instinctive fear, the sense of a threat lurking nearby. He looked down, expecting to see *Unknown Caller* flashing on the screen, but what he saw instead was Jeff's name.

"Hello?" Jed spoke into the receiver. "Jeff?"

"Hey, Jed," Jeff answered from the other end. He sounded confused, slightly wary. "Everything okay? I generally never get three missed calls from you in a row, so I thought I'd check in."

"Yeah, Jeff, everything is… fine," Jed replied, wondering how he was going to broach this subject with his old friend. He hadn't thought about that at all in his hurry. What was he going to say when Jeff asked him the reason for his strange line of inquiry?

"Uh, Jeff, are you free for a quick chat right now?" Jed asked. "There's, well, there are a few questions I want to ask you about our old days at the rehab center. My memory has been lagging a bit, and I'm hoping you'll be able to jog it up. What do you say?"

"Gee, I don't know…" The reluctance in Jeff's voice was obvious, unmistakable, and Jed couldn't blame him for it. The last time he had been with his friend, he had used him as a decoy to infiltrate his apartment and sneak a gang leader out of it, almost turning the place into a battlefield in the process. Jed had been lucky that no one had seen his face; otherwise, Jeff would have paid the price because he was the one who had allowed Jed to enter the place without arousing suspicion—something Jed's accompanying team of police officers had failed to do.

"Jeff, you don't have to worry," Jed assured him. "All I want is a chat. Nothing more, I swear. It won't be... it won't be like last time. I can promise you that. Besides, I never actually got to thank you for helping me out in the first place. At least let me do that, if nothing else."

There was a long silence on the other end while Jeff considered. Jed heard the sound of a door closing dimly somewhere and wondered if his friend still lived in that same apartment, in uncomfortably close proximity to violent criminals.

"Okay, sure," Jeff answered finally, not sounding sure at all. "There's a gazebo near where I live. It's called Mana's Sandwiches. I'll meet you there in fifteen?"

"Sounds good. See you there, Jeff. And thanks again for agreeing to meet me." Jed hung up the phone and sighed. He turned to Christie. "That terrible apartment we're staying in is finally starting to show its worth."

"Huh?" Christie asked. "Why?"

"Because I never would have been able to meet Jeff like this if I had still been living at my own place," Jed told her. "There would have been too much of a risk of being tailed and getting him involved in this mess in the process. No, I wouldn't have done it. I wouldn't have risked anyone else's life, no matter how valuable the information they had to give me."

"But you can do that now," Christie finished for him, "because there's no risk of anyone knowing where you're going."

"Exactly." Jed palmed his fist repeatedly, leaning forward in his seat, suddenly filled with an energy that made him fidgety—the excited kind of fidgety. "Take the second right from here. It's time we found out just who the hell our enemy is."

Jeff was still pretty much the same as when Jed had last seen him. His hair was long, as always, bleached blonde at the tips, and sprawled around his shoulders. He was wearing one of those hipster Bermuda shirts that Jed had seen him in at their previous encounter, along with a pair of faded denim jeans. Both clothing items were oversized and hung loosely over his tall, bony frame.

"Is that him?" Christie asked, pointing. Jeff was standing near the gazebo, looking around. He still hadn't spotted Jed and Christie inside the car, probably because he was expecting Jed to come walking, like he had last time.

"Yep, that's him," Jed confirmed. "Honk the horn and call him here."

Christie's hand hovered over the horn, touching it without pressing. "You sure he's the one? His back is toward us. And from this angle, he looks like one of those eccentric spiritual types who offer you psychedelics at raves."

Jed laughed. "Very precise description. But yes, that is Jeff, and no, he won't be giving anyone any drugs anymore because he's clean as a whistle. At least, he claimed to be last time we spoke. Seemed to be telling the truth."

Christie pressed down on the horn. It blared for a few seconds before Jeff seemed to realize it might be for him. He turned around, squinting at the Black Ford waiting a few paces away, resembling a giant block of solidified shadow in the wintry morning light. His eyes fell on Jed sitting inside, then he began to make his way forward. As he did, he seemed to realize that his friend was sitting in the passenger seat of the car. Jeff's head jerked up again in surprise, and this time, he noticed Christie in the driver's seat, watching him with a blank face.

Jed saw Jeff falter. His foot seemed to rise from the ground and sway, as if it had forgotten where it was headed mid-journey. Jeff's eyebrows scrunched, and he did a double take again at the police officer in the car. His next step was much slower than the first, the one after that even slower, more hesitant. Like a wind-up toy trying to finish its movements with a depleted battery.

The Ford's door opened, and Jed stepped out. He ran a hand over his stubble self-consciously, realizing it wasn't exactly the best look for putting his friend at ease.

"Jeff!" Jed greeted him, walking forward and embracing the bony man. Jeff's shirt smelled of salt and olives and sea-surf, as if he had just come from a vacation somewhere exotic.

"Hey, Jed," Jeff answered, patting Jed's back and smiling weakly at him, his eyes constantly flitting to the car and the fierce-looking woman who sat inside. "You didn't tell me you'd be bringing someone else with you."

"Oh, that's just Christie," Jed told his friend, waving a hand. "She's… my friend. We're… partners. Not in that sense, like we're together, but we work together. Like colleagues. But closer than that, you know? Like… anyways…" He paused and took a breath, realizing he was rambling. "Let's go inside and sit, yeah? Don't worry, we won't abduct you."

Jeff's smile widened slightly. "Thank you for clarifying that. Let's go, I guess."

Once they were inside the car, Christie showed the man he had been worrying about her for no reason. She swiveled around and flashed him her most disarming smile, which included a perfect set of pearly-white teeth.

"Hello, Jeff," Christie said to him sweetly. "Thank you for agreeing to meet us. It means a lot; I can tell you that."

"Ah, uh—no problem," Jeff stammered. "Jed and I... we go back quite a few years. Rehab wouldn't have been nearly as much fun without him."

Jed chuckled. "Look at us, huh? Who would have thought we'd be sitting here one day like this, actually calling that hellish place *fun*?"

Jeff laughed in return, more openly. "That's definitely true. I guess it means we did it. We came out of that place better men. We survived *the trials of fire*, as some of the nurses there used to call the detox process."

"We survived. Cheers to us both." Jed raised his fisted hand and bumped knuckles with Jeff. The gesture seemed to calm the man even more. He leaned back in his seat and crossed his legs.

"So, what did you want to talk about?" Jeff asked them both.

The smile slowly faded from Jed's face. That merry twinkle winked out in Christie's eyes. They both turned somber, as if their previous joviality had been nothing more than masks that had now been cast aside.

"Jeff," Jed began slowly, "do you know what the term hophead means?"

Jeff looked at Jed for a few seconds, then uttered a sharp laugh. He couldn't help it. "Are you serious? Of course, I know what that term means! I'm one of the last people on Earth you would expect to not know it!"

Jed nodded once. "Right. Obviously. My bad." He paused, and Jeff heard the sound of him inhaling deeply. "But do you remember that one guy in our rehab center who used to use that word?"

A frown creased Jeff's forehead. "What do you mean?"

"Well, you know that the term hophead isn't something people generally use, right?" Jed stated.

"Yeah, I guess," Jeff said, shrugging. "I mean, it's not the most common of terms. Dopehead, junkie, etc. are the more used titles."

"Exactly." Jed nodded eagerly. "Exactly. So, there was this one guy at our rehab center who used to use this word. Do you remember who he was?"

"Jed, I—" Jeff's frown deepened, and he let out another abortive chuckle. "I don't know what you're trying to ask. Do you want to prove that people still use this kind of lingo, or used it back in our day? In that case, you can rest assured that they do. You don't need to try and find specific examples from the past."

"No, that's not what I want, Jeff." Jed took another pause. He leaned forward, the gray of his eyes darkening, turning grave. "I want to know about the guy at our rehab center who used that specific word. I want his name, or at least something to identify him by."

Jeff shifted uneasily in his seat. "Why?"

Jed sighed. "Jeff, I never got to apologize to you for what I involved you in last time. I'm sorry about that. Making you sneak me inside your own apartment like that... I truly am sorry. I wouldn't have done it if it hadn't been absolutely necessary."

"No worries, Jed." Jeff patted his friend rather awkwardly on the shoulder. "I know you wouldn't ever harm anyone intentionally. That's not the Jed I remember."

A faint shadow of a smile crossed Jed's lips. "Which is exactly why I can't tell you my reason for asking these questions. I don't want to put you in any sort of trouble whatsoever, Jeff. I don't even want you near it. It's best you leave this car having no clue why we wanted to meet you."

Jeff opened his mouth, about to protest, but then seemed to realize something. Perhaps he remembered the apartment he lived in, the miscreants he crossed paths with every morning, the murderers, the drug peddlers. Or perhaps he simply realized that life was troublesome enough as it was, and there was no need to take on any additional baggage. Whatever the reason, he clamped his lips shut at the last moment and nodded tightly.

"Good," Jed stated, with some relief. "Now, back to my original question. Do you remember someone from our rehab clinic who ever used the word hophead?"

Jeff squinted. He gazed outside the car window, twiddling his thumbs in thought. Jed and Christie watched him quietly, trying to remain nonchalant, trying not to let him know the terrible importance of the question they had asked him, and what its answer meant to them.

The silence stretched on. Jeff's thumbs moved like lazily flapping birds in his lap. His lips twitched every now and then under the strain of his concentration. A lone gull squawked in the distance. Somewhere further away, someone hooted in vulgar fashion.

Jed and Christie continued waiting.

It felt like hours before Jeff finally turned his head back around to face them. Jed saw it instantly in his friend's eyes. Something glimmering there, like a speck of dust from a by-gone era still clinging to the coattails of the present moment, scrabbling to hold on by the very tip of its fingernails. Jeff had found something and brought it back.

"Well?" Jed kept his voice neutral, even though hope was flaring inside him, threatening to burst into fireworks. But he couldn't let that happen yet, not until he was sure he had gotten something. Otherwise, the fireworks would just fizzle out and leave everything far colder and deader than before.

"I think there was one guy," Jeff murmured, and Jed suppressed the urge to pump his fists into the air in celebration.

"Do you know who it was?" he asked casually.

Jeff shook his head. "I don't exactly remember his name. Or much of what he looked like. He used to keep mostly to himself, as far as I can recall. Was a pretty strange fellow. Wherever you went, he was always in one of the corners, sitting alone, silently watching everyone. Just watching."

"Do you remember any details about this ma—this boy, which might help us to identify him, Jeff?" Christie pressed. "Anything at all?"

Jeff scratched his chin. "I doubt that I can be of any further help to you guys, seeing as I barely interacted with anyone in the clinic apart from Jed and one or two more people. No, I think there's someone else you ought to go to for this problem."

Jed leaned forward. "Who?"

"Pedro," Jeff told him squarely. "Pedro Mascarenes."

Jed screwed up his eyes. "That schizophrenic boy? The one who always acted strangely? Who we were scared of?"

Jeff nodded. "Yes, him. He's the only one I saw hanging around your guy a few times in the clinic. Pedro, yes. If there's anyone who can give you more information, it's him."

Skepticism washed over Jed's features, flattening the hope he had been tentatively gathering there in one smooth stroke.

"Jeez, Jeff, don't you remember what Pedro was like?" Jed shook his head. "He barely gave anyone a straight answer when he was in the clinic. What makes you think he'll talk to me?"

Jeff smiled chidingly. "If there's anyone who has any experience with making people talk, Jed, it's you. You're the last person who should be lodging such a complaint."

Jed stared at his friend wordlessly, momentarily taken aback by that unexpected move.

"I guess you're right," he conceded. "Maybe I can get Pedro to… spill a few details on his rehab buddy. But where do I find him? Do you know his current whereabouts?"

Jeff shook his head. "No clue. He could be dead, as far as I know. Six feet underground, buried with all his secrets still inside his skull."

Jed groaned. "You're not helping, Jeff. I need the man alive to question him. Skilled as I may be in getting people to spill their secrets, even I don't have the power to make corpses talk."

"Look, I don't know where Pedro currently is," Jeff admitted, raising a single finger to silence Jed's next protest. "But I know someone who might. Give me a few days. I should have his address for you, if I'm lucky."

Jed nodded. "Okay, that's better. Much better than a talking dead man, at least."

"So it is." Jeff glanced out the window again. There were two men passing them by on the opposite street. They were riding motorcycles, and even from a distance, their tattooed heads were visible. Jed and Christie both tensed when they saw them, relaxing only when the duo turned the corner and disappeared from sight.

"I guess… I guess that's it, then?" Jeff inquired. "I've done the best I can, really, for you both. Hopefully it was worth something."

Christie smiled fully at him again, inclining her head in gratitude. "You've been a great help, Jeff. Thank you. Also, please don't forget to send Jed Pedro's address as soon as you find it."

"Of course." Jeff's hand went toward the door latch. "May I leave, then, if we're done?" It felt weird asking for permission, as if he were some kind of child, but Jeff was certain that the lady in the front seat was a police officer, and despite her pretty face and angelic smile, he had a feeling she wasn't someone whose bad side he would ever want to get on.

"Nonsense." It was Jed who spoke now, turning back around and buckling his seatbelt. "You're not leaving so soon. Hell, you just came. First, we're going for drinks." In the shocked silence, he turned around and grinned at the other two people in the car. "Non-alcoholic, of course."

At Jeff's direction, Christie took them to a dainty outdoor café situated next to an empty plot of land two streets down. Plastic chairs had been strewn haphazardly on the ground, and due to a lack of any nearby buildings, the wind blew in full force. It raced down their spines, nipped at their ears, and tried to worm its way inside their clothes. Jed shivered and took his seat on one of the plastic chairs, enjoying the cold despite its severity. It had a certain freshness to it, a kind of enlivening quality.

"Have you been here before?" he asked Jeff, who had taken his seat opposite Jed and seemed even more indifferent to the cold despite the thin shirt he was wearing, which rattled around on his bony frame like a flag in a gale.

Jeff shrugged. "Sometimes, when I need to clear my head. Their Malta juice is like a miracle cure for brain fog. Freshly squeezed and delicious. It reboots your entire brain in minutes."

"Well, I certainly could use some rebooting," Jed muttered. "God knows I'm going to need it."

"Me, too," Christie chimed in.

"Three glasses of Malta, then," Jeff confirmed, calling over the waiter and giving him the order.

"Are you still living in the same apartment, Jeff?" Jed asked him once the waiter had taken their orders and left.

Jeff grinned wryly. "Why, are you planning another armed intrusion with your pals in the police force?"

Embarrassed, Jed bowed his head. "I really am sorry about that."

Jeff waved away the apology with a widening grin. "You know, there are still two bullet holes on the topmost floor. They haven't been repaired yet." He paused before adding slyly, "If you ever want to come for another tour to see those souvenirs you left behind on your last visit, do let me know. I'll take you."

Jed's head continued to hang sheepishly. He rapped his knuckles on the plastic table. "Those souvenirs are actually not mine. They're... from those friends of mine, who came with me."

"Ah. Of course." Jeff's eyes momentarily switched to Christie, but he did not say anything. If he had already guessed that she had been responsible for the shooting, he didn't seem to want to voice it.

"Anyways, that's enough about me." Jed straightened up in his seat. He combed a tangle of windswept hair back with one hand. "Tell me about you. What have you been up to?"

Jeff shrugged. "Doing different things here and there, to tell you the truth. Working as a portrait painter for a school fair, currently."

"Oh, really?" Jed's voice brimmed with interest. "That's cool, man. So, what, you get to paint people for a living?"

"Yep. Turns out I'm pretty good at it." Jeff paused, then barked out a short laugh. "A few women enamored with my craft even requested that I paint them in their original forms, if you catch my drift."

Jed whistled. "Wow. Look at you. Living the life. Right, Christie?" He turned toward Christie, who was also grinning, enjoying the conversation.

"Jeff, if you really are good at painting people," she spoke, "and if you ever get tired of... painting women... there might be a position at the police department open for you."

Jeff's eyebrows quirked up. That was one response he had not been expecting at all. He leaned forward in his chair, the wind filling up his shirt, making it balloon around him.

"Are you serious?" he asked Christie. "Or are you just pulling my leg?"

"Nope. Serious." Christie shook her head. "Of course, that is if you're really good at what you do. Plus, you have to be good at drawing people from other people's descriptions, not just by having them in front of you. If you can manage that, then we always need a sketch artist working for us."

"Well—I mean," Jeff leaned forward further, elbows on the table, "I would certainly be interested. Do you think I could come by the station sometime, so you guys can assess my skills or whatever?"

"Of course," Christie told him. "Jed here will give me your number. As soon as we have an opening, I'll call and let you know."

"Great!" Jeff looked supremely pleased. "Having an extra source of income would be killer."

"See, that's why I called you here today," Jed joked. "The questions about rehab were only an excuse. I actually wanted to pay you back for last time."

"If this gig works out for me, you can ask all the questions you want." Jeff laughed, leaning back as the waiter arrived and began to place their drinks on the table. "I'll sit in your apartment with you the whole day and cater to all your queries, I promise."

They picked up their drinks and began to sip. The Malta was pleasantly sour, dusted with black pepper to give it that extra bite. Christie took a large gulp and licked her lips, savoring the strange new taste. Almost instinctively, she turned toward Jed, accustomed to sharing her culinary experiences with him. Her mouth was already half-open, ready to ask him what he thought about the drink, whether he had ever had something like it before.

But Jed was not drinking.

His glass of juice lay untouched, the wind creating ripples of disturbance on its surface. Jed's eyes were focused on it, but his hands sat in his lap. In fact, every bit of him had turned curiously still, with only his clothes showing movement, flapping around his body.

"Jed?" Christie ventured. She tapped his shoulder with one arm, almost expecting to feel the hardness of granite underneath her fingertips. But it was still Jed, her Jed, warm and soft as always, yet paralyzed for some reason. When she tapped his shoulder for the second time, he stirred. Or at least, part of him did. His face remained frozen, staring down into the drink's ruddy depths, trying to decipher some omen in those pulpy currents of orange that the others could not see.

"Jed?" Christie repeated loudly, following his gaze. She stared down at his drink and saw the froth skimming its top, the seeds bobbing at its edges like buoys, the tips of ice-cubes peeking out for a moment before disappearing again. She did not see anything else, nothing that might help her understand what had her partner so transfixed.

"I got it," Jed muttered.

Christie started at the sound of his voice. It resembled two dry bits of parchment being rubbed together.

"Got what?" she asked, putting her own drink down, suddenly wondering if it had been poisoned. Opposite her, Jeff copied her actions, his face marked with confusion.

"I know how it happened," Jed muttered, frowning as the wind swept his hair into his eyes. He pushed it back with a robotic gesture before turning toward Christie, pinning her with an intense gaze.

"I know how the murder happened, Christie," Jed told her. "I know how Sean was killed."

Realization flooded Christie. *Of course! The case!* She had forgotten completely about it after meeting Jeff and listening to Jed recount his rehab days with his old friend. Now, the worries of the present returned to seize her, reminding her of the enemy they were facing and the lives that were at stake.

"We need to go," she said to him. "We need to go back to the apartment. Finish this thing once and for all."

Jed nodded. He began to get up before seeming to realize that Jeff was there, too, staring with confusion at both of them.

Jed stood up and went over to his friend, clasping his shoulder with one hand. "I'm really sorry, but we have to rush. There's some urgent work we have to complete. It can't wait."

"Right, man. Sure. I understand." Jeff was nodding slowly. "No worries. We can always catch up later."

Jed squeezed Jeff's shoulder. "We will catch up later. I promise you that. Once this… current assignment of ours is resolved, you and I will sit together in this same spot and talk about our sorry past until our stomachs ache from laughter."

Jeff smiled faintly. He raised his glass toward Jed in a toast. "That sounds like a good idea, my friend."

Jed patted him on the shoulder one last time before leaving. "Take care of yourself, buddy. It's always good seeing you."

"It was nice meeting you, Jeff." Christie smiled, reaching forward and shaking the man's hand. "I find it comforting to know that Jed had such kind people taking care of him in rehab."

Jeff blushed. "Well, I don't think we were capable of even taking care of ourselves when we were in rehab, much less someone else, but I appreciate the compliment, ma'am. Thank you. And best of luck with whatever it is you both are working on."

They smiled and bid him farewell, heading to their car after Jeff insisted that he would walk back home.

"How did it happen?" Christie asked breathlessly, keeping pace with a Jed whose legs seemed to be motoring forward. "How was the murder planned? What did you figure out?"

Jed grinned, his teeth gleaming in the bright sunlight. "Get in the car. I'll tell you."

CHAPTER 18

"IT WAS THE ICE cube that made me understand."

Christie flashed her headlights at a trundling six-wheeler as she overtook it from the right, her foot refusing to budge from the accelerator.

"Ice cube?" She demanded. "What ice cube?"

"The one in the drink," Jed answered softly. "I don't really know how, but it must have triggered some kind of link in my mind or something because the moment I saw it, everything became clear."

"Right, you need to explain that everything to me, too," Christie said. "Because I have no idea what you're on about."

Next to her, she heard her partner take a deep breath. She almost even heard all those complex gears clanking inside his brain as he began putting together the right words for her to understand.

"Sean was stabbed," he told her, "with a murder weapon that seemed to have disappeared."

Christie nodded.

"Well, the truth wasn't very far from that." Jed sniffed. "Except the murder weapon didn't disappear. It *dissolved*."

"Dissolved?" Christie echoed. She saw a red signal far up ahead and turned right so they wouldn't have to sit in traffic. "Dissolved how?"

"Sorry, dissolved may not be the right word," Jed corrected himself. "Here's a more appropriate one. The weapon didn't disappear. It *melted*."

"Huh?" Christie blurted. "Jed, you're wrong. That doesn't really make more sense than t—" Her voice cut off abruptly, and she fell silent.

Jed gave her a sidelong glance. "You get it now, don't you?"

Christie swallowed. She pressed her lips together, wondering if the truth really could be so absurdly simple. A foolish question, considering the kind of situation they were in.

"Sean was stabbed…" She paused again, struggling to give voice to the strangeness, to dislodge it from her throat. "He was stabbed by a weapon *made entirely out of ice*. After killing him, the culprit simply left the weapon on the floor, and by the time the others arrived, it had turned into a puddle of water."

"No fingerprints, no evidence," Jed muttered. He snorted. "Sounds mad, doesn't it? Something you'd expect to see in a movie, not in real life."

"A weapon made of ice," Christie muttered. "What, like a frozen dagger or sword, or something? What's next on our itinerary of bizarreness, lightsabers?"

"Not a dagger, no," Jed answered thoughtfully. "A dagger is too impractical, too unwieldy. Besides, you're forgetting another key point of this investigation."

"Please, do enlighten me."

"The killer couldn't have brought such a weapon with him inside. One, because of the three security checkpoints. Two, and more importantly, because the thing would have just melted in the process if he tried."

"Then, how?" Christie's voice trailed off. She was out of her depth, she knew. Thank God Jed was sitting beside her, making sense of this craziness.

"The weapon never left the freezer room." Jed rubbed his hands together, excitement evident in his tone now, as he continued connecting the dots and seeing the full picture emerge. "In fact, the weapon was even formed inside the freezer room and left there until the moment to use it came."

"*Formed inside?*" Christie tried to hold back an incredulous huff, but it leaked out anyway. "What do you mean?"

"Listen, it's simple if you think about it," Jed was getting worked up now, leaning forward in the seat with his attention entirely on her. "All you would need is a mold. Like, a small container made of anything, even plastic, which our killer filled with water before leaving in one of the freezers."

"And that simple, harmless water turned into something lethal," Christie whispered, mouth hanging open. She had slowed down the car considerably because her thoughts were racing too fast for her to handle another speeding object. She felt strangely exhilarated, like a scientist who had stumbled upon a shattering discovery.

"It makes perfect sense," Christie continued, her voice almost bordering on admiration at the simple genius of the crime. "None of the guards would think anything of a small plastic container. Who would have thought that something so harmless could produce a knife?"

"Not a knife," Jed reminded her. "Something even smaller, small enough to fit into the most ordinary, inconspicuous of containers. Small enough to produce the unique wound we saw on the side of Sean's neck."

Christie thought about what such a weapon could be. The answer came to her swiftly, in less than a few seconds. Her brain seemed to be firing at twice its speed, as if it had somehow gotten into sync with Jed's own mind, and the two were racing forward in tandem, untangling the knots of the mystery as they did.

"A piece of ice, the size of a pen" Christie finally said, knowing it was the truth even as the word rolled off her tongue. "A frozen, rock-hard, needle of ice—with a tip sharp enough to kill."

"Couple that with a malfunctioning refrigerator that throws out enough mist to block out the security cameras," Jed added, "and you have the recipe for the perfect murder."

"Damn." Christie shook her head. "No wonder the guy we're up against wanted us to solve it. Even he must have been scratching his head, wondering how someone could do such a thing."

"Really makes you think, huh?" Jed leaned back in the seat, sighing. "How many crazies like that must be in this city? Using their mad genius to do harm rather than good? How many such unexplained murders are gathering dust in some forgotten archive section of some dusty storeroom in some remote police station, with the culprit roaming free, knowing there's no chance of getting caught?"

Christie was silent for a long time. "I don't know about you," she finally said to her partner, "but I'll be perfectly happy if we manage to catch our guy and no one else. Once he's behind bars, I'll have the most peaceful sleep of my life."

Jed chuckled. "Yeah, you're right. To hell with the rest; let's first solve the problem we have."

"Speaking of..." Christie pointed at Jed's phone. "You should probably text him now. Let him know we've solved it."

Jed picked up his phone and began typing. Unlike the other answers, which had been short and to the point, he typed for a long time, adding in all the details that made their theory sit soundly. Once done, he went over the message again before sending it, feeling his pulse quicken a fraction as the screen showed him it had been delivered.

"Done?" Christie inquired, braking at a red light. They were almost at the apartment now. She wondered whether Jed's phone would ring before they reached there or not.

"Done," Jed confirmed, closing his eyes and resting his head back. "Now, we wait."

Christie glanced up at the sky. Noon was burning at full throttle, turning it into scalded milk. The glare of the sunlight made it feel like it would last forever, or at least for a long, long time. Christie knew that wasn't true, though. Just a trick played by the winter on this city's inhabitants, one they fell for every year. It wouldn't be long before the deceptively permanent day began fading, dulling into twilight with an uncanny speed. It wouldn't be long before the shadows rushed in, spreading their canopied hands over the city's twisting concrete maze, burying all its secrets in darkness.

CHAPTER 19

THEY RECEIVED THE CALL an hour after reaching the apartment. Jed and Christie were both in the living room by then, idly passing the time by playing a game of checkers Jed had found in one of the cupboards. Both of them were sitting stiffly on the edges of their seats, their attention only half on the game. After each move, their eyes would flit to Jed's phone, which was lying dark and silent on the table. It still had not rung, not even once. The wait was becoming painful, uncomfortable. They wanted it to be over with, wanted the game to begin again so they could finish it for good.

Finally, the phone flashed.

Jed's fingers were on it in an instant, pushing aside the checkerboard without a second thought. He opened the screen and looked at the message, reading silently.

Christie watched him with agitation. This was the worst part for her, this tiny interim between Jed receiving the message and conveying it to her. Time seemed to stretch out during this interval, refusing to pass along, stubbornly clinging in place, almost as if to taunt her.

"He's given it to us." Jed's voice snapped Christie out of her thoughts. She looked up and found him wearing a look of grim satisfaction.

"What?" she asked.

Jed shook the phone in his hand. "We've got it. Lauren's address."

Relief whistled straight through Christie's chest and throat. She swallowed once, held out her hand. "Show me."

Jed handed her the phone, and she read the message that had been sent to him.

Brilliant work! Absolutely brilliant! I'm so happy to know that there are other minds as clever as mine at work in this city, causing some chaos of their own! How wonderful! More importantly, what an ingenious way to kill someone! My, my! Almost makes me want to use it for my next kill, you know? I wonder who it will be.

Anyway, here is your beloved client's location, as promised. You know I'm a man of my word. And don't worry, the pretty damsel is alive, though terrified out of her wits. Nothing a few therapy sessions won't solve, though. In fact, you ought to be thanking me, Gray. I just sent some business your way! Ha! Ha!

976 3RD AVE, BROOKLYN, NY 11232

P.S. I don't remember booby-trapping the place, but it feels like my memory is turning a bit faulty these days. What can one do?

XOXO

Your friend from the past,

:)

Christie was already on her feet, heading out, her keys jangling in her hand. Her other hand rested on the holster of her gun, her finger toying with the trigger as the last bit of the message played over and over in her mind.

It took them two hours to arrive. The message had not made mention of any kind of time restraints or deadline, but Christie still drove like the hounds of hell were nipping at their heels. She just couldn't take any more risks. Not after the horror they had seen in the last warehouse.

The location mentioned in the text was close to the out-skirts of the city, in an abandoned industrial zone cluttered with freight cargo and power plants. Power lines zipped above their heads like streaks of mascara in the sky. Dusk crept in quietly, stealthily, swallowing the light one morsel at a time. When they finally arrived, a smattering of stars shone directly above them. Far in the horizon, the sun was a feeble flicker about to wink out for the day.

"This is it; this is the one." Jed pointed to his right, and Christie turned and saw a large cement structure squatting next to two abandoned plots of land. The windows of the building were dark, and its gate hung ajar, as if left open by someone in a hurry. Christie's eyes went to the metal plate that had been fixed to the outside wall, and she read the address written there.

Yes. This was it.

She parked the car, and they both got out. It was quiet and cool. Only the stalks of weeds in the empty plots made some noise, whispering to each other in muted susurrations. With Christie in the lead, Jed followed, his heart a sliver of ice inside his chest, his mind filled with dark images of Maria, except now her face had been replaced with Lauren's. Gritting his teeth, he pushed aside his fears and focused on the present. He would find Lauren alive here. He had already made sure of it. His enemy knew that if anything happened to her, Jed would no longer be playing his sick games.

Once they had reached the outside gate, Christie came to a stop. Her shoulders drew together. Jed felt the tension coiling her muscles, straightening her back.

"He hinted that the place could be booby trapped," Christie whispered, even though no one was around. She turned to Jed, and he saw the fear in her eyes. Fear for him, though, not for herself.

"Jed, you should stay outside," Christie finally said. "It's dangerous. You haven't been trained to defend yourself inside a house that has been rigged. Stay here and wait until I bring Lauren out. Okay?"

Jed scowled. Even in the expanding dark, his anger was visible, a bright flame fanning his eyes.

"Like hell I will," he growled, walking forward until he was standing level with Christie. "We're going in together, and that's that."

Christie bit her lower lip but did not say anything. She made her request with a futile hope, knowing her partner would never agree to it, but still trying, nonetheless. They walked toward the building together. The door was right in front of them now, and through its tiny crack, they could see that same emptiness marking the warehouse's insides.

Except that there wasn't just emptiness waiting for them inside. Something else lay there, too—a trap created by their enemy, hidden from their eyes, waiting for them to step into its embrace.

"Jed." Christie whirled around again. The fear was in her throat, a physical lump obstructing her breath. "Jed, we have no idea what's waiting inside apart from Lauren, if she even is here. For all we know, the whole place could be rigged with explosives. There could be a lethal current running through the doorknob. Jed, we have no way of infiltrating this place safely!"

Jed's hand fell on her shoulder. He squeezed once, loosening the tightness making Christie's body ache. She felt herself unwinding in his grasp, felt some of her tension dissipating.

"Whatever it is, we'll deal with it." Jed's voice was soft and confident. The darkness had taken complete dominion over the sky now, and all Christie could make out of her partner's face were sharp angles of shadow. She focused on those twin pinpricks of gray visible even beneath the darkness of dusk and forced her heart to calm down.

"Okay, okay." She nodded once, more to convince herself than anyone else. "Let's go, then."

They returned to their typical formation, with Christie in the lead and Jed two steps behind her. Saying a silent prayer to the Gods, Christie laid one hand against the wooden door and pushed it open. It swung with a groan, its rusty hinges squalling in protest. The inside of the warehouse came into view. Dark blocks of shadowy edifice, a tiny door visible somewhere within them.

The pair went forward. Gravel crunched underneath Christie's feet as she crossed the distance at a snail's pace, her eyes scanning the environment for the slightest of movements, the barest of indications that something was wrong. But she found nothing, only that same blackness, a sea of space so dense it even seemed to have swallowed the stars speckling it.

Once they had gotten closer, Jed fished his phone out of his pocket and turned on the flashlight. He pointed it ahead of him, revealing another wooden door set into bare concrete walls. This door was closed, and its brass knob stuck out innocently, waiting for someone to grip it and twist.

Christie stopped right before the knob and paused. She withdrew her hand inside her jacket and used it as a makeshift glove, wrapping it around the knob and twisting. It moved without any resistance, with a smoothness suggesting it had recently been oiled. Christie braced herself, waiting for the current to arc down her spine and fry her to bits. Or for the bomb to activate and blow them into smithereens. Or for a trapdoor to open beneath their feet and send them tumbling into hell. She waited for something, anything to happen. For some kind of trap rigged by their crazed captor to come alive and ensnare them.

But there was nothing.

Just the silence.

They stood there for a few seconds, letting their heartbeats return to normal. Once it became clear that this part of the building hadn't been tampered with, Christie pushed open the door completely. She took out her flashlight, pointing it ahead.

They saw dust everywhere, sheets of it clinging to the walls and ceiling, the only inhabitant in an otherwise empty and uninhabited place. There was no furniture either, no light fixtures in the ceilings, no fans. Just plain white walls and a white ceiling.

The staircase loomed.

Both Jed and Christie's eyes strayed to it, and without saying a word to each other, they knew that the stairs were where they were supposed to go. Always the stairs. Always the room at the opposite end of the upper floor, as far away from the exit as possible.

"Well," Christie whispered, her voice unusually loud in the building's eerie silence. "I guess we have to go up."

"Indeed," Jed murmured, focusing his flashlight ahead and to the right. From where they stood, the stairs seemed solid, giving no hint that they would crumble beneath the slightest of weights and send the trespassers plummeting back down. "Shall we, then?"

Christie took in a deep breath. She didn't like this. She didn't like this one bit. She had been expecting a trap of some kind, but an absence of one made her even more fearful. Now, she had no clue what they were up against and no way to prepare for it.

"Let's go," she breathed, stepping forward. They approached the staircase, their flashlights revealing the cobwebs decorating each corner. No spiders came scurrying forward, however. If there were any left, they seemed content with hiding and observing the two giant intruders continue on their way, perhaps right to their own demise.

There were twenty-six steps in total. Christie counted. With each step, she made a silent prayer to God and hoped the stairs beneath them wouldn't give way. Perhaps the building had been built sturdily, or perhaps God did—in fact—exist, for they reached the top without any mishaps. Once again, they paused at the head of the stairs and cast their lights around, taking in the place before making their next move. They saw the same barrenness they had seen downstairs, encased on all sides by white walls and a ceiling. In front of them extended three rooms, two on opposite ends of the corridor and one straight ahead. All three rooms were doorless. All three rooms lay steeped in utter blackness. All three rooms lay silent as crypts. But only one room had a sign painted above it.

Jed's flashlight caught the sign first. It was right above the doorway, a splash of grisly red against the white. He squinted, nudging Christie to tell her to focus her light there as well. She did. The combined brightness revealed the message that had been left there for them.

It was a smiley face. Crudely drawn atop the doorway, without much care or concern. In a color that bore a frightening resemblance to blood.

"There," Jed whispered, a shudder passing through his whole being. "There. She's in there. Lauren's in there." He pointed with a shaking finger at the room's gaping, toothless mouth but did not take a step forward. Neither did Christie. They were both suddenly terrified by the idea of what they would find inside. After all their sleepless nights and efforts, all the risks and painstaking measures they had taken, they didn't want to stumble across another dead body. Christie shivered at the idea of seeing Jed lock eyes with another one of his lifeless clients. The first one had already taken such a huge toll on him, she knew. Finding Lauren in the same state would cause something inside him to crack, she was sure.

But they had no choice. They had come this far. They would now go all the way, right to the finish line, no matter what waited for them there.

Without saying anything to each other, Jed and Christie took a step forward in unison. Then another. And another.

The doorway grew nearer, growing in size with every step, its tarry depths remaining impenetrable. The silence rose all around them, lumbering to its feet, towering over their heads and over the empty building. A brittle, fragile, giant of a silence that felt like it would fall apart with a thunderous crack any moment

Once they were close enough, their flashlights cut through the swathes of black, and they saw the room's interior. It was bare, like everything else, the paint on the walls chipped in places. Twin trailing skid marks dusted the floor, leading right to the room's opposite corner, where the emptiness was suddenly interrupted by a presence. A shape. A fistful of shadows bulging out of the blankness. Christie turned her light their way.

They both saw Lauren.

Jed's hesitance dropped out of him like amniotic fluid from an expecting mother. He was suddenly running forward, unmindful of whether the room contained any booby-traps or not, whether the floor had been rigged with landmines or not, whether there were tripwires concealed in the darkness or not, waiting to be activated by intruders. His vision had tunneled, and all he could see was Lauren, her face clear and visible in the phone's light, her white dress smeared with dirt. Behind him, he heard Christie call out sharply, ordering him to stop, but Jed's legs did not obey. They moved with a will of their own, carrying him right inside the room and toward

Lauren, until he was standing over her, looking down with petrified eyes.

"Lauren?" Jed whispered raggedly. He leaned closer to her, aiming his flashlight on her face. For a moment, both rescuer and captive became equally still, as dead and frozen as the landscape around them. Then, a sigh of relief broke through Jed's lips. He let out a stifled moan and leaned back, one hand going to his chest.

"She's alive," he uttered in a fragmented voice. "She's alive. She's alive. Christie, she's alive."

From his other side, Christie approached. She looked down at Lauren's face and let out a pent-up breath. Yes, the girl was alive. Her chest was rising and falling imperceptibly. Her eyes were closed, her hands loosely dangling in her lap. In fact, she appeared to be unhurt, at least from what Christie could see. No wounds marked the girl's face. No apparent injuries were revealed by the light. It seemed like they had found Lauren safe and secure.

They had done it.

Christie paused. She shook her head, looking around the room again, a flutter in her chest. Butterfly wings flapped against her ribcage. This didn't feel right. Didn't feel... true. There was something else they were missing.

"Christie, what is it?"

She turned around at Jed's voice, shook her head again, and frowned. Gave the walls another suspicious glance.

"Where is it?" she asked in a troubled voice.

Jed blinked at her. "Where is what?"

Christie splayed her hands. "The trap. The one that was supposed to be waiting for us here."

Jed looked around the room, chewing his upper lip. After a few moments, he turned back toward Lauren and leaned closer to her, as if checking that she was really alive and that they hadn't been tricked. Then, he looked back up at Christie, and she saw some of her own worry crisscrossing his face.

"I don't know," Jed finally answered. He shrugged. "Maybe there is no trap this time. Maybe he was just messing with us."

Christie wished she could believe that. She really, really did. She desperately wanted to be convinced that their mission was over, that they had found Lauren and all that needed to be done now was to carry her back to the car and drive her to safety. Every bit of her was yearning for that, yearning for the end of their challenge to have arrived. But she simply couldn't accept that as the truth. It was too outlandish, considering the enemy they were facing. He wouldn't allow them to end on such a happy note—oh, no. He had implied that the building was booby-trapped, and Christie believed him with a fervor.

"Okay, okay." She paused, considering. "Let's carry her back to the car. The sooner we're out of this place, the better."

"I couldn't agree more." Jed went over behind Lauren and hooked his hands beneath her underarms. "Come, grab her legs, Christie," he ordered.

Christie fitted her flashlight inside her pocket until only the topmost edge was visible, allowing the light to spill out unblocked. She went toward Lauren and kneeled down, wrapping her hands around the girl's bare ankles. They were smooth and unblemished, milky white in the light.

"On the count of three," Jed instructed. "One, two, and three—"

They grunted and pulled, hoisting Lauren into the air. She wasn't very heavy, but their minds were already weighed down by other worries. Together, they brought her out of the room and into the corridor, taking slow, careful steps in the darkness. Christie's light illuminated the way for Jed as he walked backward, craning his head to ensure he didn't slip. It would be an ironic way to die in a warehouse fitted with traps—to simply trip on the bare floor and break your neck.

But Jed didn't slip. Nor did any hidden traps in the building activate. What happened instead was something they hadn't been expecting, something neither of them had even thought of.

The sound was low at first—a dim, distant whirr, its source hard to pinpoint. For a few seconds, Jed and Christie failed to register it, too caught up in their current predicament. But then, Jed froze at the head of the staircase, his head cocked to one side, his eyes slits of color in the dark.

"What?" Christie whispered harshly. Her arms were sagging beneath Lauren's weight. She wanted this whole ordeal over with as quickly as possible.

"Do you hear that sound?" Jed asked her. His head tilted further. Wrinkles popped up on his forehead. He adjusted his grip around Lauren's underarms but did not move.

"Hear what, Jed?" Christie asked. "I don't he—" Her voice broke off. She frowned. Yes, there was something there. Something in the air. A sound. Like a chainsaw or a generator running somewhere in the distance, getting louder by the second.

"What is that?" Christie asked. Her hands were suddenly clammy around Lauren's ankles. Her chest had turned into an aviary, thumping flutters filling it up. "Jed, what the hell is that?"

"I don't know," Jed answered. There was a note of resignation in his voice, akin to disappointment. For a second, he had almost believed that their troubles were over and they would leave this place unharmed. But of course, such good fortune could never be theirs. They had found Lauren, but the trial wasn't over yet.

They stood there for a few more seconds, listening. The sound steadily grew louder in their ears, changing from a whirr to a rattle, from a rattle to something familiar. If either of them had figured it out yet, though, they didn't say it. Perhaps because they were too afraid. Perhaps because they thought that if they voiced their idea, it would turn into reality.

"Let's put Lauren down here," Jed said in a heavy voice. Everything about him suddenly felt heavy. He leaned down and gently placed his client's head onto the floor. Christie saw that his face was pale, his jaw set tensely.

There was a small window on the opposite wall, the one which led to the staircase. Jed walked over to it. He leaned out, and Christie saw him turn his face to the side, toward the road from which they had arrived. She stood there for a few seconds, watching him, hearing that rattly roar in her ears increasing, its identity becoming clearer and clearer. Then, she went over to join her partner. As Christie leaned her head out the window next to Jed, the noise suddenly acquired a newfound clarity. Now, it was unmistakable, undeniable.

They stood there together and listened to the sound of an approaching engine. Neither of them said anything. The road before them was a strip of gray in the black landscape, empty as far as they could see. But it wouldn't be for long. Someone was coming, Christie knew. Their timing was far too perfect to be a mere coincidence. No, this someone was coming for them.

"Do you think we should rush to the car?" Christie asked, already knowing the answer to her question.

Jed shook his head. His face was still turned towards the road. "There's no time," he answered softly. "We have around a minute at best, from what I can judge."

He was wrong. They arrived in less than that, eager to get the party started. Finally, the rattle in the air and in their ears changed, revealing its true nature. A roar, the roar of engines thundering forward. Far in the darkness, they both saw a shape slicing through the shadows—no, not a shape. *Shapes*, many of them: a horde of piranhas swimming forth in a pitch-black sea, homing in on their trapped prey.

Jed and Christie leaned back, peeking through the window now, trying not to be seen. Their eyes tracked the bulging shapes which came into view, revealing themselves to be motorcycles. A whole fleet of them. On the motorcycles? Wielding machetes and guns, sporting a second skin of tattoos, their shaved heads silver lamps in the night, their faces unhinged with violent lust, were their old enemies.

Skinheads.

Jed's chest crumpled inward, and a shocked breath rushed out of him. He put one hand against the wall, letting out a small noise.

"Wha—what is that?"

Christie turned toward him, aghast. She tried to speak, but only a whimper escaped her lips. Outside, the skinheads were dismounting their vehicles, surrounding the warehouse. There were too many of them, far too many. A dozen. They began trickling in through the front gate, their weapons raised before them, their steps utterly soundless.

Jed turned around. He looked at Christie, then he looked at Lauren's unconscious form lying on the floor. He envied her in that moment, how oblivious she was to her surroundings, how completely without fear. He wished he could join in her sound sleep. He didn't want to face what was coming. He was so tired of it all, so tired of failing to protect the people he loved.

"Jed," Christie whispered. Her voice was barely audible now, lighter than the wind blowing in through the window. She withdrew her weapon from its holster. The pistol gleamed in the wan moonlight, seeming to grin. Its time was here, it knew. Blood would spill tonight, one way or the other.

Jed swallowed. He said nothing to his partner. What could he say? What time did they have? On the floor below them, the subtlest of creaks filled the silence momentarily. The front door had been opened. The enemy was here. All this time, they had been searching the building for traps, trying to outsmart their opponent. But once again, he had managed to trick them. The trap had never been inside the warehouse. It had always been outside, a net drawing in around them, cutting off all routes of escape. There was nowhere to go now, nowhere to hide. The only option left was to fight against an enemy that both outnumbered and outgunned them. Jed took out his own gun from his waistband and weighed it in his hand. It was a grotesque thing, smooth and seamless and ugly, filled with death's metallic scent. His hand shook with its weight, shook in the grip of a nameless terror. He had never done this before, had only fired the weapon at the shooting range. He realized now how futile an exercise that had been. Nothing could prepare you for a real firefight. Nothing at all.

Christie's hand fell on his own. He looked up and into her eyes. Such beautiful pools of blue, it was a shame he had never spent more time admiring them. Christie squeezed his hand once, past the point of speaking. They couldn't risk it now. She gave him a look, a look that made a valiant but unsuccessful effort to speak a thousand things in a single moment. Then, she turned toward the staircase. Jed went and stood by her side, grateful at least for the fact that if this was the end, they would face it together.

CHAPTER 20

THE WAREHOUSE WAS NO longer so empty.

There were ten skinheads in total. Two had remained behind to surround the place, and the rest had entered with their guns and machetes raised, lips barred hungrily with the thrill of the kill. They were all part of Alfonso's gang, all of them his subordinates. Ever since his unthinkable abduction from his headquarters, they had been restless for revenge, waiting for a way to get back at the ones who had stolen their leader from them.

Now, they had their chance.

The anonymous phone call had been brief but powerful. That strange voice had told them how they could avenge the injustice that had been done to their leader. They were given the address and identity of the two people who were present there. That was all they needed. They mobilized instantly, grabbing their killing instruments and arriving without a second thought, knowing their prey was inside, unaware of the trap they were in.

It was time to balance the scales.

They crept up the staircase in twos, slowly, soundlessly, their fingers caressing their triggers. Behind them came the ones wielding machetes. Their smiles were just as wickedly sharp as their blades, and their eyes snagged the thin threads of moonlight, shining with inhuman glee. The guns were just for insurance, of course. Their real plan was to catch the intruders alive, so they could take their time with them, carving them up into an example the city would remember forever. Out here in this abandoned nothingness, a scream could travel many miles and still not be heard. It would be a fun game, seeing who could make the couple scream the loudest. Especially the woman. They all knew from personal experience that a woman's tortured screams were the most delicious of all.

The landing on the second floor stood empty. But still, they approached cautiously, making no sound, taking their time. Once they were at the top, one man out of the leading pair swung around like lightning, finger on the trigger, ready to apply that final squeeze should it be necessary.

But it wasn't. There was no one in the corridor. It stretched out before them, an alleyway of shadowy outlines, still as a dead giant's gullet.

Except.

Wait.

The third man who stepped onto the landing saw it first. His name was Emmanuel. He was twenty-five years old and had been to prison three times already for domestic abuse.

After getting out the third time, he had gone straight home and strangled his wife with a telephone cord before throwing all her jewelry in a bag and fleeing to the other side of the city, where his gang had taken him in. He was particularly looking forward to catching the female police officer alive. The thought of her tied and helpless before him made him aroused with anticipation. It made his stomach grumble with hunger pangs. She had taken Alfonso from him, who had been like a mentor, a father. Now, he would bring to her a world of pain.

In the darkness of the second floor's landing, Emmanuel nudged the man next to him. He pointed straight ahead, toward the base of the doorway on the opposite end of the corridor. The man followed his pointing figure and saw what Emmanuel's keen eyes had caught, barely visible in the dim light.

A shoe. The very tip of a boot, peeking out from the corner wall. As if someone were standing there, pressed against the concrete, hiding.

Emmanuel grinned. He couldn't care less about the man. It was the woman he wanted alive. He stepped back and allowed the two men with the guns to go forward. They crept toward the room at the very end, toward the sliver of boot peeking out from behind the wall. Both men stood on the other end of that wall and paused. They raised their weapons in the direction of the owner of that boot. They paused. Emmanuel grinned. He salivated at the thought of the first kill, the first of the enemies brought to justice. It was going to be a glorious night.

They fired.

The façade of peaceful quiet decorating the place was finally broken. It was ripped apart into smithereens. Bright flashes of muzzles blinked in the black like leering eyes. A barrage of gunshots rose into the night, heard from miles away. The wall didn't stand a chance. It crumbled instantly against the force of the bullets, as if it had been waiting for someone to come and give it that final blow. Flaking bits of plaster and concrete fell to the ground in a shower of snow. Puffs of dust rose up, misting the air, hovering ghosts in the lightless space. And that shoe, that tiny bit of brown at the wall's edge, was yanked back instantly. A groan came from inside the room, a male groan, full of pain, cutting off abruptly as soon as it started.

Silence returned to the warehouse.

Emmanuel's grin widened.

The two men paused to reload their weapons. While they did, the mist began clearing before them, and Emmanuel saw them standing in front of a wall punctured with holes. Through those holes, the room on the other side was visible. Someone was there. *Standing* there.

Alive.

Just as it had arrived, the silence was driven out again, an unwanted intruder in this den of death. Gunfire filled the hallway again, different from last time. This time the bursts were staccato, sharp and precise. Both of Emmanuel's comrades were flung back, their limbs jerking like faulty marionettes, their heads hitting the concrete with a crunch. Their guns fell from their grasp and hit the floor with equal force. One of them made contact at the wrong angle and fired. Emmanuel saw its muzzle blink again, a single fiery eye staring straight at him, almost in damnation. By the time he realized what was happening, it was too late. The bullets fled the gun's chamber and embedded themselves into his chest. Three bullets, lacerating Emmanuel's sternum in a perfect arc. He was thrown against the wall, his machete slipping from his grip and impaling the floor. The last thing he saw before death took him, before his quest for revenge remained eternally unfulfilled, was a figure emerging from the opposite room, a tall, muscular man burning with wrath, his eyes granite splinters.

Jed surveyed the scene.

Three bodies were lying in the hallway. One was still twitching faintly, blood erupting from its throat in a noisy gurgle. Moonlight streamed in from the overhead window and turned the leaking substance dark and silvery, into some strange potion of magic and witchcraft. Jed came forward slowly, his gun still raised, his eyes watching the staircase. He stopped near the dead men in the hallway and bent down, inspecting their guns on the floor. Then, he began putting the second part of his plan into action.

JODI WALTER

It had been the perfect ambush—an ambush for another ambush. Jed had been the one who had come up with the idea. As the first trio of men had made their way up the stairs, he had gone into the room and hastily taken off his left boot, pulling out one of its laces and quickly tying one end of it to the boot. The other end he had held in his hand, placing the boot at the doorway's edge before slowly crawling away from it, as far as he could go, until the string connecting him to the shoe became taut.

Then, he had waited. He had waited for the men to spot his trap. He had waited for them to open fire. As the hail of bullets had arrived, obliterating the wall, Jed had yanked hard on the lace, drawing the boot back to him. It had been the perfect illusion, making the men on the other side think that they had shot their hiding enemy. To sprinkle on a final layer of conviction into his act, he had also let out a pained groan, hoping it sounded real enough. It had. The men had fallen for it enough to let their guard down for a few seconds. Then, he had struck.

Now, the second wave of intruders was arriving.

There were five of them now, four with guns and a single one trailing behind with a machete. As they ascended the staircase, they saw one of their fellow brothers lying dead against the wall, his own weapon harpooning the floor. His eyes were parted in surprise, as if he still hadn't quite come to terms with his own demise.

Miguel took in the sight of Emmanuel's lifeless form and paused. He swallowed. The rage smoldered within him, threatening to singe the walls. He hated these bastards. First, they had captured Alfonso, and now they had managed to kill three more of his brothers. He would make them pay for it. He would make them pay for every drop of blood they had spilled.

"Listen all," he rasped softly, turning around. "Careful. Be very careful. These devils are clever. They killed Emmanuel. They'll kill us, too, unless we stay on guard." He tapped his weapon. "No pausing to reload in the open. No lowering your weapon. No matter what, okay?"

In the dark, his companions nodded. Their inky, tattooed skulls bobbed up and down like wraiths fleeing through the night. Miguel tightened his grip on his weapon and continued onward. He had killed 32 people in his life so far, at the tender age of 31, and for each person whose life he had taken, he had gotten his stomach tattooed with their number. Soon, there would be no more skin left for him to brand. It was Miguel's ultimate goal in life to cause a level of carnage too vast to be preserved on the scrolls of his body.

Right at the staircase's opening, Miguel paused again. He sucked in a sharp breath. His finger coiled around the trigger, his feet readying for action. In one smooth motion, he swung around the staircase, weapon raised, shark-like eyes scanning the dark. He was fast, the fastest of the entire gang—and the most lethal. None who had ever stood against him in a gunfight had escaped with their life. Just like certain people were born with certain innate talents and capabilities, Miguel had been born to kill. He relished it, the act of snuffing out a life, and especially the complex game of calculations that preceded it. It gave him an almost orgasmic thrill, knowing he had stilled someone's beating heart. No other sport in the world could compete.

Now, he stood in the hallway, weapon raised, his tongue licking his lips eagerly. Oh, their two targets were good. Very good. They had taken down the first attacking wave. He could see the vague dark shapes of his other two companions sprawled in the hallway, blood pooling around them, their weapons thrown aside. No one else was there. The three rooms stood dark and silent. The room right opposite him had a wall sheared with holes. He gazed through them to the other side, but once again, only shadows greeted him.

Miguel grinned. This was going to be fun. The harder the game, the more satisfying the victory.

He waited for the rest of his armed fleet to join. Once they were all there, four gunmen standing in a single row with their weapons raised, Miguel gestured in the direction of the room opposite them. His lips drew back from his teeth in a snarl.

"On my count," he whispered. "One. Two. Three."

They fired. Four submachine guns exploded into life. Gleaming golden parcels of death poured out of their muzzles, too many to count, infesting the cramped space like locusts, a plague sent to wipe out all life. They struck the already weakened wall of the room and tore apart whatever little remained of its defense. The wall crumbled, bits of pulverized plaster raining down to the floor. But the gunfire did not stop. It continued. The locusts swarmed the room itself now, riddling the floor, the walls, and the ceiling with holes. Perforating the entire space, skewering the darkness until there were no more bullets left.

Then, they reloaded.

It took barely a second. They didn't take their time, like their other companions had done, much to their misfortune. Miguel dropped the emptied magazine onto the floor. His hand moved in a blur, drawing out another full magazine of ammo and jamming it into his weapon. His brothers followed with equal speed. Once their weapons were filled with fresh stocks of destruction, they fired again, targeting that same room right in front of them.

Nothing was left standing. The room turned into shredded paper. Chunks of the ceiling fell down. If there was anyone inside, it would be hard to even identify them at this point.

Finally, they stopped, breathing hard, their noses filled with smoke. Miguel licked his lips again, his heart fluttering. They were not done yet. The best was yet to come. After all, two more rooms remained.

He pointed at the two men on his right, told them to take the room on the right of the corridor. They reloaded, cocked their weapons, then began tiptoeing through the hallway.

Miguel stepped over the dark, sinewy frame of one of his fallen brothers, feeling a pang of regret. If only they had been smarter. If only they had let him lead the attack. They would still be alive right now.

The remaining two rooms were right before them now. Miguel exhaled slowly, readying himself to finish the game once and for all. He raised the gun. Paused. Hesitated. He couldn't understand why, but there was suddenly a prick of unease deep within him. His heart's excited flutters had turned into nervous hoofbeats. His pulse was racing through his palms, making them achy and numb.

He was afraid.

Miguel couldn't understand what it was. Something was preying on his mind. The same mind that had led him to countless victories in his life was now telling him that a terrible mistake had been made. A mistake he was not realizing. He paused, scrunching up his forehead, trying to figure out what it could be.

Then, it hit him.

It slammed into him like a freight train.

Sinewy frame.

A strangled cry tore its way past Miguel's lips. His companions looked at him in surprise, finding him whirling around, his weapon rising. But it was too late. It was far too late.

Behind the attackers, one of the fallen corpses had risen to its feet.

It loomed in the hallway, a nightmare brought to life.

The men screamed. They swiveled their weapons, realizing what had happened, that they had been tricked. They tried to open fire once again.

But the figure fired first.

Holding a submachine gun in each hand, Jed pressed down on the triggers, his eyes pinpricks of rage. The guns dutifully did their bidding and unleashed another fresh wave of death. The hallway exploded, the four men in it spasming as if caught in a twister. Their bodies spun left and right. Their limbs flew into the air, dancing to an unheard tune. First, the bullets punctured their stomachs and chests, slowly making their way up and ruining those perfectly tattooed faces. Spurts of ink mixed with blood splattered the walls, drew strange satanic runes on the floor. The men's weapons dropped from their hands with a thwack. One hit the floor and misfired, its bullet lodging itself in the ceiling.

Jed released his fingers from the triggers, breathing hard. He sucked in a large breath and almost gagged, tasting blood in his mouth. Whose he did not know. There were so many. So many that had died. So many he had killed.

From one of the rooms, the sound of tentative footsteps came. Jed stood in the hallway, breathing hard, waiting for her to come out. A few seconds later, she did.

Christie took in the mess with utter disbelief. Corpses lined the cramped space. There was blood smeared everywhere, still fresh and wet, trickling down the walls. She turned toward Jed and almost gasped. He was standing motionless in the hallway, a grim reaper amidst his prizes, his face cloaked with shadows and blood.

"Jed..." Christie came forward, tidal waves of emotions threatening to overwhelm her. Jed, her Jed, the kindest and softest person she knew, who could never harm a soul, had been forced to partake in this carnage. She came closer to him, seeing his face come into view. It was the face of a different man altogether, spotted with red everywhere, his eyes burning feverishly.

"No time," Jed croaked, raising a hand to cut off her questions. "There's no time. We don't know if there are more down there. I have no more tricks to pull on them. You need to take the lead. I'll carry Lauren."

"Okay. Okay." Christie nodded. She seemed too flustered to say more. Instead, she just picked up a submachine gun from the floor and checked that it still had ammunition in it, then tucked her own pistol back into its holster. Jed stepped inside the room where Christie had barricaded herself and Lauren in. He saw Lauren lying in one of the corners, hands peacefully crossed atop her chest. All that disturbance, and she still hadn't woken up.

When Jed reached Lauren, he had to stop for a second because he found that his hands were shaking. In fact, every part of his body was shaking. In his mind's eye, he kept picturing those men being flung back, making those horrible twitches as they lay on the ground.

I'm a killer.

"No time for that now, Gray," he said harshly to himself, each breath becoming an effort. "No time. Get a grip on yourself. For Christie and Lauren, if not anyone else. They're still not safe. Not yet."

Those words helped. The thought of Christie standing alone in that corpse-littered hallway infused Jed's limbs with some calm. He leaned down, slinging his arms under Lauren's legs and neck before hauling her up. The girl was light, he thought to himself—much lighter than those guns had been, at least. He could still feel their cold metal forms weighing down his hands. His heart, too, most of all. He doubted that weight would go away soon, if ever.

Christie was waiting in the hallway for him. She was looking down at the fallen men when Jed came out. He saw an expression on her face, half-hidden by the shadows, a look he couldn't quite figure out. Christie gazed at him for a long moment, her eyes taking in his form as if he weren't the same person she had walked into this warehouse with.

"Shall we?" Jed asked.

Christie broke out of her reverie. She nodded once.

"Yeah, let's go." Her voice was strained.

They descended the staircase from which they had come, Christie took the lead now, the gun raised before her. They found the warehouse's first floor empty. She swung her flashlight around, searching for intruders, but there didn't seem to be any. For the first time, Jed was glad that the place was so hauntingly bare. It meant fewer hiding spaces.

Once Christie was satisfied that the floor was deserted, she motioned for Jed to follow her. They crept through the main floor and toward the door leading outside, which hung slightly ajar. Christie kicked it open, brandishing her weapon into the night, eyes scouring the courtyard for crouching shapes, gleaming barrels.

Something moved to the right.

She twisted and fired, her body racing ahead of her thoughts, riding on pure instinct. There was a thunderous fury inside her, a fury at the fact that Jed had been forced to do what was her job all along. Fight. Protect.

Her aim was perfect, her hands steady. The moving smudge in the courtyard's corner cried out and fell back. Christie shot another flurry of rounds at it for good measure. Then, she beckoned for Jed to step out of the warehouse's cover.

They continued forward, through the courtyard and toward the gate. The night had gotten thicker, wrapped its velvety cape around the world. A sliver of the moon peered down at them, illuminating the path leading outside. Christie pushed open the unlocked gate and stepped out, ready to face anything. But only the wind greeted them, singing merrily, as if oblivious to the mayhem that had just happened. Their Ford stood at the very end of the deserted yard, half dissolved into blackness.

Christie cast another look around. This was the most dangerous part. Inside the warehouse, although they had been trapped, at least they had known where the enemies were.

Here, no such luck. There was some visibility immediately around her but too many hiding spots and shadows beyond that. She had no way of knowing where their enemies could be hiding.

"On three," Christie murmured to Jed, turning around. Outside, the blood on his face was clearer. It was a grisly sight. Tiny droplets, almost spray-painted onto his cheeks and forehead, dotting the curving tip of his chin. His eyes stared through the scrim of red. Gray like always, except now the granite had hardened into diamond. Something had been taken from them, Christie realized with sorrow, a softness that could never again be returned.

"On three," Jed whispered roughly, shifting under Lauren's weight.

Christie counted. Nothing came to interrupt her count. At three, they both ran straight toward the Ford, abandoning all subtlety, their feet pounding on the asphalt. The Ford was maybe ten meters away, at most a dozen. Slowly, it grew before them, changing from an amorphous half-shape in the night to the vehicle that would carry them to safety. Christie glanced at its tires and exuded relief at seeing they weren't slashed. Things would have gotten a lot more complicated if their enemies had planned this far ahead. Alas, luck finally seemed to be on their side. They were almost there now, almost in reach of safety. Almost at the finish line.

A shot rang out.

Jed flinched and felt something whizz past him, terrifyingly close to his neck. He grunted and said a silent prayer, running harder, his head bowed. Christie whipped back her hand and blindly fired a flurry of shots into the night. There was no time to aim now. They were sitting ducks out here. The vehicle was their only option.

More shots rang out. Almost instinctively, Jed changed his beeline course into a swerving one. It was a brilliant last-minute maneuver because it saved his life. The bullets whistled past him, brushing the edges of his body before disappearing ahead. Christie cursed and emptied her weapon behind her. In that interval, Jed reached the Ford and fumbled the handle with one hand, trying to support Lauren's weight with the other. Another bullet squeezed through the gap between Lauren's face and their vehicle. Jed cursed and flung open the door. He heard more bullets make dents in it. Throwing Lauren inside without much care, he leaped in after her, shutting the door and locking it. From his other side, Christie slid in, too, throwing the emptied gun into the road. She shut the door and turned the ignition.

They were in.

Like a sleeping hound prodded awake, the Ford's engine roared to life. Its headlights switched on, twin suns in the tarry night. They brought the assailant into full view; another skinhead crouching behind his motorcycle and firing at them.

"Sonofabitch," Christie swore viciously. She kicked the accelerator and the car surged forward, speedometer rising wildly. The skinhead realized too late that he was right in their way. Jed saw his eyes widen comically under the Ford's blinding glare. He tried to dive sideways, but like the rest of his deceased companions, he was too slow. Christie drove the Ford right into him. It hit the motorcycle, and the pitiful little thing was crushed beneath them like an aluminum can. Metal shrieked and squealed as it was pressed flat and split open. Moments later, the bike's owner met the same fate. His cries were cut short, the Ford bumped erratically, they heard a wet squelching sound, and then they were back on smooth ground again, heading toward safety.

It was done.

Christie glanced at Jed. He glanced back at her but did not say anything. Neither of them spoke a word to each other during the entire trip, not until they entered the city once again, where the lights were bright as always and the laughing streams of people suggested that nothing had changed, even though everything had.

Forever.

Chapter 21

"She's okay. A little dazed, but okay." The doctor smiled at Jed. "Someone gave her a heavy sedative. There's no permanent damage, but it's going to take some time for her to get back to her senses."

Jed nodded in relief. "Can I go and see her?"

The doctor smiled. He was a kind-looking fellow, old and bespectacled, with thin, silver hair.

"Of course," he said. "Just be careful not to overwhelm her with too much information. She's already suffered a lot."

As have we all. She was fortunate to be sedated for the worst of it.

Jed nodded again. He followed after the man, who led him to Lauren's room, where two police officers were stationed. They saw Jed and made way for him instantly. Jed paused at the door, gathered his composure, took a deep breath, and went inside.

Lauren lay on the bed, a snake's nest of wires lying close to her left arm, a heart monitor beeping steadily beside her. She smiled at Jed. It was a strong smile, even though the rest of her appeared pale and weak.

"My, oh my," she murmured in a sore voice. "Now, this is one reunion I never expected to have."

Jed went to her. He stood at the foot of her bed and clasped his hands in front of him.

"How are you feeling, Lauren?" he asked.

Lauren stared at him a moment, then laughed. It was a short, dry sound.

"Looks like we're back to the sessions, huh?" she joked before turning serious. "I'm feeling okay. A little tired. A little like my brain is on a raft adrift in the ocean, but otherwise, I'm okay. Peachy, as they say."

Jed smiled. "You'll be back to your old self in no time," he told her with a smile. "The doctor said these are all temporary side effects of the drug you were given. They'll wear off soon."

Lauren nodded. "So I've been told," she murmured, her eyes scanning Jed, taking in his stubbly face, his broadened shoulders, his untrimmed hair. Most surprising of all, his eyes. They were different from when she had last known them. Harder. Flintier. Stones forged from fire, no longer exuding the softness they once had.

"So," she spoke after a long stretch of quiet.

"So," Jed repeated, shifting on his feet.

Lauren looked back at him. She scratched her IV-tangled arm absently. "Police officers came to debrief me in the morning," she said casually. "They wanted to know if I remembered any important details from my abduction. Anything that might help them apprehend the captor." A pause. "I told them I didn't."

Jed nodded, entirely unsurprised. "That's okay. The important thing is that you are safe now."

Lauren continued watching him. Somewhere inside this muscular, unshaven man with his haunted eyes was the therapist she had once worked with. She could see bits and pieces of that older self peeking out.

"I've also been told that you were the one who rescued me," she continued, keeping her tone neutral. "Is that true?"

Jed nodded once again, without hesitation. "Yes, it is. I got you into this mess. It was only right that I got you out."

Lauren paused. Words formed inside her mouth, but she did not voice them. It didn't feel right.

Jed inclined his head, perceptive as always despite the changed appearance. "You have questions," he guessed.

Lauren nodded slightly.

"Of course, you do." He sniffed, studied the floor for a moment. "At this stage, it's best you don't know much, Lauren. Not until this case is closed and we catch this bastard."

Lauren was not surprised to hear that. In fact, she had been expecting it.

"I understand," she said. "You're going through something. You'll need help along the way, but ultimately, you're the one who's going to have to solve it in the end. I get it. I went through a similar phase in my life once, remember?"

Jed smiled faintly. More of his older self shone through. "I remember," he answered.

Lauren took a deep breath. "Go, then," she told him in a firm voice. "Solve whatever it is you have to solve. Finish whatever it is that's been started. Once you're done, come back to me as the therapist I had all those years ago, the one who helped me through my darkest times. I'll take you out for a coffee, and then you'll tell me just what the hell it was I've been involved in. Deal?"

Jed's smile widened. Some of the burden seemed to lift from his eyes. "Deal," he whispered.

"Good. Go now, and do your thing." She tried to keep the emotion out of her voice, but some crept in, nonetheless. "I expect to see you soon."

"You will." Jed went to the door, then turned around once again with his hand on the knob. "I promise."

Chapter 22

"Jed, you just received a message."

"Coming!" Jed called out as he ran out of the bathroom. Christie heard his padding steps growing louder until he emerged from his room, still dripping wet, a towel thrown around his waist.

"Who is it…" Jed muttered, picking up the phone and reading. Water dripped from his face onto the carpet, giving it its first wash in decades. "Oh, it's Jeff. He's gotten the address for me."

Christie looked up and away. She waited for her heartbeat to return to normal and tried not to peek at Jed's wet, glistening body. "U—Um, that Mascarenes guy?" Her tone was strained with a false normalcy. Fortunately, her partner was too preoccupied to notice.

"Yep." Jed frowned at the screen. "He lives in a trailer park three miles from here. Or at least, that's what Jeff's source told him."

Christie sprang to her feet. "Let's go, then. What are we waiting for?"

Jed looked at her. He squeezed some more water out of his hair, blinked out the droplets hanging from his lashes. "Indeed. Let's go."

It was the day after Jed had his meeting with Lauren, two days after they had rescued her from that seemingly impossible situation. During that time, Christie had been tiptoeing around him as if he were a person of interest in one of her investigations. She had been watching him closely and discreetly, noticing the change in his behavior. He *had* changed; she was sure. For one, Jed had been having nightmares for the past two days. Twitching in his sleep with a frown on his face, his lips muttering soundless words. She had also seen him zoning out at random moments during the day. His eyes would glaze over, and his gaze would fixate on a random spot on the wall, the ceiling, the floor. She would have to raise her voice to bring him back to reality again.

The killings were haunting him.

Christie wished she could help him. She really did. It ate away at her that he was suffering for doing something that had been her job. The guilt was immense, and no number of hot showers seemed to wash it away. Every morning, she would wake with that guilt looming over her like a shadow, the first thing to greet her as her eyes opened and the first thing to trouble her in her sleep when she dozed off.

But what other option had there been? Jed's plan could only have worked with him in it. Those skinheads would have spotted Christie instantly if she'd lain down and hidden herself among the corpses in the hallway. Her blonde hair and bright white shirt would have served as neon signs, drawing attention toward her. No, the only option had been for Jed to take the reins. Which he had. And suffered for it, too. Now, Christie was suffering along with him, burdened by the weight of her own conscience.

At least they had something to do now. A clue to distract their minds. Christie was grateful. She could already see the mist clearing from Jed's eyes, that old alertness returning to them. He quickly went into the kitchen, coming back out moments later with a blueberry muffin for each of them.

"Shall we?" he asked, combing his wet hair back with one hand.

Christie nodded. "Let's do this."

They found Mascarenes easily enough, much to their surprise. The caravan was exactly where Jeff had told them it would be, strewn out next to a pond like a piece of trash. On the other side of the pond were more trailers that made up a tiny neighborhood. Trees dotted the landscape in random spots, and a couple of motels and diners sat in the distance.

Jed stepped out of the Ford, squinting up at the sky. It was the perfect winter afternoon—cool, windy, and golden. He rubbed his hands together and hoped their luck would be good today. That's all they needed, just one stroke of good fortune in their attempts to find their enemy. Just one piece of evidence through which they could locate him.

"Are you sure this guy is… safe?" Christie asked, walking over to him. "I remember you telling Jeff that he was schizophrenic, or something like that."

Jed nodded. "He was, I think. He was definitely an eccentric fellow, if nothing else. But he used to hang out the most with our invisible enemy. If there's someone who can help us track him, it's this Mascarenes fellow."

"Okay, then." Christie sighed, jamming her hands into her pockets. "After you. Maybe he'll recognize you."

"Oh, I doubt that." Jed let out a hollow chuckle. "He barely recognized me when we were in the same building, living together. I doubt my face will ring a bell now." He stroked his stubble absently. "Especially seeing the… changes… I've undergone."

That's for sure. I have a hard time recognizing you myself, right now.

Christie bit back that thought. It wasn't Jed's fault. He was just doing his best to deal with a terrible situation, and terrible situations sometimes demanded extreme measures. Such as radically changing your behavior and personality.

And killing people.

She swallowed, focusing her mind on the present, driving away the worry burrowing its way inside her. They walked up to the trailer, and Jed rapped his knuckles on the door twice.

A pause. And then:

"Who is it?" The voice came immediately from inside: high and shrill. Irritated.

Jed faltered momentarily, unsure of what to say.

"Uh—is this Mascarenes' residence?" he asked finally.

Another pause.

"Who is it?" Repeated in the exact same tone and cadence. As if their earlier answer hadn't been heard.

"Someone… who needs your help," Jed answered. "Could you let us in so we can ask you a few questions?"

They heard a chair scraping back inside. A series of items being pushed around. Footsteps approaching the door, heavy and petulant. Childlike steps.

A bolt was unlocked, and the door swung open. Jed and Christie stared. A man stood on the other side, scrawny and short, with a beard that went down to his chest. His eyes brimmed with suspicion, and his hands were on his waist, affecting the air of someone disturbed from a greatly important task.

"What is it?" the man asked, his eyes switching between the two visitors. "What do you want?"

Jed stared at his old acquaintance. He was having a hard time believing that this man was, in fact, the same boy he had gone to rehab with. So much had changed. The hair on his head, which was almost gone now. The face, lined and weary. Most of all, that beard…

Christie nudged Jed. He snapped out of his surprise.

"Pedro Mascarenes?" Jed croaked, clearing his throat. "Are you, um, Pedro Mascarenes?"

The man nodded. His beard nodded along with him, swinging to a beat of its own. "Yes. What do you want?"

Jed raised his hands in a gesture of request. "Could we come in, please? There are a few questions we'd like to ask you."

"Come in?" The man barked sharply. "Yes, come in!" Abruptly, he turned around and went back inside, leaving Jed and Christie standing in confused silence.

He's still troubled, Jed thought. *Still as strange a creature as he was before.*

After a moment of hesitation, they stepped inside. The caravan was a mess. There were towers of dishes in the sink trying to reach the ceiling, most of them filled with crumbs of what looked like bread. On the sofa, a pretty wooden guitar lay horizontally, each of its strings cut. There were magazines and sheets of paper on the bunk bed opposite the sofa. They had been filled with strange drawings of what appeared to be figures in masks.

"Ask, now," Mascarenes said to them, standing in the middle of the mess, his arms still on his waist. "What do you want to know?"

Jed opened his mouth. "I—uh—" He struggled to find the right words, completely thrown off by the situation.

Christie stepped in. "Mr. Mascarenes, we want to know about yo—"

"Yippie!" Mascarenes yelled. "Yippie fe fi fo fum! Close the lights, close your mouth! Escape the demon of the drums! The one whose mouth endlessly runs! Hoorah!"

Christie blinked. "Um—what?"

He's utterly mad, Jed realized dully. *We're standing here interrogating a mad witness.* He felt like laughing and crying at the same time.

"Mr. Mascarenes," Christie repeated, more firmly. "We need to ask you a few questions. Can you please sit down?"

"Of course." Pedro bobbed his head eagerly. "Of course. Yes, I can. Of course. Sit down." He did not move an inch from where he was standing, though.

Jed sucked in a deep breath. Exhaustion was settling into him. He wanted to go to sleep again.

"Pedro," he repeated, "Do you remember that you went to a rehab center when you were younger?"

Pedro frowned. "Of course. You were there, too, with me."

Dumbfounded, the words were knocked out of Jed once again. What the hell was happening? This man was supposed to be crazy. How had he recognized Jed, when the sanest of his friends from that time would've had trouble doing that after all this time?

"Y—you recognize me?" Jed asked, then waved a hand. "Never mind. That's good, I guess. Maybe you'll be able to answer my question as well." Despite himself, he was feeling a glimmer of hope again. Maybe, just maybe, this could be their breakthrough. It would certainly be a moment to remember, their elusive enemy brought down by information obtained through a half-mad hippie living out of caravan.

"Pedro," Jed repeated again. "In rehab, there was a man you used to hang out with quite frequently. Do you know his name?"

Pedro nodded instantly, and both Christie and Jed's hearts soared.

"Of course!" he answered, beaming. "How can I forget Graham? He was such a great guy! We used to have all kinds of fun together. I remember once h—"

"No, not Graham, Pedro," Jed cut in, biting his lip in frustration. "Someone else you used to spend a lot of time with."

Now, Pedro frowned. He looked genuinely confused. "Someone else?" he muttered. "Who could that be?"

"The guy no one else hung out with," Jed said. He added on impulse, "The invisible man. The one no one knows about."

Pedro's face darkened. It happened instantly and severely. They actually saw the shadows moving over his skin, even though sunlight was still streaming in from one window. His hands dropped from his waist, hung in the air, trembling minutely. His lower lip quivered.

"You…" he hissed at Jed, voice changed entirely, as if a different man were speaking through him. A cowering, terrified creature. "You…" The hissing turned louder, filled the cramped interior of the caravan like a gang of rattlesnakes.

"Pedro?" Jed took an uncertain step back. He didn't know what he had said, but it felt like a mistake. A big mistake.

"What have you done!" Pedro screamed suddenly, making both Jed and Christie jump. "What have you done! What have you done! You spoke of the Demon! You let the Demon know where I am!"

"Wai—Pedro, calm down!" Jed cried out. "What's wrong? Wh—"

"You told the Demon!" Pedro continued screaming. His vocal cords were straining out of his neck, trembling like his hands. "Now, it knows! It knows about me! I was hiding from him, and now he's found me again!"

"No one's found you, relax!" Christie exclaimed, frightened by the outburst. "It's just us three he—"

"YOU SPOKE OF HIM!" Pedro bellowed, voice cracking, eyes bulging from their sockets. "He must not be spoken of! Now, he knows! He'll come for me! Oh, God, he'll come for me now!" An anguished scream tore its way out through his throat, filled the caravan, spilled out into the day.

"Jed, come on." Christie yanked Jed's arm, dragging him to the doorway.

Jed began to protest. "Bu—"

"He can't help us, Jed! Look at him!" Christie flung open the door and stumbled out with her partner in tow. Inside, Pedro was still screaming, holding the elevated pitch of his cry in place, creating a terrible racket.

"Christ, he's mad!" Pulling Jed's elbow, Christie got them both to the car and started the vehicle. They processed what their next steps would be. A few people had come out on the streets by then, motel owners and waiters scratching their heads curiously. People peered across the pond at the commotion from their trailers. Pedro's screams continued unabated, pouring into the sky like smoke, drawing everyone's attention.

"Jesus Christ," Christie breathed, gripping the steering wheel harder than necessary and pulling out onto the road. She picked up her phone a moment later and dialed a number.

"Hello, is this Weill Cornell clinical services?" she inquired. "Yes, I'd like to report a disturbance. There's a man experiencing a severe psychotic break. His name is Pedro Mascarenes, and his location is…" She paused, glanced around at her surroundings, and then rattled off the address. "Yes, please send help immediately. No, he's not any danger to others, but he still needs psychiatric assistance. Yes, Pedro Mascarenes is the name. Thank you." She hung up, sighing wearily.

There was a stretch of silence in the car, where both of them soaked in the peace, the lack of shrill shouting. Finally, after even the quiet had begun to turn uncomfortable, Jed spoke again.

"He knew our enemy, Christie," he muttered. "He clearly remembered a man from rehab who no one else spoke to."

Christie laughed harshly. "Jed, are you really going to trust a word coming out of that loon's mouth? Really?"

"He remembered me, too," Jed argued. "He remembered me from rehab all those years ago. I'm practically a different person. I should be unrecognizable."

Christie glanced at him. She paused.

"What are you trying to say? That maybe we could've gotten some useful information from him if we had stayed?"

Jed nodded. "It's possible. It is."

"Really, Jed?" Christie snorted. The sound was filled with doubt. "Did you see the way he was screaming? You think it would have stopped any time soon if we had decided to stay? It would have escalated, for sure!" She shook her head. "No, no chance. If you want, we can come back some other time, but I would advise against it. That man can't possibly be of any help to us. He isn't even capable of helping himself."

There was another bout of silence from Jed. "It's not like we have a lot of options right now, do we? Not like there's an abundance of helpful clues waiting for us back at the apartment."

"Sure, we're a bit short on luck at the moment," Christie argued. "But that doesn't mean we start clutching a—"

She was interrupted. Not by Jed's voice but by his phone, that ever troublesome device, bearer of bad news, ringing on his lap.

Jed looked down.

"Stop the car," he whispered, his voice urgent. "Park it somewhere."

"What? Why?" Christie glanced at his phone and immediately understood. Her insides were doused with freezing water.

It was the Unknown Caller.

They were on a relatively empty street, grocery stores and laundromats surrounding them on all sides. Christie parked opposite one such laundromat, which was half-shuttered, and turned to Jed. Her face was white.

"Is that...?" she asked, even though the answer was obvious, right in front of her, flashing on the screen.

"Yes," Jed muttered darkly before picking up the call with a shaking finger. He put on the speakerphone.

"Seems like you two are doing some extracurricular explorations of your own, huh?" The voice was loud, sharper than before, and even less human. As if the machine part of it were slowly taking over, devouring the humanity bit by bit.

Jed swallowed. "I—I don't know what you're talking about."

"Oh, Gray, you sweet summer child." Horrible laughter. Mechanized and harsh. Steel knives scraping against stone. *"I love it when you try and lie to me. It's so sweet."*

"I'm not lying," Jed insisted. "Why would you think that?"

"I don't think. I know." A pause. When it spoke again, the voice was teasingly chiding, a parent gently reprimanding a

disobedient child. "*Someone's been very naughty, haven't they? They're talking to people they have no business with.*"

Sitting next to him, Christie stifled a gasp. It couldn't be. How could this man have known? How? They had just had the meeting with Pedro!

Jed's hands were clenched in his lap. Sweat glistened on his neck despite the cold.

"Talking to whom?" he managed to muster. "I think you're starting to get paranoid."

"*Oh, if only. If only.*" The voice clucked. "*But unfortunately, my magic crystal ball showed me you both at Pedro Mascarenes' place, asking him questions you had no business asking. Tell me, am I wrong?*"

For a while, neither of them spoke. The car seemed to have been frozen in time, its passengers made into puppets out of some horror show.

"Yes, you're right," Jed finally admitted. His voice was flat. Resigned. "We went to Pedro's place, asking about you."

"*Now, why would you do that, when we were having so much fun in our little game?*"

Jed did not reply. There was nothing to say.

"*Well, since you love snooping around so much during your free time, I've decided to speed up your next trial, Gray. Mind you, this is one of the final ones.*" Another pause. A menacing one. "*We're almost at the endgame now.*"

Jed leaned forward, frowning. "Next trial?"

"*Of course!*" The voice turned cheery again. "*By the way, congratulations on getting Lauren out safe and sound! I didn't think you'd make it, but you have always exceeded my expectations, Gray. Which is why this next level of the game is going to be a unique one.*"

Jed did not like the sound of that one bit. When a psychotic killer thought something was fun and unique, it wasn't a good sign.

But to his enemy, he simply said: "Tell me what it is. Tell me what new brand of crazy you've thought of now."

"*Ha! Fabulous! I love the enthusiasm!*" The laughter returned, loud and painful, giving both Jed and Christie a headache. "*For this next part, I'm afraid you're going to have to dress up a bit, Gray. Time to step out of your introverted shell. I've booked you and your lovely girlfriend two tickets to a concert tonight. It's at 10 PM and one hell of a whopper, let me tell you. At least 15,000 people are attending. So, bring your A-game with you! Ha!*"

"Wait, wait." Jed frowned, irritated. "A concert to do what? I'm not in the mood for any music these days."

"*Oh, you're not going for the music, dear child.*" The voice paused again, and they felt the catch coming before it arrived. "*You're going to save someone very special.*"

It's always the same, Jed thought wearily. *The rules may change, but the game is always the same. It's always someone from my life paying the price.*

He gritted his teeth. He gritted them so hard that an ache ran through his jaw. "Who?" he managed to spit out while reigning in his anger. Unleashing his emotions right now would only delight his enemy. It was what he wanted, after all—to see Jed's control spiraling loose.

"*Who, indeed? That's the game!*" the man cried out in a hideous, sing-song voice. "*All I can tell you is that it's another client of yours. Through a miraculous stroke of luck, someone anonymous sent them a free ticket for the concert. There's no way they'll be missing this show, which means you can't miss it either!*"

Jed frowned. "You're going to try and abduct a client of mine from a live concert." He snorted. "I'd like to see you try."

"*But my dear child, who said anything about abducting them?*" In the proceeding silence, the voice tittered. "*No, the time for abductions has passed. Plus, this time it won't be me doing the dirty deed. Oh, no, no, no, absolutely not. I've hired someone else for this. Someone very special. A professional.*"

Jed's frown deepened. The cocoon of dread inside him unfurled its horrid wings. "A professional to do *what?*"

"*Why, to kill them, of course.*" Another titter. Each bout of laughter seemed more unhinged than the last, if that was even possible. As if the person on the other end were sliding down a rabbit-hole of insanity whilst having the conversation. "*I've hired a hitman, my dear friend. A professional. Cost me almost all my savings and most of my connections to pull off. He's going to be there at the concert, and his orders are to orchestrate the assassination in the crowd, whatever it takes. Now, just one question remains.*"

The voice paused. The world seemed to pause with it, holding its breath.

"Who's going to find the poor client first: you or him?"

CHAPTER 23

"WELL, WELL. IT'S BEEN a long time, Gray."

Joseph stood up from the chair to greet Jed. He embraced the man, clapping his back once. "I hope you've been doing okay through this whole mess."

Jed smiled. Clean-shaven and short-haired, he looked like his old self again, with the only remaining difference being the black leather jacket he was wearing. "Just surviving, Joseph. Just surviving."

Each of the remaining members of Christie's task force stood up then, one-by-one, greeting their old friend. The one who had been absent from the station for so long. Even Jason seemed glad to see Jed, as if he had missed having someone to fight against.

"Heard you've been staying at a different place," Jason remarked, shaking his hand. "I—uh, just want you to know we're all working hard to dig this guy up as soon as we can. So he doesn't bother you anymore."

Jed smiled faintly, cocking his head to one side in surprise. "Thank you for that, Jason. I appreciate it. I have a feeling the end is near now, one way or the other."

Once he had greeted everyone, Jed sat down in his usual seat. It felt good, really good, the familiar firmness of the cushion, the chipped armrest on one side. Like he had come back home. Back to his family.

"So, everyone." Christie stepped up to the head of the table. She glanced at Jed and held back a smile. He had cleaned himself up so that his old client would find it easier to recognize him at the concert. It was a purely tactical move. But still, seeing her partner sitting there in his usual form was a wonderful sight. Almost a sign that things were returning to normal.

"There is a concert taking place tonight," Christie continued, gesturing toward herself and the cream-colored crop top she was wearing beneath a maroon bomber jacket, "which Jed and I will be attending, as you can see from our clothing. One of Jed's old clients is expected to be at this concert, and our job is to identify them and escort them to safety."

"Safety from what?" Carter inquired.

"From a hitman." Christie took in their surprised faces. "Yes, a hitman, and apparently a professional one. He'll be at the concert, too, and his only job is to eliminate the target."

The room stirred. Their faces had been serious before, but now they were grave. Especially Graham, who was staring at the floor grimly.

"I see you all are very concerned," Christie observed, "and I'm glad to see that you are." She paused, taking in a breath. "This is no ordinary operation. We aren't dealing with crim-

inals, gentlemen. We aren't even dealing with violent criminals. Not this time. No skinheads, no other gang members.
None of that." She exhaled, the sound of her breath loud in the
room's quiet. "We are dealing with a *trained expert*. A master
of his craft. Someone who has spent a lifetime practicing
how to kill people. No matter what, we cannot let his next
assignment succeed, not at any cost."

They all nodded, murmuring their agreement. Jed felt gratitude welling up within him at seeing his colleagues there. He
didn't know how he and Christie would have faced this on
their own. He didn't have the stomach for any more killing,
any more fights. He felt like he'd had enough of them to last
a lifetime.

"This is the layout of the concert." Christie fiddled with her
laptop. Moments later, the TV's screen lit up with a sprawling
blueprint of the venue. It was convoluted, mazelike. Paths
overlapped each other, twisting around in strange ways, with
a giant oval space in the center, where the event would take
place.

"If you look closely enough," Christie pointed at the screen,
"you'll see there are 13 exits in total. We'll have men stationed
at each exit." She surveyed her team.

"All of you will be inside the venue with Jed and me,
wearing earpieces, dressed in civilian attire. We'll enter at
different times and in pairs, so we don't arouse suspicion."

They nodded.

"It was a close call, but I spoke with the superintendent, and he's given us special access. We can go anywhere, do anything, without being stopped. I want you all to comb the location for sniper perches. Find every possible spot the killer could use, then put security there. Meanwhile, Jed and I will be in the crowd looking for the target, in case the killer is opting for a more personal touch."

"I'm surprised they didn't cancel the show entirely," Graham muttered.

"I already spoke to the concert organizers." Christie waved a hand. "Told them we'd received an anonymous tip that something might go down. They were unwilling to cancel or reschedule because of the lack of specific details; they believe it to be a hoax. But they are permitting us all full access. That way, we can keep an eye on things, pin down trouble as soon as it starts."

"That's smart," Graham grunted. "It takes so much planning and effort to put together something like this. The organizers would rather break a few rules than reschedule, or even cancel altogether. Besides, if we attend the concert, at least we have a chance at stopping this murder. Who's to say that if we got the event canceled, the killer wouldn't just go after this client of Jed's at some other time, without us present?"

"Exactly." Christie consulted her wristwatch. "I think it's time you all get ready, gentlemen. We're due to leave soon."

"Wait." It was Jason who spoke this time. He had been uncharacteristically quiet throughout the meeting—and very atypically non-disruptive. "This client of Jed's. Who are they? We need a name and a picture if we have to safeguard them."

Christie smiled.

"We don't know," she replied, nodding at Jason's look of surprise. "Yes, that's the challenge. If we knew who they were, we could've just contacted them and told them not to attend the concert. We could've hauled them into protective custody to prevent the killer from getting to them." She splayed her hands. "Unfortunately, we have no clue who they are."

"Whoa, whoa, whoa." Jason leaned back in his seat. His face was lined with skepticism. "You're telling me we have to protect someone in a concert when *we don't even know who they are?*" He laughed briefly—a sharp, high sound. "How in the hell is that possible? Forget protecting the person. How in the world will Jed even identify them out of thousands of people?"

"You leave that to me."

Jed's voice was soft, unargumentative. They all turned toward him and saw him sitting calmly in his seat, one hand playing with the zipper of his leather jacket.

"I guess it's best if we do leave it to Gray," Joseph said quietly. "This is outside my forte. I'm just going to focus on what I'm good at: being a police officer."

"Smart decision." Christie closed her laptop. The screen behind her went dark, reflecting seven tense outlines of the people in the room. "We all have our own challenges to deal with today. So, let's just focus on those. Our job is to protect every civilian attending that concert and to eliminate any threats present there. The better we do that, the easier it'll be for Jed to complete his part of the mission: locating his client and getting them to safety."

The team rose to their feet. Jed watched them file out the door to change into regular clothes. Only he and Christie remained behind. In the end, it was always just the two of them, and no one else. They sat in silence, waiting for their companions to return.

"Do you know the band that's playing today?" Christie asked suddenly.

Jed shook his head.

Her lips quirked upward. She looked down at the table, tucking a strand of hair behind one ear.

"Look at us, huh?" She chuckled. "Going to a concert, and we don't even know who's playing there. What strange times we've come to."

"Strange times, indeed," Jed echoed. He absently stroked his chin, surprised at feeling smooth skin instead of rough, untrimmed hair. "Who is playing, by the way?"

"The Wanton Werewolves," Christie pronounced. She made a face. "Either I've gotten too old or they're just not to my taste because I've never heard the name before."

"I have." Jed swiveled his chair around. "They play EDM music. Mostly beats."

Christie frowned at him. "A concert with only beats? What a rip-off! Where's the fun in that?"

Jed grinned at her. "Oh, there's a lot of fun, trust me. You just need to bring the right... accessories with you."

"Accessories?" Christie stared at him, blank-faced, for a moment before understanding dawned. She rolled her eyes. "Oh, don't tell me. Drugs. Everyone will be doing drugs at this concert."

Jed laughed. "Yep. Most definitely. MDMA and alcohol and maybe even a few coke-heads." He patted his thighs. "It's going to be a fun night."

"I hope so," Graham answered from behind, entering the room with the others. They were all dressed and ready to go, wearing a wide assortment of different items, from oversized hoodies and wonky sweaters to stylish suede Jackets. The perfect blend of clothes so that no one could tell they were together.

"Right, then," Christie spoke, eyeing her team with satisfaction. "Let's get the party started, shall we?"

The concert was taking place at MetLife Stadium. Crowds of people were gathered outside by the time they arrived. Most of them were young men and women without a care in the world, eyes bright and glittery, their concert energy was electric. At the arena's main entrance, a squad of personnel wearing rainbow-colored vests were organizing the crowd into lines. They dashed back and forth around the building in bright flashes of color, speaking into walkie-talkies, ushering incoming cars in the right direction.

"Damn, don't tell me we have to stand in line," Jed muttered. He was in Christie's Ford, staring at the line which had just formed but which was already beginning to extend to the end of the block. And that was just the first. Two more were forming next to it, the scattered throng of arrivals slowly being molded into a perfect pitchfork.

"We don't." Christie parked the Ford on the opposite end of the street. "Since we're undercover police personnel, we get special access. Now, I just need to call that Simon guy…" She went through her phone and dialed a number. Seconds later, someone answered on the other end.

"Hello, yes, Simon? We've arrived, my partner and I. Waiting for you to escort us inside the premises. We're in a black Ford right opposite entrance two."

Simon came out almost immediately—a skinny, dark-skinned boy running out through one of the doors and waving at them.

"Come on, let's go." Christie unlocked the door, and they both got out.

It was chilly outside. Chilly and festive. Excited chatter filled the air, mixed with the sound of impatiently shuffling feet and random bursts of laughter.

"Hello! Good evening!" Simon greeted them both. Jed saw an overwhelmed look on the boy's face and knew he had a lot to deal with today. "If you'll just follow me!"

Simon led them both through another door set into the venue's side. An armed guard was standing there, who moved aside upon seeing Simon's colorful vest. Jed and Christie stepped inside a narrow, snaking corridor. Fluorescent lights shone above them.

"After me, please!" Without waiting for them to answer, Simon began hurrying through the corridor, his hands swinging as his feet moved. Jed and Christie followed. They took a series of turns before arriving at another pair of double doors that hung open, revealing the venue itself.

"Whoa," Jed whispered, walking through. His ears dimly registered Simon saying something to Christie before walking away. He was too distracted to pay attention, though. The venue had hijacked his eyes.

It was huge. The place was huge, a giant bowl placed on the Earth's chest, fitted with a sea of tiny red seats on all four sides. Right in the center, the stage loomed, wide and black, with state-of-the-art mics and speakers jutting from its base. All around it, an artificial turf had been laid out beneath an open, star-studded sky.

"Pretty cool, huh?" Christie nudged him with an elbow. "When was the last time you went to a concert?"

"I've never been to one," Jed replied in an awed voice, his eyes taking in the view with fascination. "I've seen pictures and videos of them online, though. Looked cool to me. But seeing one in real life…"

"Yeah, it's a whole other experience." Christie's surprise had faded, and that serious, businesslike look was back in her eyes. She was scanning the seats and the empty spaces, watching the people moving around them, oblivious to the danger that surrounded them.

"Jed, I think it's time we start moving." She tugged at her partner's elbow. "Most of the attendees are already here. The concert will start soon. We need to find your client."

"Yeah…" Jed muttered. He couldn't tear his gaze away from the massive size of the place. Plus, most of it was already filled. How in the world were they ever going to find someone here, let alone an old client, someone whose face he hadn't seen for years?

"Relax." He felt Christie grab his hand and squeeze once. "Let's do this methodically. Let's take a walk through the venue. After all, all we need to do is look and keep looking. Sooner or later, you'll stumble across that familiar face."

Jed nodded. They began to move together, their fingers twined so the crowd wouldn't pull them apart. As they did, Jed scanned the people passing by. He let every other part of him relax, channeling all his alertness into his mind. His eyes poured over the swarms of eyes, bodies, feet. Wide smiles and hoots of laughter. Drinks sloshing around in cups, spilling onto the ground. Cameras flashing and groups striking poses. Boys dancing goofily, wrestling each other. Girls standing on tiptoes to catch a glimpse of the stage, asking their boyfriends to raise them higher so they could see. Festiveness everywhere, choking the air.

The rest of the team was surveying the entire stadium, looking for places that a sniper would choose as their vantage point.

Jed and Christie went through it all. Quietly. Slowly. As if they were a couple out for a stroll in the park. They walked in a circle around the stadium, Jed searching for a familiar face and Christie searching for a suspicious one.

There were so many faces to search, though. An endless landscape of people. Most of them, Jed only glimpsed in blurs, which he soon realized was their next problem. A one-second snapshot of someone wasn't enough to identify them, especially if they were an old client. He needed to take more time, stare at each attendee longer.

But such a thing wasn't possible. One, because they didn't have time. Even if they only spent one second on each face, it would still take them around four hours to finish with everyone. Two, and more importantly, most of the people here were youngsters. Jed would look like a creep if he began ogling them all.

"Christie, this isn't working," he told his partner, his voice worried. "There are too many people here. They're all wearing caps and shades. How do I possibly recognize an old acquaintance like this?"

Christie's face mirrored his worry. "You're right, Jed, but we have no other choice. Look harder. The concert will start any moment, and then finding someone in the chaos will be impossible."

No sooner had she spoken those words than a terrific cry rose from the crowd, dispersing into cheers and applause that spread through the stadium in a wave.

The band had arrived.

The event was beginning.

Jed cursed under his breath as the lights changed, white fluorescents replaced by strobing colors. Everyone rushed toward the stage, or at least as close as they could manage, their backs forming an impenetrable wall, their phones raised in the air with flashing cameras.

Shit. We're out of time.

"Come with me," Jed told Christie gruffly, pulling her by the hand. There was a tiny crack in the fortress of bodies to their right, wide enough for them both to wiggle through. Maybe they would find his client in the area closer to t—

"Jed?"

Jed whirled around at that voice, one hand rising instinctively to protect himself. He let it down slowly once he saw who was standing behind him, though.

Alexis. Alexis, wearing a neon yellow hoodie with plastic shades pushed up on her head, her lips shaded purple.

"Alexis?" Jed exclaimed. His mind was fragmenting under the confusion, the chaos of everything. "What are you doing here?"

"Attending a concert, duh!" She came forward and shook both his and Christie's hands, grinning, her eyes wild and alive. "I've been a fan of The Wanton Werewolves forever! When I heard they were coming to New York, I knew I couldn't miss it! I preordered tickets a month in advance." She paused, taking in the sight of Jed and Christie together, surprise evident on her face. "But I didn't know you were fans, too! Wow! Especially you, Jed! You never told me you were into EDM!" She shook her head, chuckling. "Imagine that, both my ex-partners having the same music taste!"

"Y—yeah," Jed stammered, grinning weakly. "I—I thought I'd make Christie try something new for a change. She was really excited."

Christie dug her nails into Jed's palm, smiling sweetly at Alexis. "I am. We were just trying to make our way to the front to get a better look." She cast a helpless look at the crowd, packed together tightly. "But there's no way through."

Alexis threw back her head and laughed, her ponytail jiggling behind her. "Because you're still a novice concertgoer!" she exclaimed. "Come with me. My friends are up ahead anyways. I'll take you so close you'll be able to reach out and touch one of the band members, if you want!"

There was nothing more to say. They turned and followed Alexis, who went straight toward a crack in the crowd and slipped through it. Jed and Christie copied her every move, watching her skillfully navigate a forest of limbs and poking bones, muttering *excuse me* repeatedly under her breath and squeezing through the throng.

At some point during their journey, the concert began. A single beat rose into the air, washing away all conversations and eliciting another deafening cheer from the crowd. Another beat accompanied it, faster than the last one, followed by another, which was even faster. They came one after another without pause, perfectly synchronized, rising in volume with swift smoothness. The lights shifted in sync with them, flickering and strobing and swaying back and forth. Dim reds and yellows and greens careened across the crowds, brightening as the music rose, softening along with it.

Jed and Christie continued on their way. Jed's head was craned upward, and he was scanning every single face he could find. It was terribly difficult work. Sometimes, he thought he dimly recognized someone, but from a changed angle, they morphed back into a stranger. Most of those strangers were now moving, getting into the feel of the music, letting it fill their bodies with eclectic maneuvers. Their faces were awash with strobing green pulses one second, swimming in scarlet the next, overtaken by sapphire shades after that. The lights constantly changed, never retaining their form for more than a few seconds, trying to mirror the music's tempo as it shifted back and forth, slowly rising higher and higher.

It had become very difficult to speak now. The beats were too loud. They drowned everything out, demanded to be heard and understood. Jed, despite never being a fan of EDM, couldn't help but acknowledge an appreciation for the music. It had a feel of its own, one that seemed to speak directly to his body rather than his mind. He was embroiled in a terrible emergency, racing against time to save an innocent soul's life, yet his limbs were itching to move to the music. Some of it seemed to have seeped inside him. Jed could feel the beats calling out to him, inviting him to abandon all worries and surrender to the present moment. He gritted his teeth and ignored that voice, continuing through the crowd.

Further up, the bodies thickened, though still easy for Alexis and Christie to slip through. But Jed, with his massive frame, found himself struggling. He unintentionally elbowed people and jostled for space, muttering apologies which went un-heard and trying not to lose track of his friend and partner. The lights illuminated the way for him, and he half-crawled and half-stumbled his way through what seemed like tunnels of glittering fire, ice, and lightning.

Right toward the very end, the music hit one of its first crescendos, and the whole crowd raised its arms in triumph, cheering once again. Jed was caught off guard by the sudden movements and sounds. Confused, he surged forward, failing to stop his elbow from smacking into someone's ribs with considerable effort.

"Hey, watch it!" cried a voice over the music. Jed shouted an apology, stopping only briefly to reorient himself before searching for the path in the crowd he had accidentally veered away from. As he stood there, another, different voice behind him crested the beats.

"Mr. G?"

Jed's body turned around, even though his mind had failed to make sense of the greeting in all the mayhem. When he saw Max standing behind him, however, some of his senses returned.

"Max?" Jed shouted, staring unblinkingly at the boy moving toward him, cocooned in pulsing red ripples.

"Mr. G, what a surprise!" Max hollered. He was dressed entirely in black, shades resting on his forehead, a gleaming chain wrapped around his neck. "Man, you're a sack fulla shocks, Mr. G! I never knew you was into raves and all that shit!"

Jed shook his head, too taken aback to speak. First Alexis, now Max? What the hell was happening? Were all the people in his life secretly partiers?

"I'm here with a friend! She brought me!" Jed shouted back the lie once more, readying to leave. There was no time left; it didn't matter how many acquaintances he ran into.

"Ahh, thas sweet, Mr. G!" Max yelled. "Imagine running into you here, of all damn places!" He laughed, ice-blue lights crawling up and down his skin. "If I hadn't gotten a last-minute ticket, I never woulda found out you was into raves!"

"Yeah, Max, imagine!" Jed turned around, his eyes searching the crowd once again. He found Christie at the far end, standing with Alexis and—

Jed froze.

Slowly, like he was in a dream, he turned his head back toward Max, who was still standing there, grinning goofily at him. Jed swallowed. The beats seemed to travel down his throat, into his heart, reverberating in its very center.

"What did you say, Max?" Jed shouted into the boy's ear again, grabbing his collar and drawing him close.

Max leaned back, confused. "What?" he yelled.

Jed's grip tightened on Max's jacket, as if he were afraid the boy would be yanked away from him by a sudden tornado.

"How did you get the ticket to come here?" he shouted.

Max grinned. His teeth looked like they dripped blood in the crimson flashing lights. "I won the ticket! I got a call today telling me I won and how to pick up my tickets at the entrance. It's funny, I don't even remember entering a contest like this," he answered into Jed's ear. "God bless the generous people of this world!"

The world swam beneath Jed's feet.

He clenched his eyes shut and steadied himself, trying to think past that terrifically loud, perfectly harmonized music. In the blackness of his vision, the lights were still dimly visible, afterimages of exploding fireworks brightening the dark. Jed took in three deep breaths, his hand holding Max's jacket in an iron grip, refusing to let go. He couldn't let go. Not now, not ever.

It was Max.

Max was the target.

"Mr. G!" Max's voice made its way to him through an avalanche of beats. "Mr. G, you okay? You don't look too good."

Jed opened his eyes. The world rushed back in seething flashes of color. The music pounded its fists against him from all sides. Max's worried face floated before him, a mirage in this madness.

"You need to come with me," Jed whispered, realizing no one had heard him. He spoke again, forcing his voice into a shout. "You need to come with me, Max!"

"What? Why?" Max stared at Jed in confusion, offering little resistance as his therapist began hauling him forward.

Christie was standing up ahead. When she saw Jed, she pointed in his direction, her eyes widening as she spotted Max being dragged behind him. She whipped out her phone and sent a message, letting their team know they had found the person they were supposed to protect.

"It's him!" Jed wheezed, pushing Max between himself and Christie so that he was safe, at least for the moment. "We have to go, Christie! We have to leave now!"

"Yes." Christie was frowning at her phone, going through the place's layout, searching for the nearest exit. "Follow me, Jed. Keep the boy between us."

Max had no idea what was happening. Yet he did not protest as they took him with them through the crowd. There was something in his therapist's and that stern woman's voice which frightened him. It was a voice adults used when something terrible had happened—or was about to happen.

The music reached another crescendo. The crowd cheered again, the people dancing madly, blind to the crisis unfolding within their midst. Jed kept his head down and his eye out for danger, but it was impossible to properly see anything now. The music was too fast, too chaotic, and the crowd had met its rhythm. Faces were just a blur, hands and feet smudges of color, visible one second and gone the next. He kept going through them, following Christie, waiting for that door to arrive that would lead them to safety.

Something whistled past Jed's ear.

"Down!" he screamed, instantly pushing Max to the ground. Christie whipped out her pistol and turned around, but she could see nothing coherent. The passion of the event seemed to have melted and fused the lights, music, and audience into one single organism. There was no way of saying where one ended and the other began.

From the ground, Jed craned his head to the left. He saw the crowd moving, and in its midst, unnoticed by everyone, was a body. Lying on the ground. A victim of the bullet that had just missed him.

"Christie, we need to go!" Jed screamed.

Christie hauled Max to his feet, and now the three of them were sprinting, rudely shoving people out of the way, leaving a storm of curses and surprised shouts behind them. Far in the distance, through the crowd, Jed saw the exit. They were there. They were almo—

"Ahh!" He fell to the ground, white-hot agony flowering in his thigh. The grass rose to meet him, each blade a halo of purple. As if celebrating his fall, the music peaked again, and the world around Jed was drowned in deafening cheers.

"Jed!" Christie was coming toward him. Jed could see her from the corner of his vision.

"No!" he snarled through the pain, waving a hand. "Go! Go! Save Max! Max is the target, not me!"

Christie hesitated for just a second, looking back at Max, who was standing frozen with petrified, wide-open eyes.

Another shot whistled past Jed.

He heard Max cry out, heard his own heart cry out with him, and saw his client bend down, clutching a bloodied elbow.

"Christie, take him!" Jed screamed. The pain in his thigh was a throbbing beat of its own. He put one hand against the injured area and hobbled to his feet, clenching his jaw with the effort.

"Je—!"

Her voice was cut off as the beats rose again. The sea of bodies surged with them, and Christie was drowned out by the tide. Jed knew he had no time to search for her. Trouble was coming. He reached inside his jacket and drew out the gun. His gun. The one that was now tainted with the blood of so many. Jed held the horrible thing in his hands. It pulsed and strobed beneath the lights, turning into a figment from a psychedelic trip. He looked to his side, from where the bullets had been fired. Through the crowd, through the waving limbs, he saw someone coming toward him. A man in a suit, with a slick bald head and gloved hands. Skin white as wax. A blank canvas for the changing lights.

Jed faltered. His finger was on the trigger, his hand itching to raise the weapon and discharge it. But he knew he couldn't. There was no way he could have a shooting match here. If even one of the bullets missed its mark... No. He had already killed enough in his life. He would not add innocent people to that list, too, as collateral damage.

The man spotted Jed. Their eyes met. The pair stood opposite each other, an ocean of bodies between them, swelling and dipping, sloshing back and forth.

Jed saw the man raise his weapon. He knew he had only seconds left, seconds to either dodge or fire back, because there was no way he could escape from someone who was such a brilliant shot—someone who had managed to hit both Jed and Max in a concert full of people. No, it was either kill or be killed.

Jed lunged to the left and raised his hand. The gun came up in the air in a swinging arc, barrel glinting hungrily. It swept toward the man, who moved with an almost inhuman speed, standing there one second and crouching the next. But Jed didn't care. He hadn't been aiming at him. His target was something else, his plan already formed.

The gun rose, traveling beyond the man, beyond the crowd, toward the night sky. Jed closed his eyes and pulled the trigger.

Madness ensued.

The music was loud, impossibly loud, each percussive beat jostling for space in the chaos. But it still wasn't loud enough to compete against the sound of a gun without a silencer attached to it.

Jed heard the sharp, explosive crack. It ripped a jagged path through the music. Everyone else heard it, too—or at least the people closest to Jed did.

They shrieked, their cheers distorting into cries of terror, their dancing bodies transforming into a frenzy of flailing limbs. A ripple spread through the crowd. Waves of people surged left and right, forward and backward, colliding against one another and turning the already cramped area into a congregation of panicked animals.

Jed felt like he was caught in a stampede. No, multiple stampedes, each rushing in a different direction. He was bulldozed by shoulders and elbows and knees, by a swarm of humans that seemed to have no end. The pain in his thigh flared, and he put one hand against it, melding into a wave of people heading toward the closest exit. He cast a look back but could not see the bald man anywhere. He had been eaten by the crowd.

The crowd reached the door and threw it open, flooding the hallways, flitting through it like locusts. Jed followed in their midst, his gait erratic, his injured leg screaming angrily at the torture it was being put through. He reached the other end and stumbled through it into the night, back onto an empty street that was quickly filling up.

Christie? Where was she? Jed took out his phone and called her. She answered on the first ring, her voice drenched with worry.

"Jed! Oh, God, where are you? Why is everyone running out?" Her voice was breathless.

"I'm fine," Jed panted. "Where are you?"

"In the car with Max." There was the sound of Christie honking the horn repeatedly. "Tell me where you are. I'm coming to get you."

"No!" Jed cried out, wincing as a fresh bout of pain lanced his leg. "No, there's no time! Max is the target, not me! Take him to the hospital. I'll be fine."

"Bu—"

"Christie, there's no time!" Jed exclaimed. "I'm fine! I'm on the uh—west end of the stadium. Where the bank is. Tell someone from your team to come get me."

"West end? Okay, Jed, just stay there. I'm calling Graham and the others to pick you up immediately." She paused. "Stay safe. I'll see you at the station."

"See you," Jed wheezed. He was leaning against the bonnet of a Chevrolet, the gun in his left hand getting heavier by the second. People were still streaming out through the exit in droves, infected with fear, slowing down only once they had reached the end of the sidewalk.

One gunshot to empty out an entire stadium, Jed thought with a sigh. *That's how infectious a thing fear is. I doubt half these people even heard the gun firing.*

There was a honk to his left, and he turned around to find a police cruiser approaching him, Graham and Carter in the front seats.

"Jed!" The car stopped, and Graham jumped out, his eyes narrowed with worry. "Christie said yo—"

"Yeah," Jed grunted, limping toward him. "I got shot. But in my leg. I'm fine for now. Just…" He stopped to take in a breath. "Just take me to Max and Christie, wherever they are."

Graham hooked an arm around Jed's shoulder and helped him inside the car. They cut a path through the fleeing pedestrians, Carter's hand never moving from the horn, the car's sirens blaring.

"Jed, did you catch a glimpse of the killer?" Graham asked. "I doubt we'll be able to find him in this mess, but still, we need to try."

"He was bald," Jed muttered, head sagging against the seat, vision swimming. "Wearing a black suit. And gloves."

Graham took out his phone and relayed the information. Jed heard his voice as if it were coming from somewhere far away. His eyelids began fluttering, and with each flutter, the world returned a little blurrier. The pain in his thigh was only a dim sensation now, something happening to someone else, in some other time. Too weary to think any more thoughts, Jed closed his eyes and let the darkness take him.

When he awoke, he was in a hospital bed. Graham and Joseph were standing over him. In one corner, a nurse was fiddling with some equipment.

"Where..." Jed swallowed the dryness in his throat. "Where am I?"

"Mount Sinai Hospital," Graham answered in a thick voice. He looked worried, almost ill. His hair was a mess, and the top two buttons of his shirt were undone.

"You lost consciousness on the way to the hospital," Joseph informed him. He looked no better than Graham, Jed noticed. There was a sickly sheen to the man's face and a haunted look in his eyes. His left hand kept nervously playing with the hem of his shirt.

"What's wrong?" Jed croaked. A wave of fear rose within him, and his eyes fell to his leg that had been shot, almost expecting to find it amputated. But no, it was still there. Covered with a blanket and no longer aching. A stiff bandage was placed over the wound.

"What's wrong?" Jed repeated, staring at the two pale-faced men in the room. He forced a laugh. "Am I dying or something? Don't tell me I got struck by a poisoned bullet."

Neither Graham nor Joseph laughed. Not even a twitch of a smile. If anything, their expressions turned more somber.

"You're fine, Jed," Graham answered in a tone suggesting nothing was fine. "The bullet passed right through your thigh. All you got was a flesh wound."

"Then, what's the problem?" Jed asked. "Why are you both wearing those faces? What happened?"

Joseph and Graham exchanged looks. They stepped closer to Jed's bed. On the room's far end, the nurse gave him a quick glance before picking up an aluminum tray of implements and hurrying out, as if she didn't want to witness this next part. Jed's stomach coiled with dread, a nameless, formless, terrifying dread.

"What?" he whispered. "What is it? Tell me!"

Graham gave him a long, hard look. He had always been a strong man, but right then, Jed saw his lower lip quiver. A shudder seemed to envelop him, one he fought off by placing a hand on Jed's bed and steadying himself.

"Jed," Graham croaked. His voice was weak. Tired. Broken.

"Christie and your client never made it to the station."

CHAPTER 24

THE ROOM WAS SPACIOUS, with a minimalist touch to it. Only two black sofas sat in the corners, a beanbag placed between them. Other than that, there was a tall lamp and a single coffee table, nothing more. Nothing to suggest the true nature of the place, and the purposes for which it was used. The walls were pastel blue, the carpet varying shades of beige. Everything seemed to scream the words *harmless* and *mundane*, including the man who sat on one of the two sofas. He was tall and middle-aged, with long, sandy hair and a trimmed beard. His face was narrow, angular, his eyes peering out from within like incisions. A magazine lay in his lap, which he was turning lazily, adjusting his spectacles as he did.

Someone knocked on the door.

The man looked up, frowning. "Come in!"

The door handle turned almost instantly. In walked another man, as tall as the first, yet much more muscular, and with eyes that seemed to have seen too much in too short a time. The man stood at the door, looking at the other man on the sofa, studying him.

"Hello, Juan Martinez," Jed greeted from the doorway. "Thank you for giving me an appointment on such short notice."

On the sofa, Juan's frown softened. He rose slowly, putting the magazine aside. "Oh, so you must be Jed. Welcome. I was waiting for you."

"Hope I didn't keep you waiting too long." Jed went forward and shook the man's hand. He had a firm grip. "So, how do you want to start this?"

Juan cracked a small smile. "Getting straight to it, huh? No problem. You do look like you're in a bit of a rush."

The polite smile on Jed's face twitched ever so slightly at those words, settling back into place moments later. In that tiny interim, Juan Martinez thought he saw a great flood of emotion roiling beneath the man's calm exterior. He hastily stepped forward and closed the door to his office before turning around.

"Please, sit." Juan pointed at one of the sofas. Jed went for the left one. He had a slight limp in his walk, Juan noticed. Part of him was too unnerved to wonder why.

"So, how can I help you?" Juan sat across from Jed, arms relaxed at his sides, a pleasant smile forced on his face.

"I need you to hypnotize me," Jed spoke the words flatly, without any preamble. "That's what you do, right? You can hypnotize people and then give suggestions to their subconscious mind. You're one of the best in the city, apparently."

Under ordinary circumstances, Juan would have enjoyed the praise. These circumstances appeared far from ordinary, however.

"I can," he answered slowly, "but there's always a purpose behind the hypnosis. Sometimes people want to unearth a traumatic memory so they can face it fully and move on. Sometimes people want to get rid of an addiction, or treat an insecurity, or dig up a memory, or—"

"I need to solve a puzzle," Jed cut in, and Juan noticed the man looked quite impatient, indeed. He had adorned a garb of calmness, but beneath that garb, everything was in turmoil. The man was a walking nuclear reactor in meltdown, ready to go off at any moment. Juan swallowed.

"Solve a puzzle?" Doubt appeared across his face. "I don't think I've ever done tha—"

'You don't need to do anything new," Jed interrupted with that same impatience. "Just hypnotize me, and my subconscious mind will do the rest. I know it will."

Juan paused, uncertain. Rarely had patients ever come to him with such conviction. Maybe this was a session where he, too, would end up learning something new.

"Okay, then." Juan reached for the coffee table, where the instruments of his trade lay scattered. "Please lean back fully against the sofa and relax."

Jed did as he was told. He took a deep breath and exhaled, feeling his stiff muscles lighten.

"Now, Jed, relax even more." Juan's voice changed abruptly, turning deeper, slower. He seemed to be speaking from the other end of a submerged cave, his words amplified and echoing all around. "Relax. Feel my words washing over you like warm water. Feel yourself relaxing beneath them, turning lighter, lighter, lighter…"

Jed continued staring at the ceiling. A drowsy sensation stole over him, turned his eyelids heavy. His chest rose and fell with a quiet rhythm.

"Lighter… lighter… lighter…" Juan's voice seemed to be coming from everywhere now. It gushed through Jed's ears and filled his skull, warm and soft and soothing. On the ceiling, the yellow glow of the light fixtures expanded, spilled across Jed's vision. He sensed his thoughts ebbing in his mind, leaving in their wake a blank slate. Open to suggestions.

"Now, Jed, keep your focus on the pendulum. Just move your eyes, not your head. And continue to relax…" A pendulum came into Jed's vision—smooth and silver, like hardened mercury. At the base of the chain hung a small, silver orb, which began swinging left and right in lazy, almost balletic fashion. Jed followed its movements with his pupils. The orb really was very smooth. The smoothest thing he'd ever seen. Its movements were just as smooth, as if it were encountering no friction in its path. As if all of existence were shifting aside to give it space.

"Yes… keep watching it… and notice your eyelids getting heavy… heavier… heavier…"

Jed didn't need the suggestion. It was already happening. Someone had stuck chunks of cement to his eyelids. They were almost pressing down toward the ground, tugging at his muscles with an insistence he was finding hard to fight off. All the while, that pendulum continued swinging, so slow, so smooth...

"Don't try to fight it, Jed. When you're ready, let your eyelids close... descend... into peace... into the protection of your inner mind... descend..."

A deep breath surged out through Jed's nostrils. His eyes closed, and darkness filled his vision, the pendulum and the ceiling disappearing from view. He felt himself sliding down a tunnel, his alertness waning with every passing second. Before the darkness took him completely. he mustered all his strength and sent out a final, clear thought into the abyss:

Solve the puzzle.

Juan Martinez sat and stared at the man. He was in a state of deep rest, his eyes shut and his breath barely perceptible. The light falling on his face didn't seem to bother him in the slightest. In fact, it almost looked like he had died, or was about to. But Juan knew that wasn't the case. The man was alive, as alive as him. He was just in a different place. Whereas Juan was sitting in the outside world, this man called

Gray had made an inward journey, right to the very core of his mind. Juan wished him the best of luck. He wasn't an expert at analyzing people, but he had taken one look at Gray's haunted expression and realized the fellow had a very complicated mind, filled with layers and layers of memories better left untouched.

I hope you find what you're looking for.

After a minute more of fidgety waiting, Juan dimmed the lights and took a seat on the other sofa.

It looked like this would take a while.

CHAPTER 25

HE IS LOST. FALLING. An endless tube of flashing lights and sounds and images. Half-formed memories reaching out for him like ghosts, grazing his skin for fleeting seconds before being left behind. His plummeting descent seems infinite, eternal. A kaleidoscopic blur of the past he is destined to traverse till the end of time.

All the while, the truth is gathering somewhere close by.

The puzzle fitting into place.

One piece at a time.

"Jed! Catch!"

He turns around. His father is standing on the other end of the lawn, framed in sunbeams. Lips split into a smile, he throws the baseball toward Jed without another word.

It sails at him, a huge blob hungrily leaping for his chest. Jed raises his arms and catches it at the last minute. The force of the throw sends him stumbling back, landing on his butt in the soft grass. His father's throaty laughter fills the afternoon. Grinning himself, Jed hears the porch door swing open. A slender figure walks out.

"Richard, stop being so rough with him!"

A hospital bed. White sheets. Whiter lights. Whitest of all: the pain. Excruciating, unbearable, searing its initials into every inch of his flesh. Making him writhe on the sheets and cry out repeatedly.

"It's okay; it's okay. Detox can be quite painful in the beginning. Just hold on, my child. It'll all be okay..." It is a doctor's voice, soft and kind, but not kind enough to dull the pain. Not even close. It is too intense, that agony—a blade of fire digging into his guts, twisting and wrenching his innards without mercy.

He screams.

More screaming.

But not his own.

His mother's. She's standing in the living room, facing Richard, who is looking impassively at the floor. His father's face is embarrassed but determined. He has already made his decision. Nothing will change it. He is leaving Jed and his mother.

"What about Jed?" Laurie exclaims shrilly. "What about your son, Richard? Don't you have any responsibility toward him? Do you know the kind of company he's around these days, ever since you started disappearing?"

Richard's eyes remain on the floor. He mutters something. It only serves to infuriate Laurie more because she launches into another tirade, fists waving.

Jed watches from down the hall, peeking out of his bedroom door. A single tear trails down his cheek.

"HA-HA, you think you're real funny, huh?"

The words are spoken by Haley, his friend from rehab. They're harsh words, but she says them lightly, jokingly. She and Jed are sitting at the clinic's basketball court. It's early morning, bright and windy. Their clothes flutter around their bony frames. Their hair are wispy messes.

Jed says nothing. He stares up at the sky, at the black specks soaring in it. He wonders what it would be like to be as free as those birds are, to not have a care in the world.

"I like spending time with you, you know. I don't know why, but you're just easy to be with."

Again, Jed says nothing to her. He just grins her way, a cute, goofy grin which has already begun to mature into the charming smile he will possess as a man one day. Haley stares at him a moment, then takes his hand in hers and clasps it. She says nothing more. They sit and watch the birds fly. Jed's heart does its own little soaring dive, but he doesn't tell Haley.

It's the first time a girl has held his hand.

"Jed, what the hell is this?"

His mother is standing before him, livid. Red spots flecking her skin. She holds a burnt-out stub of marijuana in one hand, a tiny sachet of the remaining, unused stuff in the other.

"I asked you a question, Jed? What is this?"

Shame bursts forth through Jed in a hot torrent, sluices up his throat. He bows his head and mumbles an excuse. His dad already left last month, and his mother is all he has left. He doesn't want to disappoint her, too. He doesn't want her to leave him like his dad did. But what can he do? He likes doing drugs. They distract him from his own thoughts. They whisk him away on wings of smoke from the burden of his own existence.

"Jed." The tone is calmer now, softer. She comes toward him, lays a hand on his shoulder, and tilts his chin up. "You know you can tell me anything, right? Any troubles you're going through, anything at all, I'm always here for you. But this is not the solution."

Jed nods numbly. He doesn't say anything. He doesn't let last night's activities show on his face. All those boys, heating their poison in metal spoons before injecting themselves with it. Rolling on the mattresses afterward with dazed eyes, blasted expressions. He doesn't let her know any of that.

Especially not about his plans to try it himself next week.

A pause in the memories. A moment of relief In that tiny duration, he senses it more strongly than ever. The answer. The key to the puzzle, looming in the distance, nearly completed. The whole of his mind thrums with it, anticipating its arrival. So close now. Just a f—

The memories suck him down once again.

Not quite the past, now. More like the recent present. A coffee shop in New York. Overcast afternoon. Busy chatter.

Christie sits opposite him.

He stares at her, marveling at how beautiful she is and how effortlessly she pulls it off. Her hair is undone and finer than gold, framing her face in a halo. Her eyes sparkle, smiling a unique smile of their own as they study Jed.

"What? Why are you looking at me like that?"

Jed gives her a smile of his own and averts his gaze. He wishes he could just tell her. It would be a relief to have the burden off his chest. Maybe he should just do it right now. In fact, he decides that he will do it ri—

"Oh, Graham's messaged." Slamming down her coffee on the table, Christie rises. "He has a lead in the case." She eyes him. "Come on, let's go."

Jed sighs and rises to his feet, the unspoken confession diving back inside him.

Maybe another day.

The overdose.

Oh, he remembers this one too clearly. It's a memory he will carry till the day he dies.

He's in his room, sitting cross-legged on his bed, the duvet wet with his tears. They are flowing down his face unobstructed, a dam of grief he has been holding in place for far too long. He just can't hold it anymore.

It is too much. It is all too much. His dad leaving. His mother's sadness. The hopelessly adrift canoe that is his life, constantly tossed back and forth by the currents, having no will of its own. He wants it to end. He wants it all to end. Today, it will. He will drill a hole in the boat's center so it can finally sink to the ocean floor and lie there, motionless. At peace.

Jed's fingers hold a tiny bottle of pills. He unscrews the lid and upends it. A yellow ribbon of capsules fill his palm. He pauses, looks at them, weighs them in his hand. Almost weightless. A speck of doubt rises in his heart, the last of his resistance, and he squeezes it out of existence. There is no more room for hesitation now.

He downs all the pills at once.

Christie again. As beautiful as ever. A somber expression on her face. The two of them are sitting somewhere dark and quiet. Jed can't remember where. When is this memory from? Is it a recent one or an o—

Wait.

This is not a memory.

"Jed."

Her voice is low and toneless, as if she's afraid of putting too much energy into it. Jed looks at her and finds her staring at him, her eyes flat and lips pressed together. An unvoiced message reflects in her eyes, which he just can't seem to grasp.

"Christie?" he asks.

"We're at the end, now, Jed. Whatever happens, I just want you to know," she pauses, swallows once, fights off a wave of emotion, "you were the best partner I ever had."

Jed frowns. He's afraid. "Why are you say—"

He doesn't get to finish. The scene fragments, shatters into a million pieces. All the memories shatter, freeing him at last. Floating in the open spaces of his mind. Then, he sees it. Finally sees it. A supernova in front him, unmistakable, undeniable. His mind has finally put it together.

The answer to the riddle.

Jed's breath comes out in a rattle. Something in him shakes. He steadies it with a long inhalation.

"Take me to it," he murmurs out loud. "Take me to the answer. I wish to know."

The supernova engulfs him.

CHAPTER 26

JUAN WAS SITTING ON the sofa, flipping to the seventh page of his magazine, using a sliver of light coming in between the curtains to see, when the patient returned. His eyes shot open, accompanied by a huge gasp, as if he had been submerged underwater for far too long.

Juan was with the man in an instant, calming him down, whispering assurances.

"You're okay, sir... You're okay. Everything is okay. "

The man—Jed—gave Juan a look that clearly suggested nothing was okay. He jumped up from the sofa, his breathing still loud and irregular, his eyes disoriented.

"I need to go. I got it. I got it."

Juan opened his mouth to tell the man to rest for a bit, at least have a glass of water, but by then, he had already reached the door and was pulling it open.

"I hope the session was fruitful!" he called out weakly, knowing he had not been heard. The door swung shut, and the room fell into silence again.

Juan sighed. The world really was a strange place. He went back to pick up his magazine, saying a silent prayer for the stranger who had just left. He looked like he really needed it.

"Pick up, dammit! Pick up, Alexis!"

Jed shook the phone in his hand, as if doing that would somehow make Alexis aware of his call. His Jeep was racing down the busy New York streets toward his friend's apartment. If she didn't pick up, he would just barge in through her front door. He had no other choice. Time was running out. She was his only way out.

She had always been the only way out.

The answer came back to Jed again—the puzzle all put together after so much struggle. It made him both furious and relieved. Relieved because at least the tricks were finally over and furious because it had been so simple all this time. Nothing even close to complicated. In fact, the puzzle had just been three pieces large. Just three. Even a child could put three pieces together. He thought about it again and marveled at its brilliance.

And always chewing gum.

Escape the demon of the drums! The one whose mouth endlessly runs!

Imagine that, both my ex-partners having the same music taste!

Three pieces. Short and simple. The first had been spoken to him by Alexis, a seeming eternity ago when they had met after the demise of the witness. The second had been part of Joe Mascarene's mad rambling. Or at least, that's what they had thought. That it was mad rambling. The third had been Alexis again, running into Jed at the concert. A single sentence on each occasion. Three sentences to solve the greatest mystery of Jed's life. To give him an answer that had been staring him in the face all along.

Alexis' past boyfriend was the enemy.

The man she had dated before Jed was the one behind all this. Really, it had been so obvious from the start! How else could Alexis' phone have been bugged? How else could the killer have listened in on all their conversations? They had always mistakenly assumed that someone had somehow snuck Alexis' phone away from her, bugged it, then returned it to her without her noticing. Since such a thing was nearly impossible, their hunch had led them nowhere. Just dead end after dead end. If only they had realized that Alexis' phone had been bugged a long, long time before this whole drama started. It had been bugged when she was dating that man. It had been bugged by that man, which was why she had never found out. Who would ever suspect their partner of such a thing?

The man who chewed gum.

Jed laughed softly and bitterly to himself. Pedro Mascarenes had given them the hint. They had just refused to take it, thinking the man was crazy.

Escape the demon of the drums. The one whose mouth endlessly runs. If you took that and paired it with what Alexis had told Jed—always c*hewing gum*—the answer was so clear. Both the gum and the music. Jed put them both together in his mind and almost heard that perfect click of connection.

Always chewing gum—the one whose mouth endlessly runs!

Imagine that! Both my ex-partners having the same music taste!—escape the demon of the drums!

He shook his head at himself for having missed it. Jed looked down at his phone, reopened that message he had received an hour after waking up in the hospital with Graham and Carter looming over him. As soon as Jed had seen the message, he had yanked out the IV from his arm and hobbled out of the hospital, despite everyone's protests. He had told them to leave him alone because he had known this last stage of the game was something he had to solve on his own. Even the message had said so, as expected. He stared down at it now, read it once more, flinching at the grotesque cheer injected into its words.

Congratulations on reaching the last stage of the game!

You've been a wonderful contender so far!

Now, to reach the finish line and secure your prize (She's making quite a fuss, let me tell you. The other one's quieter.), you just have to answer one question. No more delays, no more going round in circles. No more involving the police. Just you and you alone. Just one question and one question only! The sooner you answer, the sooner this ends!

Here we go!

<u>*Question*</u>

Who am I?

(24 Hours Remaining)

Your friend from the past

XOXO :)

Twenty-four hours. Most of that time had passed by now. Jed had less than five hours left to type in the answer to the riddle. But to do that, he had to get hold of Alexis and ask her for the name. If only she would pick up the god—

Jed's phone rang in his lap right then, and he almost crashed the car into a tree in his excitement. Swinging the steering wheel hastily and pressing down on the brakes, he answered.

"Hello, Alexis?"

"Hey, Jed. You called?"

"Alexis," Jed paused to take a breath. He was close to hyperventilating with anticipation. "The man you dated before me, what was his name?"

Silence.

"What?"

"Alexis, there's no time." Impatience flooded Jed's voice, and he made no effort to hold it back. "I promise I'll explain later. But tell me: the man you dated before me, what was his name?"

"Uh, Zac Ramsay?" she answered meekly.

Zac Ramsey.

Zac.

The name did not really ring a bell. Not loudly, at least. But some part of him stirred upon hearing it. A phantom twitch in his heart, too fleeting to be noticed properly. From his professional study of therapy, Jed remembered a quote from a book that had always stuck with him.

The mind may forget, but the body always remembers…

"Thank you." Jed hung up the call. He opened the madman's message and sent his answer. The Jeep, which had just moments ago been barreling down the street like an enraged monster, slowed down with equal speed and parked at the side of the road.

He waited.

Dusk was here. Liquid shadows spilled across the sky. Streetlamps flickered to life, burning feverishly. Pubs filled up, glasses clinking, smatters of laughter tumbling out to the streets. The city was changing shape, morphing into something else entirely to face the night.

A phone rang.

He picked it up with one hand, then looked at the message. There was no cheer in it. No more hideous jokes. Seemed like they really were at the end, after all.

Come to the crossroads located past Lauren's den.

Now.

Alone.

Jed turned on the Jeep's ignition and began his final journey.

CHAPTER 27

LAUREN'S DEN.

Jed slowed down as he passed it by. The place was still empty, its gate swinging in the wind. No bodies were visible outside, no dried stains of blood scabbing the earth. Someone had come and cleaned it all up. Jed wondered who it had been, then a second later found himself pushing the question away. It didn't matter. He didn't care anymore. He'd had enough riddles for a hundred lifetimes.

The warehouse fell behind him, the road stretching onward in a single straight line. It lay empty and dark, just like it had been on the night they had come for Lauren. Except now, Jed had no one watching his back. It was just him. Just him and that man, Zac, the voice behind the phone, the master puppeteer in this whole horror show. Finally, Jed would see. Finally, they would come face-to-face.

He didn't have to travel long before the crossroads arrived. They shone a faint silver beneath the moonlight. An inverted cross, from where Jed could see—perhaps an omen of things to come. There was a warehouse standing at the road's edge, similar to the previous one, except slightly larger and made from wood and concrete.

A van was parked outside it.

Jed stared at the black van. It stood just beyond the gate, hugging one of the bare cement walls. Its windows were tinted. There was no number plate visible on the back. There didn't seem to be anyone inside, but then again, Jed had learned not to overestimate his good luck. The worst absolutely could—and sometimes did—happen if you weren't careful enough.

He parked his vehicle parallel to the van, until their side mirrors were almost touching. It was a strange way to park, considering there was ample space behind the van and in front of it, but out here in the wilderness, no one would complain. Jed turned off the ignition, rubbed his beloved Jeep's steering wheel a final time, and got out. He didn't bother locking it. Tonight was the end, one way or the other. Either he'd come walking back with not a care in the world, or he wouldn't come at all. There would be no more living in fear, no more looking over his shoulder.

The warehouse's gate hung ajar. He pushed it open and walked in, not caring about stealth anymore. He already knew he had been seen. There was no point hiding and sneaking around. His enemy was inside, waiting.

The inner door to the building hung open as well. Jed used his phone's flashlight and stepped through it. He saw an interior almost identical to the one they had seen on that other night. Everything had been stripped empty and thrown into darkness. In one corner, a set of crooked stairs reached up toward the second floor.

Jed went to them.

Each step creaked beneath his feet. The banister shook with his weight. As he climbed, he thought back to the first time he had met Christie, how he had been taken aback by that electric smile and those golden locks. He had not known, on their first encounter, how deep their friendship would go, how important a part she would play in his life. He had not known that he was in for one hell of a ride, a ride that would finally tear down all those walls he had built around him. Just one dimpled smile from her, and he would want to pour out every bit of his dark past to her, let her fill him with light. That was how it had been. She had arrived in his life like a whirlwind of good fortune and swept him off his feet. No matter what happened now, Jed would always be grateful that he had gotten to know her. She made everything worth it—all the struggle, all the pain, all the challenges they had faced together. Even during this last bit, climbing up to what could be his death, Jed had no regrets. For Christie, he would die with a smile on his face. To save her, he would hand his life over a thousand times.

He reached the top.

It was different from the other warehouse. There was only one room here, not three. It stood right opposite the hallway, doorless.

It was not empty.

Jed saw them both and felt a strange relief. At least there were no more tricks left now. They really were here. Christie's dark outline was unmistakable, slumped against a chair. Next to her was his friend and client, Max, sitting in similar fashion, with his head lolling left, as if he were asleep.

And behind them both.

Standing.

The enemy.

Jed's eyes took him in. He was just a pale bulge in the room's blackness. A ripple in the still ocean of the night. A fitting introduction, considering his ghostlike nature. He did not move. He did not speak. He simply faced Jed, waiting for him to come.

Jed did. He took a step forward and was surprised to find his legs steady, calm. Not shaky. He took another step, then another, and soon, the room came into clearer view. He saw Christie and Max's faces, eyes half-lidded and drowsy, arms and legs tied up. Before them lay something else, something he had missed earlier. A small wooden table. Cluttered with implements of some kind. It was hard to discern their identity from here, in the dimness, and a part of Jed was too distracted to try. Like a compass needle yearning northward, his eyes twitched in their sockets, rising up from the table to meet the man of the shadows, standing between Christie and Max.

Zac.

"Hello," Jed said quietly, politely. "Nice to see you at last."

The man came forward. His face broached the night. Jed saw it, and recognition flared instantly. A faulty switch flicked somewhere deep within him, releasing bolts of current. He shifted from one foot to another, let out a soft breath. Blinked quickly multiple times. Breathed in quickly, exhaled shakily.

The man was about his age, but life had wreaked an extra decade of destruction on him. Beneath the debris of wrinkles and scars, Jed could see the crawling remains of a youth snuffed out before its time. The man's face was long and oval, deep ruts running through it like trenches of war. His forehead was blotchy, scarred, the skin a grisly shade of purple, peeling in places like rotten grapefruit. Only the eyes had survived untouched. They gazed out from the blasted ruins of his features, shining opals.

"Jed Gray. We meet at last. What took you so long? You were supposed to be here an hour ago."

Whatever calamity had afflicted the man, his voice had been affected, too. It was scratchy and chopped up, as if he were speaking through a mouthful of meat. Beneath all that distortion, however, Jed sensed something else running. Something steely, unyielding. It was the man's insanity, he realized a moment later. This man, Zac, was too deranged to suffer anything anymore. He had gone beyond that point and existed only as a vehicle of destruction.

"Surprised by my appearance?" Zac smiled, causing a convulsion to grip the scarred flesh on his face. It twitched and shuddered in a fruitless attempt to imitate cordiality. "Apologies for looking this way. What you see is just a side-effect of handling—"

"The poison," Jed finished. "The poison you used to kill Joel. You got infected with it, too, despite your best efforts."

"Ah, how I love that intelligence of yours, Jed." Zac grinned at him, broken molars peeking through his skin. "Correct once again. The game is already over, but you keep solving riddles. Bravo."

Jed did not respond. He paused for a moment, taking in Christie's face. She looked peaceful, her face tilted sideways, her porcelain skin unblemished.

"You're still alive," he said to Zac, returning his attention to the thing standing before him pretending to be human, "which means you have a cure. A cure for the toxin."

Zac nodded, the grin never leaving his face. "Of course I have, my dear friend. This whole mess began with that poison, and it shall end with it. As above, so below. Isn't that what the bible says?"

Jed shook his head wearily. A dry rasp of laughter escaped his lips. "All this time…" he muttered, looking down at the ground with a bitter smile. "All this time, I kept wondering what I could have possibly done to make you hate me so much. Every night, I would go to sleep racking my brain, trying to recall my sins." He paused and breathed out slowly.

"And?" Zac asked.

"And nothing." Jed looked up at the man grimly. "I did nothing wrong. This was never my fault." He shrugged, laughing hollowly. "You're just insane. That's it, isn't it? You're completely deranged. I've been dealing with a lunatic all this time. No matter how clever your games are and how skillfully you've been tricking us, in the end, your motivations are nothing but pure madness. You have no reason for them. No justification." He gritted his teeth. "You're just a monster by design. A tragic product of nature."

Zac threw his head back and cackled wildly. The room echoed with his hideously wet and squelching laughter. On the phone, it had been metal screeching in agony. But in person, without the mechanical distortion, it was far more disconcerting. The sound of limbs being dismembered and organs being stamped upon. Jed swallowed.

"Bravo, Jed! Bravo!" Zac clapped his hands together. "A mighty fine speech, I must say! Probably designed to rile me up into making a mistake. Ha!"

"It's the truth," Jed whispered. "How is it my fault Alexis left you? How is it my fault no one at the rehab center accepted you? How is it my fault you spiraled into a life of drugs and destruction? For once in your life, why don't you start giving answers instead of demanding them?"

Still smiling, Zac simply shook his head, confirming Jed's hunch. "The time for questions is passed, my dear boy." He ran a hand over his face, feeling its bumps and pits. "Now is the time for justice. For repayment. For you to get what you have deserved all along."

Jed bowed his head. "If you had just accepted your short-comings instead of pinning them on others, you wouldn't be where you are today. You would have a life. A good life."

Something seemed to snap inside Zac right at that moment. Perhaps the last thread of his sanity, which had been pulled taut all this while. Upon hearing Jed's words, his smile vanished instantly, and a terrifying fury erupted from the craters of his face, seething like magma.

"YOU TOOK MY LIFE FROM ME!" he screamed, spittle flying from his mouth, eyes threatening to drip down his sockets. "YOU TOOK IT FROM ME! YOU LEFT ME ALL ALONE IN THAT REHAB CENTER! YOU TOOK ALEXIS AWAY FROM ME! YOU MADE ME INTO A FAILURE! YOU MADE ME RELAPSE AGAIN AND AGAIN! ALL YOU! IT WAS ALL YOU! I DESPISE YOUR EXISTENCE, JED GRAY!"

Jed stared in stunned silence. He hadn't been expecting that outburst. But now that it had come, he found himself shaking his head again, almost sadly. This man was no evil genius. He was just another regular human, too rotten to admit his own mistakes. Blaming everyone but himself.

"Whatever." Jed waved a tired hand. "Let's just get this over with. What do you want?"

For a moment, it looked like the anger on Zac's face would explode once again, but then he seemed to realize what he was doing. He sucked it all back within him, replacing it with that nauseating smile.

"Sorry about that," he apologized. "Sometimes my… emotions get the better of me. Now, where were we?"

"Your big plan of revenge," Jed muttered tonelessly. "Go on, then. Kill me. Finish the story."

Zac cackled. "Kill you? Ha! You should expect better from me, Gray. Besides, death won't be a fitting end to our story. No… I have something far more interesting in mind. After all, why would I go through the hardship of killing so many people close to you if my plan in the end was just to shoot you in the head? No, no. Alex. Maria. Joel. They didn't die for nothing. They sacrificed their lives for my master plan."

Jed's upper lip curled in a snarl. "Don't you dare say their names," he whispered.

Zac bleated laughter again. "Come on, Jed! As angry as you are, you have to appreciate the genius of my plan! The perfection of choice behind each victim! Ethan, to ruin your success story. Alex, to bring you in close contact with your lunatic father. The masseuse witness, to weigh you down with the guilt of her death. And Maria, of course, to weigh you down further. To turn your successful past into a tragedy."

"What about Joel, huh?" Jed shot back. "What crime did that poor guy commit?"

"I had a feeling you'd forget." Zac bared his teeth. "Joel was a substitute cook in the rehab we went to, my dear forgetful friend. He even allowed you into the kitchen a few times, showed you kindness. Thus, he had to go. Anyone who allies himself with Jed Gray must pay the price."

Realization dawned in Jed's eyes. The memories came back quick and hard. He shook his head, lips parting in disbelief. "You're mad…"

"Oh, enough with the crazy accusations!" Zac clapped his hands together. "They're so boring! Let's move on to the present, shall we? And what I have in store for you now. Are you ready?"

Jed nodded dully. There was nothing else he could do.

"Great! Let's unfold the final act, then!"

Zac pointed at the small table lying before Christie and Max. "*This.* This is my plan, dear boy. I'm surprised you didn't already guess it."

Jed's eyes traveled to the table. From up close, it was no longer shrouded in shadows. The implements strewn across its surface lay clearly visible, lined silver in the moonlight. Jed took them in and…

A frown.

"What is this?"

Zac laughed his hideous laugh again, bones grinding together, invisible teeth gnashing flesh, popping cartilage. "Look again, and tell me what you see. I don't want to ruin it for you."

Jed had already seen it, and he already knew what it was. He was having a hard time saying it, though, because he had never expected to come across such a thing in his life. He had only ever had occasional nightmares about it, waking up from them in a cold sweat. He should have known, though.

Some nightmares turned real.

Before him, lying on the table, were five objects. Five objects which, if seen in isolation, would not cause any alarm or ring any bells of recognition. But put the five together, and now you had a familiar mix. A slap from the past.

"You…" Jed whispered, too shocked to complete the sentence.

Zac tittered again, clapping his hands together in glee, knowing Jed had understood. Jed had understood perfectly.

His past had come back for him at last.

Lying on the table was a small lighter. Next to it, a stainless-steel spoon. Next to that, a plastic syringe. Next to that, a tourniquet. Last, but definitely not least, a small baggie filled with white powder. Its identity was unmistakable.

Heroin.

Jed gazed up at Zac. He looked down at the table. His mouth opened, but no words came out. Zac's high-pitched laughter rang out into the night, making the building tremble on its haunches.

"Exactly, my dear boy!" He cheered. "Now you know! You know what I want you to do! Pick up that spoon, and fill it with the powder! Heat up the glorious mixture, then draw it into the syringe! And then, and then, my dear boy! Ha!" He raised his head and howled up at the sky. "Inject yourself with it! Return to the past, where you belong! Return to the darkness of the old days, where your only concern was getting your next fix!"

Jed just stared, aghast. In his wildest imaginings, he hadn't expected this. Injecting himself with heroin? He knew the data well. One dose was all it took to turn someone into a full-blown addict. To transform their life into a series of unending sprints from one rehab to another, relapsing constantly. From one darkened alley to another, scrounging for the next fix. From one washroom to another, shivering, puking, suffering, wishing for death. Wishing for anything except that horrible addiction.

"I won't do it," he whispered.

Zac smiled sunnily, spreading his hands wide. "That's the only way out of this game, Jed. Crazy as I might be, and I admit I am, you know I'm telling the truth right now. Look at my face and tell me I'm lying." He turned serious, the smile evaporating. "I promise. If you inject yourself with that heroin right now, the game ends for good. Permanently." He gestured toward Christie and Max. "You can take them both home with you. You can call the cops on me." He raised a solemn hand to his chest. "I will disappear from your life forever, Jed. I swear it. No more fear. No more looking behind your back." A pause. "But. Only. If. You. Take. That. Heroin."

Jed stared at the table. His left hand twitched. A shallow gasp fluttered out through his lips, hung in the air like a parting farewell. He looked back up at Zac with narrowed eyes.

Zac smiled. "I'm waiting, Gray."

Gray's left hand twitched again. A moment later, he reached forward with his right. His fingers traveled toward the baggie of white powder, and then halfway through their journey, they made an abrupt U-turn. The gesture was so sharp and sudden that it allowed no time for a reaction. One moment, they were reaching for the packet of drugs, and the next, they were inside his pocket, drawing out a black blur.

"How about this? How about I shoot you dead, right here and now, and this game ends?"

He stood with the pistol in his hand, the barrel pointing at Zac's forehead.

Zac didn't flinch. He didn't even smile. In fact, he looked bored.

"Come on, Jed," he tutted. "You've disappointed me. Do you really think it would be so easy? You really think our final face-off would be based around something as crude as a gunfight?"

Jed stood motionless, his eyes squeezed into slits and finger quivering against the trigger. It seemed like he would stay that way forever, locked in eternal battle against his enemy. But then, he slowly lowered the gun.

"No, I didn't." The pistol dangled in his grip, muzzle facing the floor. "Tell me the final piece of the puzzle. Your last bit of trickery."

Zac grinned and bowed. "I was waiting for you to ask that. Now that we've come to the rub, let's not waste any more time..." He rubbed his hands together eagerly, then glanced at Christie and Max. "You see these two darlings of yours? I've sedated them, obviously, but that's not all I've done." A giggle seized him, violent and unhinged. "No, no, there's one more substance flowing through their veins. Can you guess what it is?"

Jed frowned. His heart shrank. "What?"

"Why, the poison, of course!" Zac exclaimed delightedly. "My own special concoction! The ichor from hell, resistant to all forms of treatments once injected! Death on a platter, served bite-sized!"

Jed's jaw fell open. His left arm twitched again. The gun shook in his other one, its barrel trying to rise up. "You..."

"If you kill me, your lovely lady and sweet little friend both die." Zac shrugged. "There's nothing you can do to save them. But if you take the heroin, if you turn yourself back into the druggie you've always been," he smiled sweetly, "I will give them the cure."

"Cure..." Jed whispered, staring at Christie, imagining the pathogen fizzing through her veins, wreaking havoc on her insides. "Where is the cure?"

"Somewhere in this building. Hidden." Zac pressed a finger to his lips. "Shhh. I won't tell. If you want, by all means, shoot me dead and find it on your own." He grinned. "But make sure you can tear apart the whole place in 30 minutes because that's how long these two have before the poison starts causing irreversible damage." He crossed his arms. "So, which will it be, Mr. Gray? What gamble will you choose?

Addiction, for the certainty of saving your loved one's lives? Or your sobriety and losing them forever, living with the guilt?"

Jed said nothing. His face was blank, a mask scrubbed clean. The gun hung heavy in his hands, the trigger no longer being squeezed by a finger. He raised it close to his face and inspected it, almost idly, before tossing it aside. It hit the wooden floorboards with a heavy thwack, spinning twice before coming to a halt.

He turned to face his enemy, his left hand twitching yet again. For a long while, neither of them spoke. They stared into each other's eyes, thinking, wondering, calculating. Or at least, that was what Jed did. Zac simply stood, relaxed, knowing a foolproof plan when he had one. His plan was as foolproof as they came. After all, he had spent years constructing it.

"Fine." Jed sighed, and his whole body seemed to sigh with him. His left shoulder twitched, his expression deflating. He looked down at the scattered instruments on the table with a resigned dread like a man building up the courage to face his worst nightmare, knowing he's fighting a lost battle.

"I'll do it. I'll take the heroin."

"Bravo! As I knew you would!" Zac clapped his hands. "Come on, now, dear friend. Hurry up and do it. Your friends don't have much time left. Besides, I've been waiting to see this sight for a long, long time. Waiting to see you admit it."

Jed offered Zac a tired gaze. "Admit what?"

JODI WALTER

"Why, that you're a junkie, of course!" Madness seethed in Zac's eyes like a rabid fever. "All this time, you've been pretending you were so good and mighty. So strong-willed! So clean! So pure!" He snorted. The smashed detritus of a nose quivered with effort in the center of his face. "Tonight, you reveal the truth. You admit that you were always just like the others. Like me. A druggie. A weakling. A *coward*." He spat that last word out.

The fight seemed to have deserted Jed entirely. His left hand twitched again. "That's what this is all about?" he inquired flatly. "You couldn't escape your addiction, so now you want to force me into another one, so you can feel better about your own lack of willpower?"

Zac sneered. "Don't play your stupid mind games with me, Gray. I'm beyond all that. Pick up the heroin and fill your insides with it. Let the demon in again. I'm waiting. *It's* waiting."

Jed bowed his head, then nodded. "Okay, Zac, if that's what you wish."

He came forward, eyes on the table, his left hand going forward, almost in slow motion. It reached for the powder. Zac watched with fascination, slavering, his eyes those of a star-struck child. This was it. This was his victory. It would happen now. His opponent would be defeated.

Jed's left arm twitched again.

The seventh time was the charm for Zac. Too drunk on his victory, he had failed to notice the previous six twitches, failed

370

to become suspicious. But the seventh one did it. Some part of his brain made the connection and informed him that Jed's left hand was twitching far too much for it to be normal. His eyes widened, and his alertness skyrocketed, readying itself for some trick.

But he was too late.

As it twitched for the seventh time, Jed's hand made an odd gesture. It reared in toward itself, fingers reaching like hungry tentacles for the wrist they were connected to. Jed's jacket's sleeve slid upward with the effort, and Zac saw what was there. In that fleeting, defining moment of his life, he realized two things: one, why it had taken so much time for Jed to arrive. And two, that in the closing lap of the match, he had underestimated his opponent.

Stuck to Jed's wrist with a strap of adhesive was a metal strip, tiny and rectangular, with a button set into its center. Jed's thumb reached for that button and pressed it. At once, the signal was sent.

Outside, in the cover of the night, standing quiet and still and subdued, Jed's jeep offered its final act of service to its owner. It exploded. The 10 kilograms of C4 attached to its engine caught the transmitter's signal and reacted without hesitation. A great mushroom of orange fire spread out in the night, carrying with it a shockwave of immense proportions. Both the heat and the terrific sound, along with the force of the blast, hit the warehouse in a deadly trifecta. The walls groaned in agony, and the ceiling shook, wooden shavings raining down. A large crack spread through the floor, zigzagging to the wall on the far end. Both Zac and Jed were sent stumbling sideways with the force of the explosion. Christie and Max's chairs toppled and fell to the floor. It all happened in a single second, a wave of overwhelming mayhem overtaking everything. In that chaos, while he slipped and fell and hit the ground, Jed made sure to do one thing.

He kept his eyes on Zac.

It had been his final weapon against his enemy, something he had learned over years of practicing and studying therapy. A feature of the human mind, a quality found in people everywhere across the world. Jed had taken it and staked everything he had on it. He had staked his whole life on it, on his understanding of human nature.

Now, he was reaping the rewards.

In a moment of unprecedented calamity or danger, during that very first second, it is instinctively hard-wired in a human being to look toward their most precious asset in life, to see if it is protected. The movement is involuntary, carried out by the body instead of the mind. One cannot stop it any more than one can stop themselves from flinching when something is thrown at them. In the event of a fire, when the announcement is first made, a mother will reflexively turn toward her child, a pet owner toward their cat, a workaholic toward his laptop, an alcoholic toward his wine cellar, a junkie toward his stash, a pastor toward his bible.

And a killer toward his poison.

Jed saw Zac's eyes flit sideways. They moved with a will of their own, racing ahead of the conscious mind before it could realize what was happening. Jed tracked their movement, saw them land on a wooden panel of the leftmost wall, centered at its lower end.

The poison. And its cure.

That's where it was.

Zac realized what was happening. He yanked his gaze back with a snarl, turning to face Jed, seeing a look of grim victory coloring his enemy's face. He knew. He had seen.

For the first time in their meeting, fear zigzagged across Zac's face. Fear coupled with uncertainty. This was one possibility he had not prepared for. One scenario he had not expected. He had been outsmarted. That, too, right at the finish line.

Zac howled and leapt for the wall, intending to destroy the cures before they could be used. But he didn't get very far. Jed came roaring at him, his body crashing into Zac's with the force of a freight train. Zac was thrown backward. Jed's elbow met his forehead with a sickening splat, sending him crumpling to the floor. Without wasting a single second, Jed whirled around and gripped the wooden plank Zac had looked at. He curled his fingers around the molding wood and pulled with all his might, heaving like a madman.

With him, the warehouse heaved in perfect sync, swaying under the force of the Jeep's detonation, its rusty hinges too weak to hold it in place anymore. The ceiling squealed, throwing down more wooden splinters. The crack in the floor widened, parting with a great shudder. A sliver of the building's ground floor peeked through from below, all cluttered debris and pillars of smoke. While the destruction ensued, Jed kept pulling, the muscles and tendons in his arms stiff with effort, his face a ball of agony.

The plank came loose. Jed stumbled backward, his feet trying to find purchase. He steadied himself by placing one hand against a wall, which suddenly didn't seem too solid anymore. Above him, the ceiling let out another terrible moan, warning him to leave before it came plummeting down on his head.

But not yet. Jed could not leave yet. He was so close now. There was a tiny compartment in the wall where he had pried loose the plank. In that compartment, a small briefcase sat snugly. Jed pulled it out and laid it open on the floor. There were four small vials in it. Two were empty, and two were filled with clear, green liquid. There were also two syringes beside them. He was going to keep his word and save them. He pulled out a vial and a syringe, coughing hard. Smoke crept into the room through the crack in the floor. Thick spurts of smoke rose like lost specters, drifting aimlessly in the empty space, turning the whole place into a blurry, gray canvas.

Jed fumbled with the first syringe, inserting it into one of the vials and drawing out the antidote. His eyes watered with the clogged air and salty tears streamed down his face. He let out another string of coughs, feeling a faintness overtaking him.

Not now. Not now, please. Just a little more time.

Rising to his feet, Jed staggered over to Christie. She was a pale husk in the room, her skin ashen, her breath barely perceptible, as if the specters fluttering all around her were slowly leeching the life out of her body. Jed grabbed her arm and gently inserted the needle in her upper arm. He pushed the stopper and felt a cold flood of relief fill his insides. Safe. Christie was safe for now—at least from the poison. The thought renewed him with energy. He went back to the second vial and filled the second syringe before returning to Max and injecting him in the same manner. Once done, Jed turned sideways and hacked out another flurry of coughs, his lungs trembling with effort. There was almost no air inside the room now. He had to leave. He had to leave with Christie and M—

"You bastard."

Jed turned around. Zac was standing on the other end, wreathed in coiling tendrils of gray. He truly looked like something that had crawled out of hell. Whatever pretense of humanity the man had been wearing had now completely fallen off. His face was a nightmarish landscape of craggy flesh where tributaries flowed—tributaries of blood which Jed had unleashed with his elbow. Zac's eyes shone like white skulls in their sockets. His mouth was a cave of jagged teeth.

He was holding Jed's gun.

"You bastard." Zac repeated the word in a gargled, choked voice, the blood flowing into his mouth, darkening his shredded lips. "Forget the heroin. I'm just going to kill you now. Enough with this. You and that blonde bitch—you both die."

Jed stared. The gun was pointing right at him, with Zac's finger on the trigger. The man was too far away for him to do anything. Was this it? All that struggle to lose in the end?

Zac seemed to read the thoughts playing through Jed's head. He smiled, a smile which oozed blood. "Shouldn't have thrown the gun away like that. Now, you die. Like the rat you are."

Jed stared at Zac. He glanced toward Christie, took in her beautiful, peaceful visage one final time.

I'm sorry. I tried. You did not deserve this.

Zac's finger pressed down on the trigger. It slowly inched inward at a snail's pace. Jed felt the grim reaper's cold gaze sliding down his back. This was it. He was going to d—

The world was ripped apart by another explosion. Just as loud and fearsome as the first. Later, much later, Jed would realize what had happened. He would come to know the almost divine stroke of luck that had saved his life.

The first explosion had been from Jed's Jeep. The second one was from the van it was parked next to, the van Jed had very purposefully parked parallel to. The van which had been on fire all this time, and like a lit fuse, had been excitedly waiting for its moment to come. As it did, the vehicle blew outward in a shockwave of fire, sound, and metal shrapnel.

Like an aged man too tired to stand anymore, the house buckled beneath this second assault. As the shockwave hit it, Jed and Zac both stumbled sideways. Zac fired the gun, and a final bullet left the muzzle, embarrassingly off-mark. It struck the leftmost wall, making a tiny contribution to the cracks already spreading across it. The floor beneath Jed and Zac let out an ear-splitting shriek before part of it caved inward. The shearing was neat, almost precise. Zac saw the cracks spider-webbing around him. Before he could do anything, nothing was touching his feet but air. He fell down, down to the first floor, which had turned into a cauldron of smoke and seething flames.

In the room, one lone man remained.

Jed staggered to his feet, throat scorched, lungs blistered, eyes swollen lumps. He staggered toward Christie, gathered her up in his arms, and slung her across one shoulder. Then, he leaned down toward Max's fallen form and picked him up in both arms. Gasping beneath the weight of both, he stumbled out of the room, each inhalation a rush of knives in his chest.

The stairs leading down did not look good at all, but somehow, miraculously, they were still standing. They were also his only way out. Jed descended, the smoke shrouding him, turning him into a grotesque, misshapen creature, six arms and legs jutting every which way. When he reached the first floor, he squinted and tried to discern where the entrance was. Everything was a flickering haze of red and gray. But past all that, to his diagonal right…

Yes.

There.

Jed went toward it, that dim square of light in the distance. The light at the end of the tunnel. The tunnel he had been traveling through for so long. He lurched and stumbled toward it, his breath hitching, his eyes furiously pumping out fluid, his heart whipping a broken body to keep it in motion.

Closer and closer that light came until, finally, he stumbled out. Out into the open. Oh, the sweet relief of clean air. Oh, how wonderful, how delicious. Jed laid Christie and Max down on the cool asphalt. A moment later, he collapsed beside them, gasping like a drowning man, feeling the fresh oxygen rushing back into his lungs. To his left, there was a great ripping sound, and he saw the rest of the warehouse finally collapse in on itself. The flames rose in place of it, greedily licking the air, hungering for the sky. Jed turned his eyes away from them and placed his head against the cool, hard tarmac, breathing hard.

In the distance, sirens approached.

CHAPTER 28

"So."

"Hmmm? So? So what?" Jed moved closer to his partner on the couch. He placed his hands on his lap and looked straight at her with solemn, open eyes.

Christie's left brow arched upward. She shook her head slightly. "Uh-uh, Jed. You're not getting out of this now. You don't get to pretend innocence."

"I'm not!" Jed protested, laughing. "I'm just waiting for you to… speak before me. Ladies first, you know."

Christie stared at him a long while, a light mix of suspicion and affection swirling on her face. Then, she let out a nervous chuckle of her own and nodded.

"Okay, fine," she relented. "I'll go first."

Jed leaned forward eagerly.

"Well…" Christie swallowed. They were safe and secure inside her apartment, but her heartbeat made it seem like she was still running for her life from a gang of skinheads. *God, why is this so hard?*

"I'm waiting, Detective," Jed urged her on softly.

Christie nodded again and sucked in another lungful of air. "Okay, so…" she began again, "as you know, we've been partners for a long time now…"

Jed nodded.

"We've fought together, solved cases together, saved lives together—heck, we've even saved each other's lives, and that, too, more than once." She paused again. Her mouth was curiously dry, her pulse whizzing through her. She took a moment to compose herself before continuing.

"Jed, I've gotten to know you better than I've known anyone else in my life," she almost whispered now, her voice falling low. "I've seen you at your best, and even at your lowest, when life was really giving you a beating. I've seen how kindly you deal with people, how quickly you can put together almost impossible connections. How bravely you walk into the face of danger just for the sake of doing what is right. How easily you risk your life for the ones you care about. How unwaveringly loyal you are to them."

Jed said nothing. He had gone very still, his stare fixed on Christie. She felt herself being heard and acknowledged in a way she never had before. It was a thrilling sensation, yet terrifying, too. Her skin prickled with goosebumps, and her stomach did a swan dive.

"So," she continued, her voice now slightly shaky with emotion, "to summarize what I've said before, you're a true wonder of a human being, Gray. The darkness within you, borne of your past, only makes your light so much more valuable. It makes your kindness and softness a true miracle, considering everything the world has put you through. I—I ca—" She broke off, the emotion overwhelming her. After a few seconds of pretend coughing, she resumed what was left of her confession.

"I can't imagine ever finding someone like you," she said. "I can't imagine having never met you. I can't imagine how my life would be without you present. And... I... I can't imagine just staying partners with you for the rest of my life."

Her lips fell shut after that, and silence reigned. Jed's face was a muffled storm of emotions. Christie could see them flickering all over his features like stray bursts of lightning. A flare of hope here, a twitch of nervousness there. He was trying his best to keep himself composed, but her speech had really gotten to him, had stirred something deep within him. Christie was glad for it.

"Well," she demanded after Jed continued to stay quiet, his gaze drifting far away. "Don't leave me hanging here, Gray! It's your turn!"

Christie's words seemed to yank Jed back to the present. He blinked and looked at her, seeing her anew. A surge of longing brightened his gaze, so intense that Christie flushed beneath its attention and averted her gaze. She heard Jed moving closer to her until their knees were touching. Such a simple touch, yet it sent currents racing through Christie's entire being.

"Detective." Jed's voice was its usual calm, deep self again. "I have to say, after a speech like that, you've set the bar so high I'm afraid I can do nothing to overcome it. Nevertheless, I'll try. As you just stated, when have you ever known me to back out from a challenge?"

Christie was still gazing shyly down at the cushions. She started as fingers grazed her chin, gently pulling her face up and forward. She found herself staring right into her partner's eyes, all else blocked out. Their noses were mere inches apart. Their strained exhalations met midair, tangoed around in excitement.

"Right. That's much better," Jed continued with a murmur. Christie felt his words heavy and hot on her face, tickling her lips. She swallowed again.

"So, as I was saying," Jed whispered, "where do I begin? What can I even say that will match your speech, which you gifted me with just now?" He clucked softly, shaking his head. "I could tell you that a part of me cracked open the moment I first laid eyes on you, on that fateful afternoon a lifetime ago. I could tell you that when I first saw you smile, I felt a kind of hope I hadn't felt in a long time. The hope that life still held some magic, some untainted beauty. That dreams did really come true after all." He shifted forward, and now they were unbearably close, their noses almost touching. "I could tell you that when I first heard you laugh, my heart danced to its sound, and I knew right then I was in deep trouble. I could tell you that when I first saw you fiercely heading into battle and taking on the city's worst to uphold order and justice, part of me was sick with worry for you, and part of me just watched on in awe. Your bravery. Your brains. The goodness within you. And not to mention that gorgeous face, the kind men used to wear around their necks in a locket before going to war. All of it has me spellbound, Christie. *You* have me spellbound by how amazing you are."

He slid even closer, and now there was barely any gap, just a pretense of it. Everything else had fallen away for Christie. Her mind had gone utterly still, too petrified to intervene.

"So," Jed breathed, "I could tell you all these things, but I'm afraid they won't be enough to make you understand how I feel about you. Instead, I'll do you one better, Detective. I'll *show you.*"

It all happened in a breathless blur. He finally leaned forward, closing the sliver of distance. Christie felt their lips connecting, and something crackled and exploded within her. A storm of fireworks, held in captivity for too long, now finally blazed free. She felt the plump warmth of Jed's mouth on hers, his strong hands sliding behind her lower back and pulling her closer, onto his lap. She felt his other hand traveling up the nape of her neck, getting lost in the tangle of her hair. She grunted, awash in an intensity impossible to explain with words. So, instead of trying, she let go completely. She forgot all her worries and descended into the moment, wrapping her own arms around Jed's neck and drawing him close. He fell back onto the couch beneath her weight, his mouth still on hers.

For a long time after, they spoke little to each other, yet their feelings were made abundantly clear as they lay there in each other's embrace.

Epilogue

It was early morning.

Soft pellets of tawny light snuck in through the window, illuminating bits and pieces of the apartment. On one leather sofa, a white shirt was strewn haphazardly, unbuttoned. On the teakwood armchair next to it, a pair of black pants, an unbuckled belt still stuck in their loops. Beyond them both, hanging precariously from a coat hanger by one strap, still swinging slightly...

A lilac bra.

Silence dominated the spaces, punctuated by soft rustles and muted giggles. They came from the bedroom, whose door was hanging slightly open, projecting a triangle of orange light on the linoleum floor.

Inside, the noise was louder.

To be fair, Christie was the one responsible for making most of it. She couldn't keep her giggles to herself, couldn't keep that stupid smile off her face. Next to her, covered up to his chest in the quilt, Jed flashed his typical, charming grin. His eyes were hazelnut and entirely free of burden. His face was relaxed, his forehead unlined. It was two weeks after that terrible night, and he was having a heck of a time.

Finally, he was a free man.

No longer single.

"Well, you're the one who said it," he protested gently now, reaching forth and brushing Christie's bare shoulder with one hand. It pimpled with goosebumps beneath his touch. "You said last night was the best night you've ever had. What did you mean by that: the conversation or the... other activities?"

Christie erupted into another fit of giggles, her cheeks turning scarlet. She tried to slap Jed away playfully, but he was wise to her tricks. He grabbed her arms and pulled her close in an instant. *Jeez, the man is strong.*

"Not until you tell me," Jed whispered, their bare chests touching. He leaned forward and pressed his lips against Christie's. Although they had been doing nothing but this for the past hour, the kiss still lit up fireworks of pleasure within her. She grunted hungrily, wrapping her arm around his neck and pulling him in closer.

A few seconds later, they withdrew, breathing harshly. Jed traced an idle finger down Christie's collarbone, his eyes watching her, alight with emotion.

"You still haven't answered the question," he murmured.

Christie paused and considered. "Well, I would say that since I've already had plenty of scintillating conversations with you over the time we've known each other, and you have opened up to me quite a bit, our... extracurricular activities were last night's highlight for me."

"Yes! I knew it!" Jed pumped one fist in the air. His other arm snaked around her back, tugged her towards him with inexorable firmness. "Your praise for my performance only serves to motivate me, Detective. I reckon it's time for us to begin our second round."

"No!" Christie squealed, fighting against him, but only half-heartedly. Jed pinned her arms to the pillow and slid on top of her. His soft eyes filled her vision, her entire world. She smiled up at them, watching them grow larger and then envelop her completely as Jed's lips met hers.

Outside, silence returned to the apartment's living room, the laughter dying away. Those few specks of sun glinting through the window also withdrew, as if offering the inhabitants their privacy. On a nearby tree branch, a bird trilled merrily, welcoming the unfurling dawn. It looked like it was going to be a glorious day.

A start to new beginnings.

Want to learn why Jed was chosen for this partnership with Christie over any of the other qualified therapists? Claim your copy of **Origins of Gray** when you sign up for Jodi Walter's newsletter and learn more about how Jed came to know Ethan. https://dl.bookfunnel.com/qikjjxz4u7

Stay tuned for fresh adventures of Laurie Gray as she leaps into the next stage of her life of a travelling author. Sign up for my newsletter to get updates: jodiwalter.com or https://thirteen-pages-btxdiq.mailerpage.io/

Honest reviews of my books help bring them to the attention of other readers, who are more likely to read something from a new-to-them author if it has more reviews. You can quickly and easily leave a quick rating or brief review on the book page https://bit.ly/JedGray5. Just scroll down the page and on the left side click on "Leave a Customer Review". Reviews are the lifeblood of little authors like me. Thank you! Or you can just scan this QR code to take you to the book page.

FATE OF GRAY

ABOUT THE AUTHOR

JODI WALTER WAS BORN and raised in the Western Prairies of Canada. She spent her childhood enjoying nature and animals on the family farm. She continues to volunteer with animal rescues and has adopted two rescue dogs that she shares her home with today.

Jodi went through some difficult times in her early thirties when her marriage broke down and she became a single mom of a fantastic young son. After picking herself back up and succeeding in whatever challenge she faced, she became a firm believer that "we are never put in any situation we can not handle". Her newest endeavor is to write mystery thriller stories for you to enjoy. Delving into her subconscious, she creates characters she hopes will connect with you. Jodi has experienced a profound amount of catharsis by putting her pen to paper and releasing her characters into the world.

Jodi's website: jodiwalter.com or https://thirteen-pages-b txdiq.mailerpage.io/

Jodi's Facebook: https://www.facebook.com/jodiwalterau thor

Jodi's Email: author@jodiwalter.com

www.ingramcontent.com/pod-product-compliance
Lightning Source LLC
Chambersburg PA
CBHW021129260626
47169CB00005B/1516